Sign up for our newsletter to hear about new and upcoming releases.

www.ylva-publishing.com

OTHER BOOKS BY LOLA KEELEY

The Music and the Mirror

MAJOR SURGERY

LOLA KEELEY

DEDICATION

For Lande.
For her generous soul, and for being a better friend than anyone deserves.

ACKNOWLEDGEMENTS

Thank you to everyone who has chatted, provided caffeine, listened to me ramble, and offered feedback during this busy process of a second book.

Thanks to my wife, Kaite, who always finds time to encourage and support. Who inspires me with her own hard work and dedication. Thank you for surrounding us with books and cats, and for showing me what a writer is capable of.

Lee, thank you for getting the wood out of the trees and keeping me on track. This story is infinitely better for your guidance and correction. Astrid, thank you for continuing to let me unleash words on the world.

As always, my first line of idea bouncing and feedback are my writing buds: Sus, Luce, Rach, Marissa, and Rachel. Thank you for playing in the same sandbox every day.

JJ, Gabby, Laura, Sarah—thank you for making me laugh and sharing in the salt. Thanks to the Woolf pack regulars for showing up and for being an endless source of wisdom.

Haley, thank you for making my dream come true!

Big thanks to my parents for supporting me in so many ways, whether it's my old bedroom to crash in, or tracking down the best lunch in Lanarkshire.

My dear bezzer, Lisa-Marie, not least for always providing the tunes.

Finally: to all four cats, without whom this book would have been ready sooner and with much less wrestling over the keyboard. Franklin, Orlando, Nora, and Collins, you are a bunch of adorable idiots.

CHAPTER 1

THE KNIFE COMES AS SOMETHING of a surprise.

Not because they're in a busy central London hospital, where knives of every blade and sharpness are a common accessory to any number of plunging stab wounds or aggressive patients refusing to be treated. Not even because they're in the entrance corridor of the Acute Medical Unit, first stop for non-trauma patients being admitted after rocking up to Accident & Emergency. Which is the actual spiritual home of knives, expected and otherwise. The sharps bins there overflow with cutlery as often as they do used needles.

No, the unexpected nature of this knife is that it's being wielded by a slender blonde woman, in her late thirties. Where Veronica's own complexion retains the brown hues of her father and grandparents, lady-with-the-knife is porcelain pale.

The knife itself isn't even especially tricky. Who knew anyone still carried a Swiss Army knife? Though the famous red casing seems to have considerable mileage on it, the chosen blade is immaculate as it gleams under their sickly fluorescent lighting.

"Stop right there!" Veronica barks, an order that would have any of her foundation-year doctors scurrying for cover. The blonde, who's currently straddling an injured cyclist lying on a gurney, drops the blade next to the injured man's arm. Order restored.

Except her next move is to brace herself and pick up the knife again. This will not do.

"Put. That. Down." Well, at least there's a pause before the re-enacting of *Psycho*. "Pauline, call security. Lea, can you find out whether Mr Wickham is planning to grace us with his presence anytime soon?"

Peter Wickham, her second-in-command, should be off preparing to face his promotion panel today, but his sporty strength does come in handy at times. Veronica intends to get best use out of the consultant she's trained since he first emerged, blinking, from the hallowed halls of Oxford.

"There's no need for security." Veronica's surprised when the woman finally speaks. Her voice is like aural lidocaine, smooth and comforting, entirely unflappable. It's the bedside manner Veronica's been trying to capture for more than fifteen years. "There *is* a distinct need for an emergency splenectomy."

Veronica's head says she's some kind of fantasist, but her gut recognises a fellow professional.

"Last I checked, the Swiss don't include a ten-blade."

"This is for the Lycra."

She promptly snags the collar of the man's cycling leotard—Veronica assumes it has a considerably more butch-sounding proper name—and slices it like a strip of wallpaper, straight down the middle. Pulling it apart, she starts to palpate the upper left quadrant of the patient's abdomen. Despite being mostly out of it, he hisses through his teeth at first contact.

"See? And a moment ago he was clutching his shoulder." The blonde looks triumphant. "Where's your nearest general surgeon?"

"That would be me, but I'm not in theatre today. Let's get him to Imaging—without a passenger if you please. Then we'll see who's on the board."

"He doesn't have time."

"You're not a CT scanner, so you can't possibly know that!" Veronica's notoriously short patience is close to snapping. "So if you could get off our bloody patient, Dr...?"

"Taylor," she corrects, spine straightening. "Major Cassie Taylor, in fact. Trauma surgeon. But I'd much rather get him open and see if we can't save part of this spleen, rather than letting him bleed out until we have to remove the little bastard."

"But...you can't do that!" Veronica is relieved to see the two bumbling security guards from A&E, a modern day Tweedledum and Tweedledee in scratchy black wool jumpers, ineffectual rubber batons clipped to their belts. At least they're built like brick shithouses. This slip of a thing won't be a match for them, Major or not. Which branch, anyway? Army, navy, air force? Veronica blinks a few times to stop picturing her in uniform. Or Action Man fatigues.

Patient. Spleen. Intruder riding his gurney like a hobby horse. Focus, Veronica chides herself.

"Ms Mallick?" Lea comes sprinting back, Peter Wickham in tow. He's wearing one of his nicer suits, Boss or Armani no doubt, and his sandy blond hair is ruffled already. "Mr Wickham's here."

"I can see that, Lea. Peter, if this woman—sorry, Major—won't get off my patient, I'd like you to lift her. Bodily."

"I wouldn't try it," Cassie Taylor warns, her pale cheeks getting pinker. "But someone can wheel us into the nearest available operating theatre, and get me some scrubs."

"Oh, I don't think so—" Veronica begins.

"Since none of the surgeons here seem interested in much other than paperwork," Cassie accuses, nodding at the stack of files under Veronica's arm and then the papers in Peter's. "Listen, I've got my GMC card in my bag, so if someone wants to root around in there, I can get on with this." Sure enough, there's a nondescript black leather bag by her foot.

"Listen—" Peter tries turning on the charm, moving close, but Cassie turns away in apparent disgust.

"You!" She barks at a passing orderly, one Veronica only vaguely recognises. "Get a hold of this trolley and get us into the surgical wing. Can you do that?"

The orderly, six-foot-something and muscular, looks at the gaggle of doctors and nurses, before shrugging. He positions himself at the head of the cyclist's portable bed and starts wheeling them off, at pace.

"Did she just..." Peter watches them go. "Steal a patient?"

Veronica is half-inclined to chase after them, but the surgical staff will soon deal with it. She gestures for security to follow them, and they huff and puff, but they do it.

"Do you really care?" She cranes her neck to look after them. Should she go and physically intervene? All the training says don't engage, but Veronica will be damned if patients can be picked up on a whim, like takeout coffee. Still, no point in stressing out Peter before his hour in the spotlight. "How's the panel prep? Ready to be grilled?"

"Well, that's the thing; she's just come out of the panel." He points after the patient-pinching Major. "She must have been first up."

"That lunatic is up for Head of Trauma?" Veronica looks at him like he might have lost his mind, too. "Well, I'd say that makes you even more of a sure thing, Peter."

"Taking it a little personally, Vee?" says a familiar voice behind her.

Veronica turns to see her brash and brilliant best friend, Edie, whose attention has already switched to Peter.

"Best of luck, darling." With a kiss to his cheek, Edie dispatches him back to wherever the panel is being held.

"Thanks. I'll just check that someone has actually verified her," Peter says. "Do me good to stretch my legs before I face the firing squad." He lopes off, those easy athletic strides of his eating up the long corridor.

"Edie." Veronica greets her properly with a brisk hug. "You choose the worst Monday mornings to show up like a bad penny, you know that?"

"Well you were all standing around staring as I approached. Who was putting on a show? And was she your type?"

Veronica dismisses Edie with a wave. Forever trying to set her up, regardless of who the other woman actually is in any given equation. Just when the morning can't get any more frustrating, the new Deputy CEO comes barrelling along the hallway towards them. Veronica has got to stop hanging around at the intersection of hospital corridors. These interruptions happen less when she's tucked away in her broom closet of an office.

"Oh Christ, here comes Travers," she groans, patting Edie on the shoulder. "You should run while you still can."

"Ms Mallick!" Wesley Travers shouts at Veronica, as though she can't see him charging towards her like a bull separated from the herd at Pamplona. If bulls wore tweed and too much spiced cologne. "Have you seen my email about—"

"I'm just getting in, Dr Travers." Despite outranking her in the management hierarchy, Wesley never trained as a surgeon. In fact, some days Veronica has her doubts as to whether he finished his medical training at all before jumping wholeheartedly into management. She quite fancies his job title for herself one day, without the 'Deputy' in front for good measure. She intends to get there with the understanding and experience of a great surgeon under her belt. "I'll respond just as soon as I'm at my desk."

Veronica ignores completely that she's usually glued to her phone and could respond just as readily from there. She learned long ago to set boundaries with superiors and direct reports alike, lest they try to tell her how she should be spending her time.

"I don't believe we've met." Wesley turns the good-old-boy act on Edie, offering his permanently clammy hand to shake hers. While they both share the redhead genes, his is a weak sort of strawberry blond, the few strands hanging on arranged in a combover of sorts. Edie is the fiery red of Ireland-via-Hollywood, salon perfect on every strand.

Veronica seizes her chance to cause trouble, because frankly why she should be the only one on the receiving end?

"Oh, this is just one of Peter's one-night stands we can't seem to get rid of," she says, poker face firmly in place.

"Yes," Edie confirms, energetic in her handshake. "Only that was about nine years, a wedding, and two children ago. Dr Hyatt-Wickham. So pleased to meet you, Dr Travers."

"That name does ring a bell," he says, smarmy smile firmly in place as his beady eyes dart back and forth between the two women. "But you're not on staff here?"

"No, God no! Just visiting." Edie corrects him with her fakest, tinkling laugh. She withdraws her hand, discreetly wiping it on the hip of her pale grey Burberry trench coat. Despite the two children under five situation, she's rarely anything other than spotless. "But if Veronica here is too much trouble, you just say the word and I can have her sectioned."

"Ah, psychiatry," he replies, clearly pleased to be in on the joke. "Oh no, we need our Ms Mallick. AMU wouldn't run without her. I suspect she's keeping certain other hellscapes from spilling over too. Still, must be getting on."

He turns back to Veronica, who is preening just a little at the unexpected compliment. It's true that she does her share of standing up to, and babysitting, the lawlessness of Accident & Emergency. Still, that sort of thing is acknowledged about as rarely as a female director at the Oscars around here.

"Look forward to your email reply!" Wesley strides off.

"Shouldn't you be overcharging someone to talk about their dreams?" Veronica diverts Edie back over to a calmer exit, one that avoids A&E

altogether. "Don't worry about Peter; between the pair of us we've primed him perfectly. He'll be the next Head of Trauma here, and everything will settle."

"It better." Edie sighs. "He's so cheerful about his backup plan. Fancies himself a Dr Kildare, dishing out Valium and rabies shots in the countryside, while the kids go frolic with lambs and take lessons in a one-roomed school."

"It's just the stress talking," Veronica reassures her. "I'll have one of the keener juniors talk him into a squash game or something this evening, keep his mind off it."

"You know, when we met I didn't think you'd become my partner in keeping my marriage on track." Edie almost looks wistful. "Speaking of the old days, I was talking to Angela—"

Veronica cuts her off right away. "My darling ex has already been on my case, thank you very much. I'm more than willing to take on my share of weekends and after school, but I won't force our son to spend time with me when he doesn't want to."

"You're being too hard on yourself," Edie says. "He's a good kid. Let's have lunch this week, okay? You can tell me what happened with this mystery woman today."

"Assuming she hasn't been arrested yet. Peter would have called by now if it had gotten out of hand, right? You think you've seen everything in this madhouse, and then people start jumping on patients." For all her cool exterior, Veronica couldn't help worrying about the injured cyclist. Still, between Peter, security, and the operating theatre staff, she had to trust in the system for now.

"What team does she play for?" Edie interrupts her fretting.

"I didn't get a chance to check her sexual preferences while she was trying to perform surgery in the hall," Veronica points out, feeling about as reasonable as she's ever been. "She had an actual Swiss Army knife. What next? Sticky-back plastic? Anyway, I think I'm free Wednesday, but you're buying."

"Make it somewhere with a decent wine list and you're on."

Edie runs her own practice, so it's easy enough for her to agree.

Veronica waves her off before turning back to the Monday-morning hum of her department. The paint might be institutional pale yellow, flaking in the corners, and the floor might have the squeak of linoleum worn down by too many trolley wheels and sensible shoes, but it's her kingdom, her domain.

All around her the noises of the hospital continue. The low buzz of the lights overhead, the faint beeping of thousands of monitors, the constant murmur of traffic on three sides of them, and the vibration of trains running underneath.

Another week is starting. Time to get this show on the road. No amount of mysterious military blondes can get in the way of that.

CHAPTER 2

CASSIE DOESN'T EVER INTEND TO get herself into these situations; they just have an uncanny knack of happening to her anyway.

It's not that other people won't eventually see the same things she can—Cassie is no savant—but for most of her career "eventually" has been a luxury her patients could ill afford.

And sure, there are other ways to make a point beside climbing on people. But the critical lack of urgency in this department is what the attractive, dark-skinned doctor, with her perfect hair and her tailored pantsuit, should be yelling about. Not Cassie's well-intentioned attempts to save this man's spleen.

It's a shock tactic of sorts, grabbing the nearest able-bodied helper to wheel them away, but Cassie has little choice. It's been a bad introduction, anyway, and only going downhill from there. There's not much chance of restoring her credibility, other than by getting this bleed under control. Still, there's a defiant little part of her that wants to wave at this Mallick woman like Cassie's the captain of a cup-winning football team on an open-top bus.

An even cheekier part would like to flick her the Vs, but there's something almost too suggestive about that.

Still, at least the theatre staff are more cooperative. Maybe it's Monday-morning lethargy, but when sufficiently barked at, they stand back and make room. They're not entirely subservient, Cassie discovers as she goes about the business of quickly changing into the supposedly unisex scrubs that, in her size, make no accommodation for hips nor bust. She debates whether straining seams or another change is more irritating, only for another officious woman in a skirt that makes her walk like a penguin to come storming in.

"Look," Cassie interrupts before she can receive her institutional scolding. "I'm a trauma surgeon and I've pulled bomb fragments out of more people than you've had hot dinners, so instead of twenty questions, why don't you give me something to sign that gives me temporary privileges?"

"Well, our insurers—"

"I've just interviewed for a job here, so believe me when I say I'm qualified. And the man they're covering in blue sheets over there will likely die by the time you find someone else. Which do you think makes a bigger financial splash?"

"This is highly irregular," the woman answers with what can only be called a harrumph. "As Surgical Manager—"

"Oh, you must be Jean." Cassie sticks a hand out, though she'd rather be sticking it under a tap and getting scrubbed in. "I was sorry to hear I hadn't snagged you for part of my interview panel. Major Cassie Taylor."

They shake hands, and Jean looks pleased to be recognised. The managers always are, especially when they're non-practitioners.

"There is a form for extenuating circumstances," Jean says, rifling through her stack of papers. "And since we're technically on emergency standing, what with the winter overload…"

She drones on as Cassie snatches the proffered form and signs it without looking. Nodding along to Jean's explanation, she backs up into the scrub room and taps the pedal to turn the tap on. From her vantage point she can see the anaesthesiologist arrive and take his seat, surgical cap untied and at least one night of no sleep in his weary expression. Fantastic.

The team turns out to be solid, though. As soon as Cassie steps out in her too-tight scrubs, her gown is slipped on. While one curvy, middle-aged scrub nurse ties the loops down her back at regular intervals, another slight young man is snapping a brand-new pair of latex gloves into place over the sleeves. Mask in place, Cassie steps up to the table and watches her patient settle under the full strength of the anaesthetic.

"For those of you who don't know me," she begins, reaching for the tray of instruments and selecting a ten-blade. "And I suspect that's everyone here. I'm Major… That is, *Ms* Cassie Taylor. I came in today to interview for the Head of Trauma, no doubt competing with some people that you all like and respect. That said, all that matters right now is the life in our collective hands, are we agreed?"

Nods on every side, some more tentative than others.

"I'm going to work very quickly," she tells them, her hands doing exactly that as she opens the abdomen just far enough. "And there's no time for laparoscopy, I'm afraid. Every minute we delay, more of this spleen is compromised. Not only could this man lose his life, but even if we save him, delay means a life of being immunocompromised for no bloody good reason."

A layer of subcutaneous fat—not much; the cyclist is clearly in good shape—gives under Cassie's knife as she continues to make quick deft cuts until her splenetic ground zero is fully revealed. The team move to retract and pack the open incision, absorbing blood even as suction starts up.

"Who's my, uh…helper?" she asks, at a loss for the correct terminology. A man opposite her, the one applying suction with great care, raises his free hand.

"Well, I suppose I'm your registrar," he replies. "Don't have any F2s in yet; they're at some training meeting or other this morning. It's why there were no scheduled surgeries for another hour."

"Really? You can't operate without your grunts? I'm assuming that's what an F2 is?" Cassie asks, raising an eyebrow.

"Well, we have F1s and F2s—they're foundation-year doctors. You know, juniors, House Officers? They do the grunt work—holding things, standing for hours. It's important for their learning to start with the dull, repetitive tasks and—"

"Thanks for the explanation. But surely you must still remember how? Besides, you've done a great job already with holding the suction."

"No, of course, but—"

"Between us and these very competent nurses, I'd say we can handle a little spleen, surely?"

"Absolutely, Major."

"Really, 'Ms' will do fine," she replies. "Going to have to get used to civilian life sometime. Now, hand me that retractor, because this one isn't going to get the job done."

It's easy work in the end; she's more than used to impact injuries. Nobody questions her decisions, simply hands her what she asks for almost quickly enough.

Only when it comes to closing does her registrar clear his throat behind the white surgical mask.

"Usually I do that for the consultant," he explains, almost apologetic.

"Oh, right." Cassie is used to racing through each procedure, start to finish. She doesn't generally have a fleet of waiting juniors. On the best days every pair of hands is usually occupied with CPR and halting bleeding. This is going to take some getting used to.

Assuming she even gets the job, which is looking far less likely after her spree of rule-breaking. She must still be a little demob happy, missing the structure to bounce against.

Scrubbing out doesn't take much time in comparison, throwing everything disposable in the bin and seeking out the nearby surgical locker room to change from scrubs back into her interview suit.

Which, in a fantastic development for an already challenging day, has blood on the jacket and what appears to be bike oil smeared on one thigh. Her blouse hasn't fared much better, but she pulls it all together as best she can.

Cassie has never been one of those women who looks effortlessly put together, outside of uniform which makes it easy. She washes her hands one more time, using damp fingers to try and tame her hair again. Blonde wisps are escaping in too many directions, just like every other time she's tried to fix it herself.

Buttoning her jacket, she's just about to leave when the locker room door swings open.

Of course, it's the woman from earlier. She doesn't have a huge stack of files this time, but she does have that inscrutable "in charge" vibe that Cassie more readily associates with a general.

"Well, if it isn't the gung-ho army medic. How's your patient, Major?"

Is it a plus that she actually remembers the rank? Paying attention for hints of an accent, Cassie hears only that sort of BBC Home Counties polish so beloved of those in a certain social class. Cassie doesn't fancy her chances in a war of words with this one, so she nods towards the operating theatre door instead.

"Yes, I came that way and a very competent registrar is closing," the woman continues in the face of Cassie's silence. "I can assume that means I'm not putting a plus one on the mortality rates for this quarter?"

A bureaucrat. Of course. Makes perfect sense, since they're always the first to get squeamish at the prospect of someone actually taking action.

"He survived. And kept what I'd estimate to be forty percent of his spleen. Enough to spare him a life of drug regimens and avoidable infections."

"Yes, well. I wouldn't make a point of raiding the admission wards for stitching practice. We do actually have processes here. Ones that keep patients alive and people employed."

Jean, bless her and her bustling, comes barging in at that very moment.

"Major Taylor, that was a wonderful job. We were expecting the theatre to be booked out another half hour at least, but I see they're already clearing out. Ms Mallick," she adds in acknowledgment.

"Just lending a hand," Cassie replies, trying to skirt around both women to get to the door. "It seemed like your other general surgeons were all busy."

Jean gives a disapproving glance at the Mallick woman, confirming another suspicion.

"Ms Mallick here doesn't operate on Mondays unless it's emergent. It's not on the schedule."

"Well, I don't think our patient scheduled his bike being clipped by the number twenty-seven bus either, but I understood this was a hospital, not a spa."

"I actually have an entire department to run," Mallick cuts in. "Time in surgery is something that does have to be scheduled. I thought you would have known that, being up for Head of Trauma and all."

"That might be how things run in... Sorry, what's your department called again? Minor Injuries Unit?"

Well, that one lands. Mallick absolutely bristles at the condescension, dark eyes flashing under the stale fluorescent lights.

"The AMU is the first point of admissions for everyone who comes through A&E. I don't suppose you glanced at an organisational chart?"

12

"The way I understand it, non-emergent cases from A&E go to you. The real cases go straight to Trauma, and more often than not straight to theatre."

Jean steps in as voices and tempers rise in tandem. Shame. Cassie could do with a good barney to let some of the day's steeped tension out of her muscles. "Well, we all play a vital role," Jean says. "I'm sure if you do end up in Trauma—"

Mallick snorts.

Cassie isn't going to give her the satisfaction. "I'm sure I've ruled myself out with prioritising the patient this morning, but it was very nice just to be considered."

"Yes, well, you'll be hearing from Mr Travers one way or another," Jean replies. "Do you need a hand getting back to the car park, or…?"

"I can find my way, thanks." Cassie is done with chatty. She lets Jean leave, in case she does want to walk-and-talk her out of there. It's more of a surprise when Mallick doesn't go, too.

With a steadying breath, Cassie makes her way towards the locker room door. She's stopped by an unexpected hand on her forearm. Getting this close to Mallick wasn't intentional, but now she is, Cassie can't ignore the tantalising notes of perfume, something floral and summery despite the drizzling autumn grey outside.

"Don't feel too bad about the job."

"Oh?" Cassie bites back a more sarcastic reply.

"We have a terribly strong internal candidate. I trained him myself, so he's practically hand-picked. Just in case you were holding out hope."

"I'm a big girl; I think I can handle their decision, Ms Mallick."

"Very well."

Mallick releases her grip, and Cassie almost stumbles with a sudden burst of momentum. That's quite enough hospital politics for one day. For a supposed fresh start, this place is making her long for Basra.

"Well," Cassie says, fresh out of witty retorts. "Good-bye, then." At least she doesn't default to "nice to meet you", since it so clearly wasn't.

She strides out into the corridor before waiting for a response, if there is one, and focuses on getting the hell out of there.

13

CHAPTER 3

GOING TO CHECK ON THE interloper is a prime example of Veronica's worst instincts, the nosiness and impetuous decision-making that she's spent years trying to train out of herself.

And yet she does it anyway.

Worse, she lets the kamikaze commando have the last word, which would surprise just about everyone in this building that Veronica has gone toe-to-toe with.

Bustling out of the surgical locker room, she heads straight for the solace of her office. It's one of the larger ones in this wing, two small offices knocked into one quite by accident and never put right. Aside from her desk, a master of bland Scandinavian whiteness that's ergonomically sound in five different ways, there's not room for much else since the meeting table and chairs dominate half the space. She's done what she can to liven it up with some Klimt prints and a few well-stocked bookcases. Her last attempt at cultivating a green thumb has been mercy-killed by the cleaners, so no plants clutter the surfaces.

The laptop she left to boot up before her morning meeting has finally blinked into life. Sunday is always a strictly no work day, the one attempt at disconnecting in her otherwise screen-filled life. Unfortunately that means every Monday morning the thing takes longer to revive than the average drowning victim. There's a requisition form in for a new computer. It might be granted sometime before all their brains are uploaded to Skynet and robots are doing the surgeries.

The bad mood has settled behind Veronica's eyebrows like an incipient headache, and she knows frowning isn't going to chase it away. The brief meetings with this new doctor, this intruder trying to steal Peter's place and

Veronica's plan away, keep replaying on a mental loop. Each time, Veronica thinks of a wittier or sharper remark she might have made, frustrating her afresh with every round.

She's saved from her own obsessing by a rap of knuckles on her firmly closed office door. Lea, barely five foot nothing in her royal blue nurse's tunic. It's only three years since Lea moved to London from Manila, passing the rigorous nursing conversion exams with flying colours. Her glossy black hair is braided tightly, and unlike a lot of staff with a twelve-hour day ahead, she's made the effort to apply lipstick and mascara. Warpaint, she calls it.

Veronica is glad to see her at the best of times, but especially so when Lea has two travel mugs of coffee in her hands.

"It's like you read my mind," Veronica says. "I was too busy snooping over in theatre to swing by the cafeteria."

"Cafeteria?" Lea scoffs. "I'm not that cruel, not on a Monday. I took the scenic route to the Greek place."

"You're brave, fording the stream on Praed Street at this time of day." Veronica takes a first sip, the milky coffee still hot enough to sting lips and tongue just a little. "Sometimes I think why fight it? I should just pick a vein and have you start an IV for me."

"You can take a number." Lea sets her charts down but doesn't take the other free chair. She glances back towards the corridor, as though on the lookout for spies. "Were you checking on your army doctor?"

"She's hardly mine. I just had the misfortune to try and stop her opening abdomens in the waiting room."

"But they let her operate? Only I heard that Jean marched down there to put a stop to the whole thing, finds the woman already scrubbed in and ready to operate. Signed a bunch of forms with a pen between her teeth, just to stay sterile."

Veronica wonders where the impenetrable NHS bureaucracy is at moments like this. She can't order the wrong kind of pens without it being an insurance problem, a budget issue, and a political shit-storm all at once. But now they're offering a walk-in operating theatre to any passing surgeon.

"So you can what? Just waltz in and cut, as long as you know your way around the tools?" Veronica asks Lea. "Sounds more like a hairdresser than a hospital."

Lea shrugs as though she's seen worse. "How was the surgical meeting? People are still chafing at cancelling everything but emergency surgery. The backlog's getting harder to handle."

"Electives have been cancelled because we're overstretched," Veronica reminds her. "And we can't operate on people if we don't have anywhere to put them afterwards."

"I know this." Lea's reminder is gentle. "But there's a lot of unused space. You don't get off the ward much, but we all see it."

"Well, I've made my suggestions." Veronica has finally gotten access to her email, and amongst a hundred needless circulars there's the promised missive from Wesley Travers. She takes great delight in not clicking on it, knowing he'll be on his way the moment he sees the read receipt.

Lea smiles at someone in the corridor before taking a swig of her coffee. "Mr Wickham," she says, stepping out of his way. "I should get going."

Peter comes in to take his habitual spot in the visitor chair, long legs stretched out in front of him as he drops his briefcase to the floor with more theatricality than usual.

"Sorry to bother you before," Veronica says, and he's one of the few subordinates to ever get an apology from her. "I thought I was going to have to rely on your muscle, and you know how I hate to do that."

"Well, gives me an excuse to keep up the tennis." They both know he spends more time on the golf course lately, and the nineteenth hole at that. "Did your blonde spitfire get arrested in the end? It looked pretty close to assault from where I was standing."

"No, in their infinite wisdom, management waivered her into surgery. I assume someone, somewhere has checked her credentials. Don't worry, though, I told her she doesn't stand a chance of the job while you're in the frame."

"I don't know about that." He scrubs a large hand over his face, ruffling his neat hair and making a scratching sound across his designer stubble. "I've had enemas more pleasant than that round of questioning."

"Vivid, thank you. Still, I insist on buying the first bottle of bubbly when you're appointed."

"Now, come along, Veronica. No use putting the cart before the horse." He leans forward, flicking idly at the files on her desk.

"I trained you myself, Peter. There's no better endorsement, remember?"

"Did Edie get off to work all right?"

He's changing the subject. *Uh-oh*. Veronica hides a grimace at the thought of him saying something stupid to blow the whole interview. Unfortunately, it wouldn't be without precedent. "She did. We're having lunch later in the week, if you want to tag along."

"And interrupt you both talking about me?" Peter says, with a lazy grin. "Unlikely, boss."

"Not for long," Veronica wonders again at whether he's blown his big chance, with a little less confidence this time. "We'll officially be peers when you get this."

"You know sometimes," Peter says, apropos of nothing, "I wonder if this isn't all some grand plan, to have your people in place so you can take over the world."

"Is that what you wonder?" Veronica teases, not giving away how close it is to her long game. "Just get the damn job, Peter."

"Yes, sir." He stands to leave, ready to go about his day again. "If you'll excuse me, I have a crop of foundation-year doctors to traumatise into being better at medicine."

"I'll see you out there in a while."

Checking her watch, Veronica sighs that the face is out of sight again. Tugging on the thin gold strap to pull it back into place, she turns to the emails she can ignore no longer. If they're going to get back to full service by next week, it's going to take some wrangling and ingenuity on her part.

It must be done, and it will be.

The sudden burst of optimism is so unexpected she considers checking whether Lea spiked her latte.

"Let's see what Travers wants," she says to her now-empty office with a groan. She's barely five words in before realising her boss wants to offload some work onto her. Typical. That said, picking up another committee place will look good when she's going for his job in the relatively near future.

And as she predicted, he appears in the doorway before she can get around to clicking on 'reply'. He must have been lying in wait somewhere nearby, because she's never seen him break into a run. The executive block isn't far, but as with most places on this hospital campus, "not far" can still be quite a hike. That's not counting their two other sites, the smaller community hospital farther west, and the terribly impressive university that technically owns the whole Trust now.

If Veronica still struggles to keep up with the organisational structure, she can't imagine how unfathomable it is to outsiders. Except Major Taylor, who doesn't even look for rules in the first place, before blithely breaking them.

How does that woman keep sneaking back into Veronica's thoughts? She won't give credence to Edie's earlier teasing, even if it has been rather a while since she dated anyone for more than a string of rescheduled dinners, mediocre wine, and the odd ill-advised play somewhere that prided itself more on being trendy than on hiring people who could act.

"Veronica?"

In her distraction, she realises that she hasn't heard a word he said. "Yes, Wesley," she answers blindly, hoping that's the right choice. Given how he beams at her, it seems to be.

Swiping at his nose with a plain cotton hanky, he picks up from wherever he left off. "Now, we won't let the committee cut into—oh, that's good, *cut* into—your operating windows. I'll make sure it's only the boring admin this interferes with. Scout's honour and all that. Dib dib."

Veronica gives a tight smile, glad her stapler is out of her line of vision, or she might be tempted to staple his gaudy school tie to his forehead.

"Just let Marjorie know when there are dates—she runs my calendar."

"Of course. I hear we had a bit of excitement this morning with one of the admissions from A&E?" He's fishing, and clearly knows exactly what happened already, judging by his smug expression.

"All handled, I understand. Though more Jean's issue than mine, if you need anything for the insurance."

"Oh, we've spoken. Seems Major Taylor has impressed the panel and the staff today."

Veronica snorts. She's staff, and certainly unimpressed.

"I think we have steadier pairs of hands in waiting, Wesley. Don't you?"

"Ah. Well, in theory." He swipes at his nose again, grumbling to himself. "Let the chips fall where they may, et cetera." Travers is the only person Veronica's ever met who actually sounds it out like two separate Latin words.

"Yes, let's." She turns back to her coffee and the screen. "Now, if you'll excuse me, I really must crack on."

CHAPTER 4

BY THE TIME HER TRAIN crawls into the platform at Paddington, Cassie is about three shallow breaths away from seizing the emergency hammer and breaking the window glass to get out. Even as the doors shriek that they're finally opening, it takes an eternity for the mass of bodies around her to turn, gather their coats and bags, check their phones, and fix their ties, before she finally gets to spill out into the relative fresh air of the station. It's about ten degrees cooler for a start, and her overheated cheeks are grateful for it.

Standing out of the flow of commuters, she feigns interest in a timetable board that's not in anyone's way. Fumbling a little past the collar of her coat, she finds the familiar circular discs tucked away on their chain. She turns them over and over between her fingers and waits for a lull.

Before long, the seemingly endless crowd has reduced to a trickle, and Cassie strides out towards the exit. She attempts to pull her ticket from her coat pocket, only to discover it isn't there. With a sigh she begins the ritual turning out of all pockets and her handbag, unearthing coins, thread, three paperclips, and a receipt for a film she doesn't remember seeing.

She doesn't waste a smile and a flustered expression on the soulless bureaucrats who have heard every excuse under the sun. Whether she's paid for her ticket and lost it, or is simply scamming the ticket inspectors, they'll charge her for a full-price single ticket regardless. A punishment for being scatterbrained, and she's been racking those up since primary school.

So long as it doesn't make her late for her bloody first day. Cassie can't quite believe they still offered her the job. She'd given a good account of herself at the panel, and her references were impeccable. Despite the resistance from that Mallick woman, a spot of patient pinching hadn't killed Cassie's chances after all. Part of her was already giddy at the thought of building a formidable trauma centre, one equipped for every eventuality. It would be a blessing after years of making do in the field.

"Can I get a return from Swindon?" she asks the much younger woman at the gate, taking in her shaved undercut hair style and varied piercings. Cassie feels a pang of envy at that self-expression. Even if she had the courage while in the army, most of her superiors would have personally removed all that metal with a handy fridge magnet given half a chance.

"You should really get it at the station," comes the standard reply. "I mean, you could get fined for traveling without a ticket."

"Well, I had one, but now I can't damn well—"

The girl's expression changes from bland indifference to wariness. How many irate passengers turn on her every day?

Cassie's righteous indignation is halted in its tracks. "No, right, I'll remember that. But I'm more than happy to pay for the ticket now."

Maybe it's the way she bit her tongue, or maybe it's the way Cassie maintains eye contact a fraction too long and smiles just right, but there's that flicker of recognition, followed by a sigh.

"Just this once," the girl says with a wink. "I'm here every morning this week, so I'll know if you chance it again."

"Duly noted," Cassie says in appreciation, shoving her wallet back in her bag and rushing forward onto the concourse proper. She glances back and, sure enough, Miss Ticket is watching her walk away. Not bad for a Monday morning. Cassie's not ashamed to admit it puts a little spring in her step and definitely brings a dash of colour back to her face.

What she needs, though, is a large infusion of caffeine, preferably accompanied by its close personal friend, sugar. The nutritionists would have a field day, and while Cassie knows that she should be chasing down a smoothie made up of something green and fruity, her heart just isn't in that kind of good behaviour today. Less physician-heal-thyself, and more physician-treat-yourself.

Besides, new resolutions made on a first day never stick. The sheer bureaucracy of it all still intimidates her, but there should be ample opportunities to keep operating. As far as she could tell from her brief tour of St Sophia's on interview day, their usual idea of trauma is simply the gnarlier car crashes and the worst cases who'll end up in the specialist Burns Unit.

No, that isn't entirely fair. She remembers watching the coming and going on the news, after the bombings ten years ago. The doctors and nurses, who'd also just been on their way to work like any other day, tending to the wounded in bombed-out train carriages and on the ground, had the bearing of grim competence. What London lacks in roadside IEDs and active war zones, Cassie's sure it can make up for in stabbings and occasional flurries of shootings. Whatever this city throws at them, she intends to shape a department that can handle it.

As a Liverpool girl born and bred, she isn't overly familiar with this part of London. Not that she knows the city that well at all. Apart from six months in Albany Street barracks with the Logistics mob, she's only ever been passing through for a few days at a time. Luckily, Cassie has an inbuilt sense of geography, an unshakeable inner compass that settles just as quickly in Kabul as it does in Kensington, but London is uniquely overwhelming in its seemingly endless rush hours.

There's a surge of people on the concourse again, although the crowd is dense but not particularly unruly as they flood mostly from the overhead to underground trains. She's able to bypass the worst of that by making a break for the pedestrian exit and spilling out onto Praed Street.

Through the impressive wrought-iron gates, Cassie sees the hospital's main entrance. Gothic statues welcome and warn all who might enter here. It's crazy that this is her life now, but she can't help feeling it's already a good fit, despite the fizzling knot of first-day nerves wriggling around in her stomach.

There's no nagging temptation to jump on another patient just yet, but knowing her luck, she'll only go and get a reputation for it.

Since she's at least an hour early, Cassie has the luxury of wandering plenty of empty halls. She catches her reflection in some glass doors. No-nonsense grey suit, creamy blouse, low black heels. It's as femme as she gets, and it won't look quite so neat in a few hours. A cursory attempt at first-day make-up, her hair pulled back in the low bun that's served her so well for years, though with every cut, holding it back requires more pins. She's beyond tempted sometimes to shave it all off, but the window for experimentation like that seems to have passed her by.

21

There's a small coffee shop in the last corridor before A&E, which is where she can branch off to her own department. The other fork leads to the Acute Medical Unit, domain of one disapproving Ms Mallick. Perhaps fences could make good neighbours after all.

Cassie orders a dirty chai, something she read about in the free newspaper before the train got entirely packed at Reading. It sounds quite appealing, the cinnamon and other spices she likes in tea, with the shot of espresso to sharpen things up a little.

Secretly she likes the way the barista doesn't flinch. It makes Cassie feel urban, almost sophisticated, to order something that isn't on the painted menu above the counter. It's bloody nice to get a scalding hot drink that doesn't have a faint trace of sand around the cup's edge, without coffee that's been stewing for four hours at a time.

The junction outside A&E is where she foolishly pauses. Cassie knows this bit of the hospital better than anywhere else, and some silly part of her likes that feeling. It's been a long time since anywhere felt especially like home, and she wonders if this is going to be it for her.

"You know, if someone comes out of there with a trolley, you're going to be right in the way."

Great. Just who she wanted to run into before the caffeine had a chance to circulate. Cassie inhales through her nose a little too sharply and turns, extending her free hand.

"Ms…?" She knows fine well, but the hell is she letting this bossy woman think she made an impression.

"Mallick, but we're quite informal in these parts. You can call me Veronica. Everyone else does," she tacks on, presumably just in case it should come across as friendly.

"Cassie, then."

"Not Captain?"

"Major, actually. You just demoted me. But the titles don't matter much when you're dealing with civilians."

"I'm sure."

They've been shaking hands a little longer than strictly necessary, so Cassie drops her hand with minimum fuss. She takes a chance to really look at the woman opposite her, like something out of a classy boutique display with her fitted dress. The bold patterns in all sorts of reddish colours are mesmerising at first glance. Not afraid of real heels either, though the toes are so pointed that Cassie almost winces in sympathy. The pearls on Veronica's necklace match perfectly with the single studs in her ears, but no wedding ring is in evidence.

"I suppose you're not exactly thrilled to see me," Cassie blurts out. This is why she tries not to talk too much. She's really not very good at it. "With your boy and all."

"I'm not going to hold a grudge if that's what you're suggesting," Veronica answers, looking appropriately offended. "It'll just be a shame to have Mr Wickham operating below his full capacity on my ward for a while longer, but things change quickly around here."

That feels more like a veiled threat than the truth, and Cassie feels the prickle of warning at the base of her neck. "Well, I'd really better get on." She steps around Veronica and heads down the fork in the corridor that leads to the Trauma department. "I assume it won't be long before my first surgery."

"Oh, you won't be on rotation this morning," Veronica corrects, taking a step or two as though to follow. "All department heads have the surgical planning meeting."

"Surely that's optional?" Cassie can't believe they're going to ensnare her that quickly.

"Not if you want your department to know what the hell's going on, no. We've cancelled all electives for the past few weeks, for example, which affects a lot of your secondary procedures."

"That's...insane."

"You're welcome to make that point to our bosses and the people who hold the purse strings. See you there."

With that, Veronica disappears down the opposite fork to her beloved AMU, heels clicking. Clearly she doesn't care if Cassie knows where this all-important meeting is. Fine. She can play it that way. Cassie turns towards her new domain with a sudden reluctance. She has made the right call on her future, hasn't she?

Beyond the swing doors she sees beds, monitors, some partly drawn curtains. Everything she expected, as she draws closer step by step.

Despite that, she has the unsettling feeling that nothing about this will be how she expected at all.

CHAPTER 5

PETER IS TAKING ROUNDS WITH the F1s, or foundation-year-one doctors, still a little rowdy and nervous in their little cluster. By the time they progress to foundation year two, garnering the equally uninspired title of F2s, they'll have splintered off by specialties and formed their cliques around who hasn't slept with who yet. At least on this part of their rotation, the opportunities for hijinks are tempered by the on-call rooms being perilously close to Veronica's office. After hours, though, it's apparently fair game, and she tries very hard not to know anything about it.

Gathering her tablet and frowning at the little crack in one corner of the screen, Veronica decides she needs a fresh coffee to face her weekly surgical meeting. They've been running on fumes, resources wise. Plugging vacancies like the head of Trauma can help, even if Veronica vehemently disagrees with the choice.

The trouble is having to give a bunch of departments allocated amounts of theatre time, meaning valuable surgery hours are wasted every week when they're not needed. Then the departments overflowing in surgeries find their patients pushed and pushed. Someone needs to stand up to the bureaucrats who think running a hospital is more to do with a balance sheet than actual medicine.

It could be worse, Veronica knows. She did a fellowship in the States, and while the facilities were almost science-fiction quality at times, the reality of refusing patients who couldn't pay, or bankrupting them in exchange for health care, turned her against that kind of system for good.

God, when did the biggest excitement in her life become fantasising about being the big boss? There used to be no thrill like the first surgery of the week, and now she rarely gets to cut before Tuesday afternoon. Which is usually palmed off on someone else while she puts out an administrative fire somewhere else.

Still, it's the plan. Some people are content to become a senior consultant and use that, coupled with private practice, to see out the rest of their careers. Veronica has plans to shake this place up. She hasn't put in all the time and effort on conferences and training courses not to want to turn it into the best hospital in London. The kind of place they make splashy TV documentaries about for NHS anniversaries, to be horribly populist about it. Let them mistake her as just another pen pusher, just long enough to get the big job in the first place.

At the entrance to the conference room, her happy world-domination reverie is disrupted by that goddamn army surgeon again. They've already met this morning, proving beyond reasonable doubt that the woman really doesn't have a clue what she's getting into. If she thinks the job is all crash carts and daring surgeries, they'll soon kick that out of her. The volume of paperwork alone should have the major running for the hills soon. Although she has at least found the right meeting room.

"Ms Mallick," the woman—Cassie, that's it—greets her. "Nice to bump into you again."

"Veronica, please. Major Taylor, wasn't it? Nice to see another woman at one of these things. Apart from Jean—you met Jean—we're rather outnumbered a lot of the time. I'm sure *that* will give you whiplash after the army. I hear it's a real feminist paradise."

Well. Where the hell did that 'all girls together' solidarity come from?

"Oh, absolutely. Happy to take one for the sisterhood, then," Cassie replies, in an almost conspiratorial way. "Any kind of rank to the seating? Or just hungriest go closest to the pastries?"

"We let Jean take the head, of course," Veronica says. "And then we just seat ourselves as we please. Wouldn't worry about the pastries though; they have a tendency not to be fresh."

Cassie picks up a pain au chocolat anyway, taking a hearty bite as though Veronica hadn't warned her at all. She doesn't even frown. Usually the only decent grub is when the upper echelons are involved. They've been cracked down on for using outside caterers for anything but the executive wing.

Veronica strides around the long, oval table, situating herself at what will be Jean's right hand. Not a bad visual to impart to everyone else, and it's force of habit now more than anything else.

To her instant discomfort, Cassie follows her and takes the free seat next to her. In a room full of otherwise still-empty chairs.

Veronica's irritation is interrupted by other familiar faces trickling in. She makes a point of waving or nodding to everyone in turn, sparing a smile for one or two of the more competent department heads with whom she gets along.

Before long, the presence of Cassie is reduced to the peripheral. The meeting descends almost immediately into its usual territorial pissing contest and adult children squabbling over resources when they should know better. That distraction from Cassie, unfortunately, doesn't last long. She's soon throwing herself into the fray.

"Sorry?" Cassie seizes on a momentary lull. "I'm sure this is all very important, but are we going to be back to full surgery rosters this week, or...?"

The bluntness of the question astounds even Jean, who's heard every complaint in the book as their overseer. Every eye in the room is on Cassie, including Veronica's, but she doesn't wilt despite a pink tinge to her cheeks.

"Funny you should mention that, Ms—" Jean tries to take back control.

"Taylor," Cassie finishes for her.

"Right. Trauma. Typical. Never happier than with some viscera spilling out on the table, you lot. You'll be pleased to hear that we are, in fact, resuming surgery, other than cancer and emergent cases this week."

The room erupts, thrilled instead of disgruntled for once. Jean shushes them with her glasses in one hand, her dark short hair bouncing with the brief exertion.

"That does not mean you schedule everything all at once. Ramp it up, ladies and gentlemen. Anything complicated, you still need the requisite permissions and sign-offs. This is *not* a free-for-all."

Cassie stands, despite the meeting being barely five minutes along. There's a surprisingly helpful urge in Veronica to yank at her wrist and insist that she sit back down.

"I didn't mean start now," Jean adds, her tone just short of wry.

"Well, is anything else in the meeting relevant to Trauma?" Cassie challenges.

"It's not about individual…" Jean actually wilts at Cassie's raised eyebrows. "Although it's more of a general picture, I suppose you can get the gist from minutes. If you have somewhere more pressing—"

Cassie nods and strides right out of the room. Everyone watches her go, like she just stood up to the head teacher and talked her way out of a certain detention. There are murmurs and wistful looks as others contemplate doing the same.

"Right." Veronica is the one to pull their attention back to the front of the conference room. "So how gradually can we get back to full surgical capacity?"

With that, it's just another Monday morning, and the familiar old arguments start breaking out from every corner.

Peter's the first one to notice. They're in Veronica's office and she's just found the words to console him about not getting the job, to be followed up with an offer of a regrettable amount of red wine at the venue of his choice. But then he greets her with, "Is it just me, or are we terribly light on juniors?"

He's right. Where there would usually be a core of at least six on this shift, Veronica spots only one set of pale blue scrubs.

"Skiving? Striking? Locked themselves in a janitor's cupboard again?" It would be nice if all three scenarios weren't equally plausible with this bunch. Veronica's still struggling to remember their names or tell them apart after a month, which is unlike her.

Still, it's days like this that remind Veronica why she's spent her life working towards being in this position. She makes the tough decisions, finds solutions, and watches her team flourish under the pressure. These junior doctors will be no exception, no matter how badly they've been treated with contracts and everything else she didn't have to worry about. Once they come through the doors of AMU, they're her people, and Veronica works bloody hard to send them on in the world as better doctors.

"I'll ask the child left behind," Peter offers, striding over to confront the trembling young doctor, who was quite competently dealing with a patient until a boss showed up. Peter looks the part, in his striped shirt and coordinated tie, the grey trousers clearly tailored. Unusually for this part of the hospital, he still bothers with a white coat over it all, even though it makes the fussy plastic aprons they all have to wear during treatment even more annoying to tie. Not to mention that the shirt sleeves hygiene policy means rolling up both the shirt and the lab coat to the elbow.

This is why Veronica sticks to bare arms or the very shortest of sleeves. Doubly wise given how warm the hospital always is. People think of these buildings as huge and draughty, but the rebuilding over previous decades has made it an insulated shell within a shell, and she could swear that the staff in Facilities keep it warm year round on purpose, if only because it keeps the patients—and possibly the staff—more docile.

Peter takes off for the shortcut through to Trauma, and Veronica follows with a sinking feeling in her stomach. Whatever the juniors are up to, it had better be medically relevant or she's going to boot the whole bloody lot of them to maternity and out of her hair.

Only, when they open the swing doors into the back end of the Trauma ward, there's more activity than even A&E tends to generate. Shouts. Metal clanging. Monitors beeping at maximum volume.

Absolute chaos.

And who, of course, is at the eye of the storm? Cassie Taylor, barking orders, clapping her hands, and even occasionally whooping in encouragement.

Juniors are running from bed to bed, cheered on by the patients awake enough to observe them. Most, given the nature of their injuries or conditions, are mercifully unconscious, and those are the people Veronica decides she's jealous of.

Peter tries to ford the stream of juniors, but he ends up being handed a stack of crepe bandages and is soon lost to the fray. There's only one way to get control of a circus, and that's to charge down the ringleader.

"Ms Taylor?" Nothing. Veronica tries again, but there are so many people clamouring for attention, and every other second Cassie turns around to update figures on a whiteboard. "Cassie?"

That gets her, finally.

"Oh, Veronica, how nice of you to join in! I knew you must be missing surgery, stuck in all those meetings. This will sharpen you right back up."

"Please tell me you're not letting them perform surgery on an open ward."

"What? Oh no, we're running drills. Scenarios, you know. Livens things up for the patients too, instead of lying there waiting for the next drugs trolley. They learn how to triage, and how to cope with sudden deterioration. Mr Sharpe!" She's shouting at a dark-haired man in bed three. "You're currently deceased, sir, don't give them any help!"

"You've stolen my F1s." Veronica gestures to the ones she thinks probably belong to her. The supposedly dead patient lies down with a sigh, apparently sorry to be excluded from the fun. "They have duties to perform, patient care to follow up on."

"And tons of paperwork too, no doubt," Cassie counters, whiteboard marker waving vaguely. "Listen, I don't want to step on any toes, but they're bright kids and they leapt at the chance for something more hands on than chasing down samples and doing rectal exams."

"It's a rite of passage," Veronica argues. "It's how I was trained, and it's all about learning humility. Too many god complexes walk in here. Didn't you have to learn the ropes that way?"

"I went straight from uni to the army," Cassie explains. "We're big fans of hands on there."

"Well, this isn't Chelsea barracks, so you can stand down, Major."

"Chelsea?" Cassie scoffs. "You do know that's the pensioners, right?"

Veronica couldn't give even half a damn. "Send my AMU doctors back to their own ward. Don't make me come looking for them again."

"Or what?"

"Excuse me?"

Cassie nods towards Peter, who's waving an abdominal surgery pack over the head of a short female junior for some reason. *Rosie*, that's it. Definitely one of Veronica's lot. "I'm just not sure what your threat's supposed to be. Anyway, he seems to be in the spirit of things. Do you want your consultant back as well?"

"All of them." Veronica turns on one uncomfortable heel and marches back to her own domain. The nurses clearly recognise the mood and scatter instantly, making sure they're far too busy for eye contact or conversation. Snatching a chart from the nurses' station, Veronica turns her attention to the patient in the first bay.

"Mr Wilson, I understand you're waiting for surgery," she greets him, brusque and professional. She checks the theatre boards on her tablet, confirming her suspicion that Theatre 3 is clear for the next few hours. "Well, it's your lucky day because I'm going to tend to this pesky bowel problem of yours myself."

She clicks her fingers at the first F1 to come scurrying back from Trauma. "You. Prep Mr Wilson for his surgery. I want him in theatre and with the anaesthesiologist by the time I'm changed and scrubbed, understood?"

"But isn't that later with Mr—"

"Did you not *hear* my instructions?"

"Yes, Ms Mallick. I'll get that done."

"Rosie, isn't it?" Veronica demands, barely waiting for the nod in response. "You'll scrub in to assist."

The girl lights up like all her Christmases came at once. Veronica remembers that feeling well, even if she doesn't entirely approve of the long blonde hair streaked with blue. At least it matches the scrubs.

The most efficient surgical prep in recent memory begins in earnest, and Veronica heads for the locker rooms to get ready.

It's bad enough she can't be the fun parent to her actual son, but damned if she'll be the stick-in-the-mud at work, too. That'll show Taylor who's the real teacher. Once word gets round that Rosie's scrubbing in on a complex surgery, they'll all be vying for it. No amount of party games can compare with the real thing, after all. Not to the ones who have what it takes.

As she kicks off her heels and pulls her trusty Nikes from her locker, Veronica startles a little at the thrumming feeling in her veins. She feels rather like she could sprint the entire hospital grounds, possibly hurdle a few benches on the way to boot.

Competition, she realises. Well, isn't that something?

CHAPTER 6

GOD, THIS PLACE IS A killjoy sometimes. Mallick must have complained to someone, because the rest of the week is constantly disrupted by inspections and managers and a minor royal being shown around the ward. Thankfully the nurses are as competent as any Cassie has ever worked with, and they don't need three chapters of backstory to get cracking with patients in need.

The registrars are a solid bunch as well, though they don't have much to do with the F1s and F2s if they can avoid it. Cassie knew on taking the job that this was a teaching hospital, but at their age she'd already been off to Sandhurst for Officer Training. It's frustrating to see them so hesitant, so reluctant to act without permission.

It's not fair to speculate how many of the people around here would cope in a tent somewhere near Kabul, but Cassie can't deny the internal sense she has for sorting her colleagues into the sink-or-swim categories.

"Morning, Major Taylor," Pauline greets her. She's a recent transfer in from Veronica's ward, part of the infinite shuffling and reallocating of resources that seems to go on in this place.

Cassie would prefer to build a team of Trauma specialists, but she knows that it's more important to have capable people in general. Nurses like Pauline are an exceptional asset to any department, so it's very pleasant to have tempted her over to resume the Trauma career she first trained for.

"You look desperate to get into theatre," Pauline continues.

"When am I not?" Cassie replies with a wry smile. She's still in her running gear, having caught an earlier train and changed up her dull route near home for the far more pleasant paths of Hyde Park, a stone's throw from the hospital.

"Only you might have to skip theatre more this week," Pauline suggests, already sorting the charts back into a usable order. "Budget time, all the department heads are groaning about it. Hope you brought your calculator."

"Oh, well, Mr Travers said they had most things in place for Trauma for the coming year. I just need to see if anything's missing and sign off."

"Really?" Pauline raises an eyebrow and purses her lips in a way that never fails to make Cassie laugh. "I wouldn't go telling the others that. Might make you unpopular."

"Unpopular?" Cassie says with a faked gasp. "Oh, how would I live? I'd have to flee the country. Would they take me in Ghana, do you think?"

Pauline pretends to consider. "I don't know, you got any experience living abroad?"

Cassie smacks her forehead. "I knew I should have travelled more. Ah well, I'll just have to stay here and face the music. I think you might have put in a good word for me on the Ghana front, though. I'd love to go back to Accra."

"I might still, but for now I suggest that you get your skinny legs out of those running tights and get ready for the day. It's all very well being Usain Bolt before breakfast, but that's no good to me in the Trauma bays, is it?"

"You make a fair point," Cassie admits. "Try not to admit anything juicy until I've had a shower?"

"I make no promises."

Cassie jogs to the locker room, irritated that her brand-new trainers are squeaking against the linoleum. Not properly broken in, then. It's barely even a detail, but it feels like one more way in which this new life doesn't quite overlap her edges correctly. She isn't prone to panic, but there are isolated moments in this place when she wants to sit on the floor with her head between her knees until the strangeness of it all passes.

It's better, she knows that. No sane person would long for a battlefield. When she changes into her scrubs, she'll feel a little more grounded. She can put her squeaking shoes back on, but she checks her surgical pair is in their plastic bag in the bottom of her allocated locker. Coincidence, of course, that it's the one right next to Veronica Mallick's.

That woman is a piece of work, there's no denying it. She's also incredibly good-looking, in a way that Cassie often finds is wasted on a straight woman.

Also a woman who doesn't put a padlock on their locker. Well, that's incredibly trusting. Cassie knows better than to sneak a peek, at least at first. Nobody ever found a scintillating detail in a room that smells faintly of stale sweat and feet, even though the disinfectant and deodorant do their best to cover it.

Oh, to hell with it.

She eases the door open as though a creaking hinge will summon someone else. Comparison, she tells herself. These established surgeons will have efficient tips and tricks that Cassie and her "one duffel bag fits all" existence could learn from. Even though Cassie's own locker is as neat as it always was for barracks inspection, it's fun to see how the other half lives.

It's not even that exciting. Two silky blouses hanging more or less on the hangers, still in their dry-cleaning bags. Pastel-toned running shoes, new-looking Nikes. So the mighty Mallick does come down from her teetering heels occasionally. A few toiletries, some antibacterial gel in a clear bottle.

There's a little disorganisation in the toiletries, like they've been placed back any old way, but barely a personal touch to be seen. Only on closing the door does Cassie notice the picture tucked into the locker's door frame. A younger Veronica, in a hospital gown of her own. Baby in her arms, taking up her entire attention.

Well. That's nice.

Certainly not disappointing, no sir. Cassie doesn't much care one way or another. Sure, Veronica has captured her attention, and there's a certain *frisson* when they clash over the right way to work, but that doesn't mean Cassie automatically finds her attractive. Well, okay, she's objectively attractive, but that doesn't mean anything. Just the aesthetic. Presuming queerness is a bit like asking for trouble, especially since Veronica looks at her as if everything Cassie says is akin to suggesting they burn the hospital down.

Footsteps outside. Cassie slams the locker door harder than she meant to, shuffling back the few inches to be in front of her own.

The steps keep going, fading as they go down the corridor. Cassie exhales, leaning her forehead against the cool metal in front of her. She can't stay this much on edge all the time, but neither the running nor the busywork on the ward are helping.

It's going to take surgery. A few focused hours of slicing and suturing with nothing to worry about beyond cauterising the next bleed and the steady drone of the monitors.

Trouble is, wishing for surgery as a trauma surgeon technically counts as wishing untold horror on an unsuspecting human body. Even in her worst moods, Cassie wouldn't want that for anyone. What she sees happen to people who never, ever deserve it, has a shocking and permanent effect on perspective.

There's a song stuck in her head as she showers and changes. She splashes out the drumbeats against the tiles, humming where she doesn't know most of the words. The air, something about the air tonight. Even with her patchy and awful knowledge of pop culture, Cassie knows it's something that would be classed as an oldie by now, but it puts the spring back in her step at least.

Then she's dressed and back on the ward, and the surgical gods are smiling after all, because the tight frenzy in the air says they have a heads up from A&E. The most critical and badly injured cases come in that way from the ambulance. Instead of the sedate admissions process and a couple of hours' wait, these patients are express delivered to Cassie's domain.

It's not a tent now. She has staff and facilities beyond even her reckoning, new tech that she's itching to get trained on as well. The more she can do, the more she can help. It's that simple. The registrars have been summoned from the Sister's Office, the ward's unofficial break room, and Sister Pauline isn't far behind them, her expression all business.

"What do we have?" Cassie demands, pulling on her plastic apron and tying it hastily at her back. The buzz amongst the staff heightens second by second, all eyes focused on the swing doors that bring fresh meat to their trauma bays.

"Male, 33, RTC," the first paramedic announces, wheeling his patient right to her. The acronyms are different, but already Cassie is more than familiar with road-traffic collisions; they're some of the most frequent fliers on her service. "We've stopped most of the visible bleeding, but cracked ribs and uneven breath sounds on the right side."

"Let's get him stable and then..." Cassie makes her visual assessment and realises they have some time to work with. "We'll need a CAT scan." She palpates his abdomen. Definitely fluid, but no bruising to indicate that it's blood. A groan from the patient on inspecting his ribs confirms the impact.

It's time to test her team. She has to be able to trust them. They have enough bodies to cope with the incoming patients, and nobody seems panicked or out of their depth.

"Pauline, I'm taking my patient over to Imaging and probably straight into theatre from there. Make sure a scrub team is ready, but get me back here if anyone's patient starts to slip, understood? Oh, and page the on-call general surgeon. I'm going to need an extra pair of hands."

She feels the worried glances from her doctors and nurses as she departs first, but Cassie knows she has to let them sink or swim. It might be nice, in this manageable number of patients, to focus on just one for a change.

Nick is her patient, she learns on first glance at the chart. It's barely filled in, waiting for her to find out exactly what's wrong.

She's busy with that chart as Nick is transferred onto the CT scanner, ready for his internal close-up.

"I was paged?"

Great. Veronica Mallick. "Must be a mistake," Cassie suggests, not looking up from her clipboard. "Got it, thanks."

"Well, I am the general surgeon on call this morning." There's that haughty tone again.

Cassie doesn't feel the same fondness over blouses and a slightly messy locker now. "And this is my patient. Don't let me keep you—plenty of other injuries out there, Veronica." It feels cheeky to revert to first names, even though the invitation was extended to.

"Well, indulge me. What are you looking at with this fine young man? Another RTC?"

"They come in batches, so I'm told." Cassie resents explaining, but it can't hurt to show off her expertise. She checks the screen. "Confirming broken ribs on the right side, and that looks like a small pneumothorax to me, where the third rib is intruding. There's a liver lac, but nothing too dramatic, and that appears to be some free fluid in the abdomen. Repairs won't take long."

"Repairs? We're talking about a man in his thirties, not a Volvo." Veronica reaches for the chart, but Cassie pulls it away.

"I'll be in theatre, there should be a team ready by now. Anything else?"

Veronica looks her up and down for a long few seconds. "No, I don't suppose there is. Best of luck, Ms Taylor."

"Thank you," Cassie replies, quite insincerely. She motions for the orderly and nurse to get their patient back on the move, but just then his monitor starts beeping.

Cassie charges straight through from the observation area, but Veronica beats her to it. Usually a nurse would be on hand with a crash cart, but Veronica goes straight to it, confidently yanking it across to their patient's side.

"He's unresponsive," Cassie says, a brisk warning. This is her field of expertise.

"He's in respiratory arrest," Veronica says by way of clarification. "I'm intubating, now."

"Now, isn't this the point where you'd usually say procedure calls for an anaesthetist?"

"So you do know the protocols." Veronica sounds a little peeved, but the look she shoots at Cassie is almost…teasing. "Thank you," she says to Ana, the nurse who's stepped up to hand over the laryngoscope.

Cassie is itching to get in there and take over, but from the cursory inspection, Veronica is tutting under her breath.

"Okay, blood and swelling here. I can't see the glottis, so we can't go in this way."

"Now, wait a minute—" Cassie tries to interrupt. If they're talking about emergency airways already, this really is her area.

Veronica is having none of it. "Get that bag ready. We're going to need a surgical airway. Size 7Q, and a cricothyrotomy kit, please."

By the time she makes the incision in Nick's throat, Cassie is reduced to standing a safe distance from her elbow, ready with the bag that will squeeze air into their patient's lungs. With the crike incision made, the plastic airway inserted, all that's left for Cassie to do is attach the bag with minimum fumbling.

A few steady squeezes later and Nick's stats start climbing, the portable monitor finally easing back to a steady beep.

"I'll take over, Ms Taylor," Ana says, short blonde hair falling over her face as she leans from the other side of the patient's gurney.

Cassie is quick enough to give it up.

"Thanks for the assist," Veronica says, and Cassie must be hallucinating because that almost looked like a wink. "We'd really better get to theatre."

With that, Veronica stands back and lets their small team leverage the patient back onto the gurney and out into the hall. Small, swift, steady movements. The patient keeps breathing and his portable monitor remains happy.

That went well, all things considered, but as she follows them down the hall, Cassie has to admit she's recalibrating her opinion of Veronica Mallick. Underneath all that officiousness there's a real field doctor, one with good hands and a cool head.

Cassie just wishes those qualities weren't some of her very favourites.

CHAPTER 7

THE KNOCK ON HER DOOR is soft, but when Veronica doesn't answer, it comes again. Persistent bugger, then. Sitting back in her chair, she pulls off her reading glasses with a sigh. Lea almost caught her wearing them last week, and a little bit of vanity persists about the simple fact of weakness in her sight.

"Sorry to disturb." Of course. Hurricane Cassie. Turns patient care into some kind of reality show try-out, and lets the overgrown children masquerading as real doctors call her by her first name. Honestly, Veronica would rather she didn't come visit AMU at all.

Any two doctors having more than one conversation with each other is gossip fodder for the sex-obsessed junior doctors who view the rest of the hospital as their own private soap opera. Although she's discreetly out at work, Veronica can't stand being part of the rumour mill. With Cassie being so… Well, Veronica is sure there's some wonderful new acronym for it all, but she calls it soft butch… It would be putting two and two together to make five.

"I was just heading out," Veronica lies smoothly. "Haven't escaped this bloody desk all day."

"In that case, can I buy you a coffee?" Cassie shoves her hands in the pockets of her scrub trousers. Ever since that first day, Veronica is yet to see her in anything but scrubs. Perhaps she misses the army uniforms and is trying to replicate all that sameness. "Only I think I might need to pick someone's brain, and as my nearest senior colleague…"

Veronica assents by standing, swiping her handbag from under the desk, and ushering Cassie out of the office before her. They make it halfway down the corridor before a brief commotion and a crash cart distract them, but the staff on duty have it handled.

"Thought we were going to have a reprisal of our fun day with emergency crikes for a minute," Cassie says, attempting a joke.

Veronica just nods in acknowledgment. She watches Peter run the code for a moment, barking orders at everyone around him. He really would have been good in Trauma.

"So, the brain picking?" Veronica urges when they set off again. One thing she has learned so far is that the bulk of the conversational burden is going to be on her shoulders. "I suppose you're knee-deep in next year's budget as well?"

"Mmm," Cassie seems to agree. "I don't mind numbers, I really don't. It's everything that comes with it. Lot of forms, don't you think?"

Veronica gives her a sideways look. It's a whole-body exercise in control not to spit out a withering "you don't say". Biting her tongue, she fishes around for a diplomatic answer as they approach the coffee shop with its over-roasted beans and under-filled cups.

"Actually," Veronica says, because decent coffee is a human right, especially for doctors, "come with me."

"Oh?" Is all Cassie can say, before falling into step as they take a side door out of the long corridor, and she keeps pace easily in her rather new-looking running shoes—the better for vaulting over counters or whatever they've been doing in Trauma today.

In her heels, Veronica regrets the shortcut across the little quad, but the ground is hard enough that she doesn't sink too badly.

"We use the hospital coffee shop as a sort of fork in the road, you see," Veronica explains as they duck between two huge buildings out onto the street. "If you're genuinely knackered, it'll do. Not great, but drinkable. Now on a better day, when you've still got some juice in the tank, you use it as your landmark to cut through here and be good to yourself."

She sounds like a fucking travel agent. Veronica doesn't want to speculate as to why she can't just act normally around this woman. It's like being a junior again, trying too hard to make an impression.

Cassie gives the Greek café an approving nod. The scent of well-roasted coffee envelops them as another customer darts out of the door with a cardboard carrier of steaming cups. Cassie seems to think that's encouragement enough and barges right ahead to the counter.

"I haven't eaten," she explains when Veronica appears at her elbow. "Not quite used to having this many options all in one place. Anything you recommend?"

Veronica smiles at Eleni behind the counter. "I'll have my usual double shot latte, and Ms Taylor here will have my lunch special."

"To go?"

"Oh, I've got time to eat here," Cassie says. "Just some water for me, for now."

"You're not one of those people who actually gets their two litres a day, are you?" Veronica can't help teasing.

"Force of habit." Cassie waves it off, taking a seat at one of the handful of small tables in the place, right in the corner of the two huge windows. Veronica has little choice but to follow. "You get good about hydrating when it's not exactly reliable."

"You were in Afghanistan, then? I mean, sorry," Veronica catches herself. "Wading in like this is the salon and I'm asking where you're going on holiday. I appreciate it may not be something a person wants to discuss over lunch. Or even any of my business."

"I was in Helmand for a while, yes. Basra before that. Where there's action they need medics, so... What about you? I mean, you were a steady pair of hands during that emergency crike the other day, but how come every question I have at St Sophia's, I'm always referred to the all-knowing Ms Mallick?"

Veronica pretends the compliment isn't affecting her. It might be nice if her colleagues ever spoke to her that way, but that's just not how the world works. She knows soon enough when they're blaming her for something, at least. "They just know I rarely leave a job undone, that's all."

"Not a bad quality in a surgeon." Cassie pauses to thank Eleni for bringing over a plate of moussaka. "Oh, I'll let you order for me again. This looks delicious."

Veronica feels a little regretful she didn't order some for herself, and they're hardly at the two-forks-one-plate level of acquaintance. "Better than camp rations, I'll assume? Less sand?"

Cassie takes her first bite, eyes fluttering closed in something that looks a lot like bliss. "Just a bit."

"It's funny, I only hear the Scouse come through very faintly." Veronica winces when it sounds like an accusation. There's that blush on Cassie again.

"I've been away from Liverpool a long time. We can't all be posh, you know."

"Hardly," Veronica dismisses with a sip of her still-too-hot coffee. "Just Cambridge rubbing off. Always been a bit of a sponge that way. Comes from not wanting to sound like my parents. You know how it is." A shrug— the end of the topic, hopefully.

"Not to downplay...anything...but isn't medicine the one place where an Indian background is sort of, y'know..."

"Wow, deftly handled, Major. You should be in HR with that tactful discussion of race. I get a fair amount of people assuming my surname is Patel, if that's what you mean. Otherwise? You're right. We're sort of expected to be doctors, especially second generation like me. Ironically, my dad is the one who didn't want me to pursue medicine."

"Really? Old-fashioned sort?" There's no malice behind Cassie's question, more a quiet sort of sympathy if Veronica's reading it right.

"No, he thought it was too strict, too much like selling out. He was a frustrated novelist, for the most part. Always thought he might be the next Salman Rushdie, but then without my mum there was so much to do... Still, he said any daughter of his should have the soul of a poet. We're still waiting for evidence of my first sonnet, unfortunately."

"You lost your mother young?"

"Young enough," Veronica says, though this isn't a part of her history she prefers to share. "She passed when I was seven."

"Sorry. You'd think I'd be better about that, since I was twelve when I lost mine. Didn't have a dad around to disapprove of me, though."

Veronica lets that rest for a moment, watching Cassie stab at the side salad with her fork. She's already shared more than she usually would, so asking Cassie the same in return is a commitment of sorts. It's much harder to ignore someone when you know them as a person. "You live nearby?"

"Not yet," Cassie says with a more pronounced frown than earlier. "You read about London and housing in the paper, of course, but it's horrendous

41

out there. Still, even a Dickensian hovel would be an upgrade on commuting for over an hour each way from Swindon."

"Yikes, yes," Veronica agrees. "Why there?"

"My great-uncle's place. My inheritance, I suppose. He took me in after my mum... He's the reason I went into the Forces. When he finally shuffled off at ninety, I thought it might be time for me to try the real world."

"Regretting it yet?"

"Things blow up less, that's a plus. Otherwise? Jury's still out."

Veronica's just about to make a terribly witty remark about judge, jury, and executioner when the café door jingles open. Normally that wouldn't be enough to distract her, but she's always been a little spooky when it comes to sensing her son's presence.

"Daniel?"

"A'ight, Mum?"

"I hope you've got a very good reason for why you're not still in double something or other. I want to say Maths, but I hear it's French you've been skipping lately."

"Yeah, *merci*," he cracks, sitting his gangly frame in the empty chair next to her. "Can I get something to eat?"

"Are you coming to mine for dinner?" Veronica asks. "Only I haven't seen you in two weeks, so a little notice would be nice. And if you are, you're not spoiling your dinner, so get your eyes off that display case."

He rolls his eyes at her, turning his attention to Cassie. "You new?"

She shrugs at him, eyes shrewd. "Might be."

"Daniel, behave. This is Major Taylor, and she's running the Trauma service at St Soph's."

"Major?" He lights up like a skinny Christmas tree. "No way, you're army? No, wait, when did they let girls in the Marines?"

"How do you know I'm not navy? Or RAF?" Cassie questions him, quickly scooping up the rest of her side salad, watching him the whole time.

His hair is getting too damn long, Veronica notes with a frown. He gets the glossy dark hair from her, and though a donor makes up the rest of his DNA, Veronica could swear she sees a hint of Angela in his big brown eyes and plump lips. Maybe every parent assumes their own child to be the most gorgeous of his peers, but Veronica would swear it under oath. It's been the case ever since he was toddling. She never understood why Angela didn't like to focus on compliments about his appearance. Then again, not understanding things like that is part of why they're not together anymore.

"Because the ranks are different, innit?" Daniel sneaks a glance, but Veronica won't give him the satisfaction of wincing. "Like, when I'm flying bombers in a couple of years, I'll be going for Squadron Leader, not Major."

"A couple of years?" Cassie sounds sceptical. "You must be cramming a lot in, with a degree, and officer training and all."

"Okay, a few," Daniel corrects with a sigh. "Oh! You can be my referee, right? When I do my forms."

"Danny, please. Let Cassie finish her lunch, and don't be so presumptuous. She doesn't even know you, let alone the fact that this phase of yours will be over in six months, just like dinosaurs and supporting Arsenal."

"To be fair, everyone should get over supporting them," Cassie teases. There's that Liverpool bleeding through again.

Veronica doesn't have the slightest bit of interest in sport, though she'll sometimes put the Radio Five cricket commentary on while she works on a weekend, a rare bit of nostalgia.

"So what is it you're really here for?" Veronica doesn't mean to sound so harsh, but there's a long day still ahead of her. Having to cut out early to order a takeaway and listen to fibs about how much homework has been done wasn't on the agenda. If she was really annoyed, though, she'd cook for him. "Cash, food, combination of the two?"

"Feeling the love there, Mum. I came by the ward, but Lea said I just missed you. Figured you'd be here."

"Danny... I have to get back. Are you coming to mine tonight? Because you'll have to wait for me a little bit, unless you've got your key."

How did he get so grown up, shuttling between parents on his own? Hopping buses and Tubes like any other streetwise city kid, his free travel card burning a hole in his pocket at the best of times. It was only a year ago they decided he needed his own key for both houses, their nagging parental guilt overwhelmed by the need to know he could always get inside, to safety, should the unthinkable come to pass.

"Nah, I'm back at Mum's. You're safe."

Cassie chokes on something—the last of her lamb, presumably.

"But I ran out of stuff to read again," he continues.

"London still has libraries, last I checked. I appreciate they might not for much longer with this government, but still…"

"Mum…"

"I'm giving you ten pounds, and I will check what you bring home with you, so don't even think about fried chicken and loitering, or whatever it is this week."

He swipes the crisp note from her hand barely a second after it leaves her purse, circling the table to plant a sarcastic kiss on her cheek. "Thanks, Mum. See ya."

They both watch him go, and Cassie pushes her cleared plate aside.

"Nice kid. I didn't know they read anymore," Cassie says when the silence stretches out too long.

Their table is cleared by Eleni, who takes one look at Veronica and doesn't ask if she'll be sticking around for seconds. Since her purse is out, Veronica puts down more than enough to cover them both, which only sends Cassie scrambling to pay her way.

"It's on me," Veronica insists, rubbing at her temples once she puts everything back in her handbag. There's the threat of another stress headache, and that's the last thing she needs with the afternoon she has ahead. "Did we ever get to the problem with your paperwork?"

She stands to leave, which isn't entirely fair of her. It's not really inviting Cassie to unload her issues now.

"You know what?" Cassie stands, too. "It's best if I go as far as I can on my own. No point dropping it all in your lap."

"Well, if you're quite sure—"

"And what your boy said about the references… I mean, come the time, if it helps…"

Veronica snaps before she realises it's happening. "Daniel won't be joining the military, thank you very much."

"You say that like—"

"I really must be getting back. Now you know where the good coffee is, so enjoy that."

Veronica doesn't wait for the rest of the polite protest, booking it out of there as fast as her heels will take her. She must look like one of those uptight waddling people who do marathons without actually running.

She's not going to think for one more second about why she might be so flustered. There's work to be done.

CHAPTER 8

"Do you need another pair of hands, Ms Taylor?" Pauline asks as Cassie and her team greet the arriving gurney from A&E.

The Trauma Team page went off seven minutes ago, and it's felt like a bloody lifetime waiting for their patient to arrive. It's time Cassie's traitorous brain fills with fleeting thoughts of Veronica Mallick and her rudeness. In the face of Cassie offering a sincere favour—to help Daniel pursue a military career—it had been thrown back in her face like she'd said something offensive. Even though Cassie has given the damned woman every opportunity for a quick word, possibly an apology, Veronica has sailed on by. The only upside from that whole personal conversation has been a new reliable source for Cassie's caffeine habit.

Finally the patient is brought in, and the Trauma team quickly add to the strapping and supports the paramedics have used to immobilise their fall victim. There's some discrepancy on where exactly their man fell from, with competing reports saying he went right off Waterloo Bridge into the Thames, but it seems more likely he went over one of the concrete stair landings on the South Bank, given that he's almost bone dry.

"Do we have ID?" Cassie barks at whichever nurse is fumbling with clothing for a wallet. Then she sees the glint around his neck. Just when she'd almost gotten out of the habit of checking there first. "Never mind! We've got dog tags."

Cassie grips the table with one hand and touches the battered steel on a chain with the other. The patient is intubated, clothes being cut from him, but they're definitely civvies. The metal is warm from being between his skin and the light sweater, and that first contact is enough.

She closes her eyes.

Not now.

Sound fades out, the shouts garbled and distant enough that they might be talking in Arabic. The world reduces to the heartbeat beneath her hand, and she only knows they're all still in motion because she stumbles over her own feet.

Then a hand on her arm. Pauline, concerned now. "Ms Taylor?"

"We'll need an orthopod standing by." Cassie grasps at the visible problems first, and broken bones are not the priority unless they're poking anything valuable. Any spinal involvement is mostly neutralised, and they won't get to investigate that until any bleeds or threats to breathing are neutralised. "Neuro and cardio—put them on a warning, but it's too many cooks right now." As the shirt comes off, a badly distended abdomen shows where most of the damage is done. "General. Get a general surgeon into theatre with me, now."

The short, stocky paramedic to her left chimes in then. "Definite abdominal bleed, we had time to do the portable ultrasound."

"Thanks, um…"

"Alan," he supplies. "Heard we had ourselves a GI Jane working here now. Think he'll make it?"

"That depends on the next thirty minutes," Cassie explains. "Check back with the desk and they'll give you updates. Or so they tell me."

"Then let me get the hell out of your way," Alan finishes, stepping aside as they get the trolley rolling. The dash to emergency theatre is mercifully short, and they move the patient as gingerly as possible.

"We need at least five units of A-pos," Cassie barks, pulling the chain of the dog tags free and handing them to a gloved nurse before ducking into the scrub room. "Service number is on there, get it looked up for medical history."

She doesn't need to relay the other details: the surname and gender identifier are self-explanatory and little help for operating. Hopefully the last bit of information on there won't be necessary, because the RC for Roman Catholic suggests they'll need last rites if it comes to that.

But it won't. Cassie's pulled patients back from much worse than this, and with a lot less to work with.

The on-call anaesthetist is already at work, and the intubation switches from the manual bag to ventilator. Cassie runs the brush hard over her

46

skin, the antibacterial soap stinging in its pleasant way. Impatient though she is, she gives it the full three-minute scrub, before jogging out to the waiting gown and a double-gloving that the nurses bundle her into with consummate care. They're good; this is a good team.

The spare surgeon won't be long and, regardless, Cassie is going to have to get in there and stop the bleeding one way or another. She steps up, and the scrub nurses look at her for guidance on which part of the patient to cover and which to expose to the scalpel's blade.

"Just top and tail for now," she instructs, and the blue sheets are adjusted accordingly, leaving a surgical field from nipple to hip. Of course he's fit; Cassie clocks the six pack and defined obliques. A glance at his passive face above the neck brace, the buzz-cut ginger hair. The sheet is unfolded further, taking him out of view. Not a private, she has the distinct impression. Sergeant feels a better fit for him somehow. Sergeant Baros it will be for now, until the service number brings back the rest of his details.

A couple of F2s arrive, ready for the holding and catching duty they're always stuck with. The blood is delivered, and the first pouch hung in readiness. Cassie holds out her hand, and the scalpel is perfectly placed within a second.

She could get used to this kind of efficiency. The speakers have the hiss and low crackle of being turned on without sound playing through them, but eventually the strains of classical music start to seep through.

"Who's playing that?" she asks.

The anaesthetist pops up sheepishly from her stool. "I don't think we've met," she says in a hurry. "Dr Hamann. The techs gave us Bluetooth access, since most surgeons like some background noise?"

"Well, this one does." Cassie has to keep her eyes on where she's cutting. "But something with a bit of life? This is what I put on when I can't sleep."

"Sure, got a request? I've got everything."

"What's that song..." Cassie feels the twitch in her hands to drum it out. "The air tonight?"

There's a sudden, awkward silence before Dr Hamann replies. "You mean, like, Phil Collins?"

"Maybe?"

"O-kay."

There's a snicker from the F2s, so Cassie shoots them a glare that usually makes subordinates a bit jelly-like in the knee region. It works, too.

Moments later, the familiar song is coming through the speakers and Cassie is through the subcutaneous fat and ready to check organs for damage. Of course, even the first experimental prod has an unpleasant sloshing of blood, something that doesn't bode well for how much has been lost already.

Cassie looks at the monitors. Heart rate has stabilised with the anaesthetic, but nothing's in a particularly promising range. She calls for suction, and it's ominous how quietly it works. No air and blood to make it noisy, just blood to suck up and lots of it. Damn.

"I was summoned?"

Of fucking course. Who else would the on-call general surgeon be on a Friday afternoon, more than two weeks since they last spoke directly?

"Ms Mallick, I'm going to need you in here." Cassie manages to summon some professionalism in the face of wanting to ask for just about anyone else. The damage is considerable, but at first glance it can be salvaged. It means working quickly—she's already reaching for the cauteriser.

Making space on the opposite side, Veronica is quick to plunge her freshly gloved hands into the fray. That alone is shocking. Cassie expected to have to explain or argue for a course of action, but it seems jumping in for a collapsed airway last time out was no fluke. The queen of paperwork is the real deal when it comes to surgery.

"Bloody hell," she says, meeting Cassie's eye over their surgical masks. "Spleen, liver, and I don't like the look of this either. You zap, I'll stitch?"

"We've hung some blood—"

"Can someone get the salvage machine up and running, please? It should be already." Veronica manages to order people around without entirely taking over. "It cleans the existing blood and makes it ready for re-transfusion. We'll need fewer bags of blood."

"Oh." Cassie has learned a lot about the advances while she's been working mostly on portable kit, but that's a nice upgrade. "Well, isn't it nice to have new toys?"

They work instinctively, the blood flow slowing with each minor save they make. Once or twice their hands bump, the nature of the beast in something as limited as an abdominal cavity. They direct and redirect mostly through murmurs and nods, working around, over and under each other until the suction nozzle finally starts to encounter air and not just a pool of blood.

It takes a considerable shift at the coalface, but by the time Cassie is ready to hand off to the paged neurosurgeon and orthopaedic surgeons, she's buzzing as though she'll never be tired again.

Scrubbing out, she can't keep still at the sinks, lightly bouncing from one foot to the other like she's in a very small boxing ring. It earns her a quizzical glance from Mallick.

"You were good. In there." Cassie fumbles the compliment, but she means it.

"Wrote me off as a pen pusher, even after last time, didn't you?" Veronica says. "I did tell you, I love surgery when I get the time for it. You've got incredibly quick hands."

An innocuous comment, professional appraisal from a colleague. And yet Cassie's cheeks are burning a little. She wishes she still had the paper mask to hide behind, but has to settle for turning away while untying her scrub cap. The safety she felt on presuming Veronica straight was obliterated over Greek food, talking about the son's other mother. Now there's the possibility that saying just the right thing—or in Cassie's case usually the wrong thing—could be construed as flirting, or showing an interest. That is far more than Cassie's surgery-hyped brain can process.

"Never really had time to be slow, I suppose."

"He's one of your lot, I heard?"

Cassie tenses. Their last conversation about all things military hadn't exactly gone swimmingly. She nods, not trusting herself to say more yet.

"Well, they'll have his information by now. No doubt a family will come rushing to his side. Strong lad like that, he might even walk out of here." Veronica leads the way back through to the locker room, looking less than polished for once with her formal skirt and comfortable running shoes for surgery.

Cassie doesn't need to change, confident her scrubs were well protected by the gown. For the sake of something to do with her hands, she trades out her own running shoes for the lighter pair in her locker.

Pauline bustles in then, smiling at each of them.

"We found your boy. Reached out to his unit, but apparently he doesn't have much by way of family. They'll send someone over tomorrow, assuming he makes it through." She hands a folder over to Cassie, the start of his patient file.

Cassie opens it greedily, needing detail to chase away the impending sense of dread. Steven. Steven Baros, rank of sergeant. She'd been right. Thirty-three years old. No spouse, no children. Parents deceased and no mention of siblings. A copy of his army medical records sits tucked in behind the biographical data, paper still with a trace of warmth from the printer.

He'd seen active duty, then, and picked up a couple of bullet wounds for his trouble. There are some scratched notes about shrapnel with abbreviations everywhere that will mean little to civilians. Cassie files each detail away as a check to make later, before handing the paperwork back.

"We got the bleeding under control, so the others have to do their part now," Veronica explains for both of them.

"He's in the best hands," Pauline agrees, before taking her leave.

Cassie spends a long time on her second shoelace, almost forgetting how to tie a knot in the first place. In the thick of it all, the familiar role of treating a fallen solider had been routine, almost welcome in its familiarity. Now she has the queasy feeling of two worlds colliding, of the army still reaching out to her despite her decision to walk away. Especially since this isn't even the nearest hospital. There must have been some hidden forces at work on this one.

"Is all this okay?" Veronica asks, sitting on the bench next to Cassie and slipping her heels back on. The black pencil skirt comes with a crisp white blouse, and it seems somehow miraculous that it can escape surgery without even a drop of blood.

Part of Cassie wants to have blood on her hands now, all the better to smear that pristine surface with. "You don't look like you're struggling with the horrors of war or anything, but I think we both know appearances are usually deceiving on that front. Just thought I'd check."

"No, I'm just grand." Cassie doesn't want sympathy from this woman, not when it's so close to pity. Her hand goes to the chain around her throat, the same chain that holds two identity discs of its own, just like Steven's. "I promise if I become a gibbering wreck and start playing *Ride of the Valkyries* too loud, you'll be the very first to know."

"Right. Well."

"Yes," Cassie agrees to nothing in particular. "How's Danny? Onto a new phase yet?"

Veronica frowns. "Alas, no. Seems meeting a real-life army medic has only spurred him on. My ex is thrilled with me, I can't tell you how much."

"So sorry," Cassie says, grinning.

"What about that paperwork of yours? Did you ever figure it out?"

"Fine, I think. It's all these codes for things that take up the time. I know where the duodenum is, not what an AFSR2001 stands for."

"You definitely don't want that one. There's a starting hint for you."

"I'm pretty sure it's in there already," Cassie argues.

"Well, I hope you haven't been paying your supply runs in cash, because that's for advances. Same in every department."

"Oh, then I've remembered it wrong," Cassie says, annoyed that her usually flawless memory would choose now to go AWOL on her. "Anyway, back to it. Thanks for the assist."

"See you around, Cassie," Veronica says, watching a little too intently as Cassie fusses with her key on its chain. "Just let me know if you need me to scrub in again."

"Will do." Cassie is the first out of the door, turning towards the safety of her Trauma ward. They should be getting ready for Baros. There's no way they'll be able to move him to a lighter-staffed ward, not for weeks, probably.

She forces herself not to turn around at any point, just to catch Veronica walking away. No matter how good an assist, or how thoughtful Veronica had been to check on her, Cassie is not going to be anything other than professional. Who knows what she'll do next to piss off Veronica? There's no point in getting invested.

Her resolve holds until the corner, and she turns in time to see those shapely legs lead the other surgeon right back into the AMU.

CHAPTER 9

IT'S BEEN A WEEK SINCE they operated on that squaddie together, and Veronica still finds herself daydreaming about the near-perfect surgical experience.

It's taken a frighteningly long time to reach the top of her game as a surgeon, and indeed for many years of the training she had that seemingly universal experience of being trusted to do very little. In the rare time she catches one of those American medical dramas, it always makes her laugh to see everyone looking like a model, with more lovers than they have hairstyles—always a lot of both. They show people barely old enough to complete her foundation programme jumping in to perform complex surgeries single-handed. Even now, when completely in control of an operation and responsible for the patient, a small part of Veronica still expects a more senior surgeon to come in and take over the fun parts.

She finds herself replaying that surgery far more than any of her recent ones. Usually it's her own nitpicking that does it—fixating on the one thing she didn't do quite perfectly, moments where she lost control of a bleed, or some unexpected complication.

It was different this time. Working with another surgeon is almost never that smooth right off the bat. There's usually a clash of egos or too much politeness. Being in each other's way or arguing over the best approach. Yet she and Cassie had worked as though they had agreed every move in advance. That compliment about her quick hands was the minimum appreciation Veronica could let herself express; Cassie was exceptional from start to finish.

It's a quality that has done very little to diminish something Veronica is having increasing trouble denying: Cassie Taylor is damned attractive.

And, unless Veronica is mistaken, she's batting for the same team as herself. Veronica knows better than to read every short hairstyle and sportiness as queer, but there's something undeniable about Cassie that Veronica just recognises.

This strapping young sergeant is hanging in there at least, though he's had spells under with the spinal experts and a brief panic with his heart that's taken the self-professed 'cardio gods' two attempts to stabilise.

"You okay?" Lea cuts through the fog of distraction, handing over a bottled water that matches her own. Grateful, Veronica twists the cap and takes a long swig. "I think Peter's looking for you."

"Isn't he in surgery?"

"No, the locum took it—she's vascular too. He's been out somewhere, maybe it's about that."

"Well, tell him to wait in my office, I just need to check on a patient in—"

"The sergeant is stable so far today," Lea fills in. "Trust me, there's a line of nurses and orderlies checking on him. Not to mention Ms Taylor. She actually let someone else take a surgery yesterday and stayed at his bedside doing paperwork."

"Will wonders never cease." Veronica knew that already, but she'd rather get caught up in the narrative of the stricken Action Man than have her staff and friends notice that she's particularly interested in the actions of Cassie Taylor. "I'll get back to my office, then. Let Peter know where to find me."

Peter strides through the open door a matter of minutes after Veronica situates herself, preventing her from getting lost in a journal article from the list creating angry red unread notifications in her app. The trouble with reading them on her tablet is that she still sees all the alerts for everything else, and rarely gets more than a page without interruption.

"Don't tell me you've been off checking on our fallen soldier too?" He collapses into the visitor chair with the muscle relaxation of a man who's just run a half-marathon. "I'm all for a bit of heroism, but you'd think you people had never seen multiple ruptured organs before."

"I believe it's more the nature of the cause," Veronica points out. "Saving an old lady from a mugging, only to be tossed off a concrete staircase?"

"Yes, bad enough the little bastard traumatised the old woman, but he couldn't have just run instead of hurting the only one who stood up to him? You really think you've seen the worst of people, and then…"

"Yes. And then," Veronica says in agreement. "Despite all that, you seem to be in a suspiciously good mood?

"I am, in fact." Peter clasps his hands and leans in a little. "I've found a way to get over my little disappointment about the Trauma job."

Oh goody, he has something to confess. Veronica has been here before, from him not studying for his Primary exam to become a Fellow of the Royal College of Surgeons, through to him proposing to Edie without a ring.

"Turns out I'm leaving you after all, darling," he continues.

"Won't you think of the children?" She gestures vaguely to the ward, where harassed juniors are scurrying from bed to bed, each looking more sleep-deprived than the last. "You're not serious? I'm sure Ms Taylor is pleasingly dramatic, but there's no way she'll last here under this kind of scrutiny. She thinks paperwork is an optional extra in the NHS. I mean, come on…"

"She's good, Vee. I know it, you know it. Any chimp with a typewriter can get to grips with the admin sooner or later. Or find a willing subordinate to palm it off on. She keeps up the action teaching, and reviving people that A&E have written off, and there's no one who's going to dislodge her."

He wags a finger in her direction, putting her back up for once. "Not even you, so you can stop plotting against her if that's what you're doing. I hope it goes without saying that I appreciate everything you've done for me over the years. And, uh, well, if that continued just long enough for a top-notch reference, my new bosses over at the Kensington would appreciate it."

Oh. Well, that stings. Some hospitals are especially equipped for certain types of surgery or have additional splashy facilities the others don't. It's another twist of the knife in Peter not getting the Trauma role like he was supposed to.

Bitter? Veronica doesn't know the meaning of the word.

"I see." She tries to keep the bite from her words, but it's futile. "Well, I'm sure you'll have fun there. Edie will be glad you're not fleeing to the countryside at least. So what will you be running there? The One Direction in-grown-toenail ward? Getting into the Richard Branson cafeteria line?"

"Don't be like that, please?" Peter is instantly wounded, and it honestly seems as though his pale grey shirt might start seeping blood, so convincing is he in his complaint. "They're still fighting the fight like the rest of us. It just…wouldn't be horrible to look at something other than chipped lino floors and badly painted patient rooms?"

"If interior design is your deciding factor—"

"Veronica, they've got the senior spot and St Sophia's doesn't!" Peter raises his voice, which is almost unheard of. "That's what it comes down to. Please, try to understand. You'd move on if it helped your career. Cassie has the job, and I don't."

"Cassie now, is it?" Veronica asks. Surely Cassie hasn't been on a charm offensive to win over even her competitors? Veronica can see where they'd get along, though. Peter fancies himself a bit of an action hero in the way too many men do.

"Oh, come on, she's hardly my type," Peter says, in that slightly bored way he has. "Speaking of my type, though, Edie is thrilled I'm not dragging her to the countryside, and she wants you to have dinner with her tonight. I do too, since it means she can then take you to whatever museum it is tonight, instead of me."

"A little culture really won't kill you, Peter. If you'd ever set foot in it, you'd know that the V&A is—"

"I'm sure that both Victoria and Albert would be proud of it, but it's still a museum full of dresses and who knows what. So, can I tell her you're game? I know it's short notice, but I have a pile of forms to get through, as you'd expect."

"Fine, but dinner's on her."

"Fair. She'll text, I'm sure."

Veronica stands when he does, ready to see him out. Despite her hurt at him leaving, she does the friendly thing and walks around the desk. Where others might make the mistake of going in for a hug with her, he gives her a strong, enthusiastic handshake instead.

"I knew you'd see it my way eventually." His smile is pretty relieved for someone who claimed to be so certain. "Have fun with my missus."

"How could I not?"

They eat at a middling Scandinavian restaurant where the chef's idea of authentic Swedish food begins and ends with herring. The wine goes down well, and Edie links her arm in Veronica's once they step out into the late summer evening, heading down for the extended hours at the V&A's newest design exhibit.

Truthfully Veronica has never been one for museums and galleries, although it's always been the done thing on every city break. Even then, she steered Angela and groups of friends on those weeks and fortnights towards ruins and crumbling temples, finding more interest in castles that contained a thousand years of living history with real people, rather than the canvases and marble of a few rich people who would otherwise have been lost to the sands of time.

The trips to the British museum with her father hadn't helped. His favourite habit, as an amateur historian, had been to tour the endless halls and corridors with conspiratorial whispers about what had been stolen from which part of the old Empire, and how much blood had been shed.

Maybe that's why the only museums she can tolerate, often for half a day at a time, are the surgical and medical ones that others find macabre. Edie certainly keeps teasing her about how many disorders that might be a symptom of.

So tonight: impossibly gorgeous dresses once worn by minor royals. The craftmanship can be admired, if nothing else. Plus, Edie is a member or a patron of just about everywhere interesting, so that means plentiful wine and lots of semi-scandalous gossip.

They're walking down the wide expanse of Exhibition Road, still rehashing Peter's decision, when Edie suddenly stops.

"Isn't that her?"

Veronica cranes her neck, trying to look in the same direction as Edie seems to be. She doesn't recognise anyone, hardly unusual in the sheer scale of London crowds.

"Your GI Jane," Edie adds for clarification.

"How do you know what she looks like?" Veronica demands.

"Didn't correct me on the 'your' this time," Edie announces, suddenly triumphant. "And because I looked her up, once I found out she was the

56

competition. No social media—another one of you Luddites. But she's certainly made the papers a few times. No wonder the panel were all over her."

Veronica feels a little trapped. She's barely spoken with Cassie since they operated together, other than a splash of small talk between meetings or nods in the corridor. It would be the easiest thing in the world to carry on blithely down the road, with the bustling London footpaths there's no reason to see a familiar face in the crowd.

And yet she veers across three lanes of determined commuters and evening diners alike, just to put herself in sight range.

"Ms Taylor." *Well, shit. What's with the formal greeting now?* "How nice to bump into you." *Nope, abort conversation. Retire to far-off land, relearn social conventions and art of small talk. Now.*

"Veronica?"

Oh God, is that actual concern? I must look like I'm losing my mind. Time to use Edie as a human shield. "Edie, this is the famous Cassie Taylor. Cassie, this is Peter's wife—"

"Dr Hyatt-Wickham," Cassie finishes, practically diving in to shake Edie's hand. "I saw your talk on post-traumatic therapies a few years back. Absolute game-changer."

"Oh, well aren't you a charmer?" Edie holds the handshake longer than is strictly necessary. "How's life in Trauma? Had any limbs thrown at your head yet?"

"… No?" Cassie looks downright disturbed.

"I had a traumatic rotation, you might say," Edie half-explains. "It's why I stuck to the more bloodless kind of medicine, in the end. Having fun working with Veronica? Don't let her ride you the way she does all the other department heads, now."

Veronica's choking sound sounds mercifully like a regular cough, but it still leaves her wanting to strangle Edie for each Irish-lilted word. Time to redirect. "I heard you've been babysitting the sergeant. Any news?"

Cassie beams. "He's awake! In considerable pain, of course, but we're managing it. Not sure he grasps the extent of his injuries, but we'll have time. I was just heading out to meet a friend from the same unit. Put all their minds at ease, since we can't have much in the way of visitors yet. Infection is still the biggest threat."

"Well, that is good news."

"Yes, isn't it?" Edie interjects. "In fact, if you want to really get up to speed, we're heading to an event just down the road. Plenty of free wine before you have to go and face that tough conversation."

"Cassie clearly already made plans to visit the soldiers," Veronica points out, starting to steer Edie away as she addresses Cassie. "See you tomorrow? You're on shift?"

"Yeah, yes," Cassie says, moving off herself. "See you then."

Veronica lengthens her strides, practically dragging Edie along with her. It's only a matter of time before the inappropriate comments come, and she intends to be well out of earshot.

"Well, well, well," Edie says, as they approach the traffic lights to cross. "Looks like someone's finally back in the game."

"Don't be ridiculous!" Veronica knocks it back just a fraction too quickly, cringing as she does. "One, no confirmation on the queer front."

Edie is incredulous. "Yeah, right. I got the once over and you certainly got more than that. That woman likes women."

"Two. Unprofessional. I don't...*you know*, where I eat. And yes, I'm anticipating any joke you want to make right now about eating. Three? I'm fine, just as I am. I have work, I have Danny, and I have a bunch of certifiable friends. No further complications required."

"Fine." Edie holds up her hands. "There's nothing there. Consider it dropped. Only... Actually, it doesn't matter."

"Only what?" Veronica asks.

"You do realise that you've looked back in her direction about ten times while telling me all that, don't you?"

"I didn't..." Veronica catches herself doing it, even in the midst of her denial. "Fine. She's not entirely unattractive. Satisfied?"

"Oh, darling," Edie says, words wrapped around a tinkling little laugh. "There might just be hope for you yet."

CHAPTER 10

"COME ON, SERGEANT." CASSIE SAYS it gently, a coaxing more than a command. "Up and at 'em."

A grunt in response. Not quite the chats they've been having over the past few days, but it all counts at this stage. The last of his surgeries is booked for tomorrow, vital signs permitting. Most patients would be transferred to ICU by now, but Cassie has fought to keep her soldier, at least until the last of his traumatic injuries are treated.

He's given them more scares than a horror movie in recent days. For every repair made or wound stitched, Steven has managed to develop a new complication. The pulmonary embolism had been the nastiest surprise, but at the moment there's no immediate concern beyond the low-grade fever.

As has become her routine over the past week, Cassie takes a chair at his bedside, along with a stack of charts to sign off, and a steaming cup of coffee. She's grateful to Veronica for sharing the secret of her caffeine fix. It's truly the only real coffee within walking distance.

"Don't you have other patients, Major?" Steven asks, his voice rasping after the last few hours of sleep.

"I'm right here if they need me. But not everyone in here got hurt defending someone else from a mugging."

"Sure it's not just that you fancy me, Doc?" He grins weakly, the bruising on his face spoiling the effect a bit.

"Down, boy," she warns. "Now, I went to see your old CO and we had a chat about your time in Afghan."

"You can't have been in Lash Vegas," he says, referencing the British Army base at Lashkar Gar. "I would have remembered you, that's for sure."

"No, I was stationed at Butlins most of the time," Cassie corrects him, knowing his lack of deference is more about the large doses of morphine lodged in his system than anything else.

"Talking in code again?" Alan says, tutting as he passes. The paramedic's in his usual green jumpsuit, the waterproof green and fluorescent jacket clutched in his hands like a bullfighter's cape. "Only you lot could name an army base after a holiday camp."

"It's a lot like the NHS in that sense," Cassie defends them automatically. "Dark humour for trying times? Something like that, anyway."

"Don't let the major drag you down to her level, Steven," Alan says, patting his arm carefully above the fibreglass cast. "I'd better get back on the rig, but I just wanted to make sure this lot were looking after you. I mean, we did the hard bit on the scene, me and you."

Steven nods gingerly in acknowledgment. "Well, the food's a bit shit, but then they're still giving it to me through a straw. I've definitely had worse all the same."

"Any luck with finding someone to contact?" Alan persists. "Not that you want them visiting you yet. Wait for one of the comfy wards upstairs."

"Just my unit, and Major Taylor here has sorted that," Steven replies. "I suppose if I'd had a big family I might not have run off and joined the army, eh?"

"Exactly," Cassie agrees. "You've still got plenty of time to start a family of your own when you get out of here. If you like that sort of thing."

"You know, Doc, you scrunched up your face just then like someone suggested public whipping. Not the settling-down type?" Alan is teasing, but Cassie knows the buzz of the rumour mill is frustrated by lack of detail on her personal life. It seems even the paramedics are in on it here, even if they're mostly passing through. Even in the busiest parts of the NHS there's always time for a cup of tea and some gossip.

"Maybe for the right woman," is all she'll say, and Alan's beaming smile suggests it's exactly what he suspected. "But kids? Pfft, I get enough snotty noses and questionable life decisions from my staff, thank you."

"At least I know now why you don't fancy me," Steven interrupts. "Here I thought I had lost my charm along with half my liver."

"I'm sure your pride will mend, Sergeant," Cassie says. "In the meantime, you let me know if anything hurts more or feels different. I'm going to do everything to get you home from here in one piece, okay?"

It's the same promise she made to every conscious casualty brought to her medic tent. She found the strength more than once to repeat it as a blatant lie to soldiers bleeding out in her lap, freshly pulled from burned out vehicles. Every time she said it, the sentiment was true. Cassie would have given just about anything to send them all home, hale and hearty. The ones she couldn't at least died with a few moments of comfort and all the pain relief she could provide.

"Now, is there anything else you need?" She should start checking on other patients at least.

"A six-pack and a decent film would be a start," Steven says, smiling again. "You sure I need this other op, Major?"

"Only if you want to walk again."

Alan departs with a cheery wave, and Steven gestures for Cassie to lean in. She does, feeling a little apprehensive. Quiet conversations with the badly injured are rarely a good sign.

"Major, I need a favour. All these forms, next of kin and that? I ain't got anyone, not local. Can I... Would you do it for me? Just if it comes to it."

"You're getting better by the day, Sergeant," Cassie reminds him. "There's no reason to start panicking now."

"I'm not, I swear. It's just, you know how it is. Before you face the big guns, you've got to put your own affairs right. I'd feel better going under again if I knew you could call the shots. You know more than I do, for a start."

Cassie considers. There's probably an NHS policy against it. Or at least a specific St Sophia's one. Still, her gut says to do it. The way she promised to call a dozen unspecified exes or estranged family members. That doesn't mean she's betting on Steven to die after all he's already been through. She's simply giving her patient peace of mind, and isn't that the care and compassion she promised to practice with?

"I'll see what I can do," she promises, already picking up his chart. She's interrupted on her way back to her barely occupied office by Wesley Travers, bustling about and trying to look important. How the Deputy

CEO hasn't melted in those heavy tweeds is beyond her, but then her uncle was always the same.

It's so strange to be living in his house without him, everything boxed up and mothballed, apart from the guest room she's been staying in since her childhood, the nearest bathroom, and some functional parts of the kitchen.

"Major, you're looking purposeful."

"There's plenty to be done." She doesn't mind when other people use her rank, even to mock her a little. But coming from him it sounds disrespectful, as though he outranks her in military terms rather than in their relative jobs. A little rude, given he hasn't served a day in his life. He probably has a home full of military portraits and second-hand medals, but Cassie has little patience for the historical voyeurs. Given her way, anyone who wants to pontificate on the trenches of World War I should have to pass basic training first. That would weed out a few of them at least.

"I hear you've got yourself something of a star patient?"

"You know how wards get with a bit of drama. Place has been crawling with the Met for days, and you know police don't stick around hospitals if they don't have to."

Travers strolls around her office, pausing only to look at the empty message board, the lack of adornment on the windowsill.

"They catch the little criminal yet?"

"No, sir. They suspect he hangs around the area, though, so just a matter of time." Cassie wishes she shared the confidence she speaks with. The bastard who flipped a good man off a thirty-foot concrete staircase will be just another statistic by the time the next spate of stabbings comes along to soak up time and resources. "Did you, uh, need anything?"

"You know, you're not in barracks now, Major. No demerits for bringing in a plant or something. I know the other…women have a fondness for those splashy art prints. What they're supposed to signify, I have no idea, but they do seem to insist on them."

"Not much of a green thumb and I don't know much about art," Cassie counters. "I'm sure I'll find something to make it more homey." Maybe she should just drag the few cases and boxes stacked at home in here instead. She might have some energy left in the day then to unpack the damn things.

"Budget coming along okay?"

"So far so good," Cassie lies. What she doesn't know, she's determined to work out. The acronyms and codes are nonsensical, and she's done actual cryptography. "It's not due just yet, is it?"

"What? Oh, no, no. Still a while yet. I got AMU's budget this morning; put the notion in my head to ask around." Of *course* Veronica got hers in before the deadline. Cassie isn't sure she's been less shocked in her life. "You know, I wouldn't offer to just anyone, but with the timing of your appointment and all. Let's just say my door is always open, should you have a question or two."

"That's very kind." Cassie is actually trying to like him, but it's off-putting the way he rifles through the few sheets of paper on her desk. For a moment it looks like he's going to tap the keyboard and bring her screen back to life. If he's that interested in her unread email, he's welcome to it.

Pauline saves the day, having finished her rounds. "Ms Taylor?" She knocks even though the door is open. "The sergeant's due for his next round of scans. You okay to let him go down?"

"Make sure they're careful with the left shin this time," Cassie warns. "I don't need Ortho bitching that they need to align it again. Why they don't just splint it is beyond me."

"I'll leave you capable ladies to it," Travers says, slinking out into the corridor, no doubt to get under someone else's feet.

"Let Steven know that I've done his form, could you?" Cassie turns away from the sight of him retreating and pats Pauline on the shoulder. "I've just been reminded I'd better crack on with the budget. Otherwise you'll all be farmed out to other departments and we'll have no plasters."

"I don't mind as long as it's back to AMU. It's a pain in the backside, having to walk over there just to gossip with Lea and the boys."

"Oh, we'll have to set up a livestream, in case you all miss anything."

"Yeah, you can float that one to Ms Mallick," Pauline suggests, with a grin. "I'll have them send Steven's scans straight to you as well as into notes, yeah?"

"Perfect, as always."

Cassie wishes the rest of her nurses had the same bustling capability as Pauline. If she hadn't been reassigned, the rest might be a bit too wet and hesitant for trauma. It's hard, trying not to compare them to field medics, but even the A&E lot seem more hands on from the little Cassie has encountered them. Maybe they should merge departments in the long run. No, just the thought of how many committees and panels and budget documents that might take is enough to make her dizzy.

She'll make it work; she always does.

———— ⇥⇤ ————

A while later, her eyes almost crossed from the nightmare spreadsheet of doom, Cassie gets up to stretch her legs. There's a flurry of activity around a new admit, but they seem to be handling it. One to keep an eye on. The first shout that's too tense, equipment clattering to the floor, and she'll be right over. For now, Cassie has to learn to trust her team and let them work.

Steven is drifting back in from a nap when she approaches, offering a brief smile. No need to get sentimental.

"Heard you've been flashing the girls down in Imaging again," she teases. "It's not enough we gave you a gown that opens in the back, you have to show off your liver as well?"

"I reckon I showed them more than that. Pauline said you'd done the thing?"

Cassie nods, patting the top of the clipboard that holds his charts. "It's all in here. But you listen to me, soldier. You're not going to need that. The worst is already over, and I'll check your scans myself to make sure of it. Once the bone docs do their magic, it's just a matter of time before you're in physio, and walking again."

"They keep telling me it's a miracle I'm not paralysed."

"Apparently you're very adept at falling. Managed to protect your spine. Luck of the gingers, eh?"

Steven sticks his tongue out, though his lips are still dry and chapped. "Something like that. Been a bit scary, all this."

"It can be." Cassie doesn't patronise him by talking of taking fire or crashing choppers. She knows what decimates these young men most of all is the realisation that they're not invincible, that so much of the body can break and betray them at once. "I've got some meetings, so behave yourself until I'm back. Stop telling my nurses they're pretty."

"To be fair, Major, that Adrian is a bit of a looker."

"You must have been the comedian of your unit."

He winces through the next smile, and without thinking she's upping his morphine a notch. Steven settles when it flows through his bloodstream, sinking back into the pillow. Conversation is going to be too much effort for a while.

"I'll check on you before your next op," she says, a promise she won't make any other patient, but to hell with the double standard.

She glances back just the once before heading to her general surgery weekly meeting. This one she actually wants to go to, because there are some terrible inefficiencies that need to be stamped out. They're going to just love her.

CHAPTER 11

"Ms Taylor."

Cassie makes no sign that she's heard, continuing to massage the heart manually, almost elbow-deep in the chest cavity in order to get a grip on it.

"Ms Taylor!" An absolute bark from Peter this time. Veronica can't remember the last time she heard Peter raise his voice. He's usually so softly spoken that the secretaries transcribing his post-operative notes curse his name.

He can't see what Veronica can, in her privileged vantage point beyond the glass. Cassie's eyes are unfocused, her breaths coming high and shallow in her chest. Peter has already conceded defeat, dumping his surgical gown into the waiting waste bin, letting the nurses flurry around him. Heaven forfend a consultant surgeon actually dress or undress their operating garments in this hospital.

Only Pauline holds back, watching Cassie like a hawk. She's ready with the tray, with fluids, with a handful of other useless remedies that budget and common sense say should no longer be wasted on the deceased.

Because, despite Cassie's frantic efforts, the sergeant is gone. The monitors don't lie, and the monotonous long beep has been piercing even Veronica's eardrum out here in safety. Then she sees Peter about to make his mistake, one they can ill afford in a room full of sharp implements.

Veronica has only a second to act, and reflexes are on her side. She barges the door with her hip, the sanctity of the surgical field moot now, in practicality if not in procedure.

"Cassie, stop."

Mercifully her words halt Peter in his tracks, but Cassie's rhythmic movements continue. There's really nothing else for it. Title alone might not be enough, so Veronica's going to try sheer irritation. "*Captain* Taylor. Stand. Down."

Finally Cassie's muscles obey where her brain has been rebelling. She pulls her hands free with the elongated slurping and anti-climactic pop of pressure releasing.

Countless years in operating theatres and Veronica has never found that definitive noise to be anything other than slightly cringeworthy. It reminds her of overenthusiastic teenage snogging, all vacuum sealed and messy, ending with what sounds like the slap of wet clothing against a tile floor.

On unsteady legs, Cassie takes one step back, then two. Her body is trembling, but her posture is as rigid as any steel girder.

"Mr Wickham, we can handle this from here. Don't let us keep you from your dinner plans."

"Is she—"

"I said," Veronica turns on him then, doing very little to hide the panic that must be screaming across her face. If he touched Cassie, tried to overpower her or pull her back, this could have ended terribly. "We can handle this. Have a good evening."

He leaves, after what feels like a short eternity, muttering under his breath something about women and their moods. It's strange, the things she didn't notice about him while she was grooming him as her protégé. Like that supposedly ironic streak of sexism, overlooking the considerable privilege that let him walk into medical school and his job without breaking much of a sweat.

Or is it only now obvious by comparison to Cassie, with her rough edges and the way she approaches every job, major or minor, as though she'll be kicked out of the door for failing. Veronica knows it still runs beneath all her confidence and achievements.

The call had panicked her, a frantic F1 sent to find the nearest responsible consultant. Luckily or not, that had been Veronica. It's an almost unerring ability she has, to be the closest port in a storm.

That just leaves cleaning this scene up. Turning to Pauline, Veronica is able to summon a smile. "Pauline, if you could be a dear? Get yourself organised now and have our dedicated F1—Adrian—here step in to close up. Then it's the usual arrangements until we can contact the sergeant's family."

"He doesn't have any." Cassie's voice is cracking, and she doesn't look at either of them. "He told me, on the ward. It's why he joined up."

"Nothing for him here, it's a common enough story. All the same, we'll have to check the paperwork for whomever he did name next of kin because—"

"Me." Cassie finally looks over at Veronica then, the single word an accusation and a defence.

"Right, well," Veronica hedges for time, out of both her depth and her element and fairly sure that it shows.

Pauline steps out to give them privacy, having disposed of her surgical scrubs and dragged Adrian along with her. They're alone, for the first time, and Veronica's overwhelming urge to care for someone in such a broken state takes over.

Veronica lays her hands on Cassie's shoulders, the one part of her definitely free of blood and viscera, starting to steer her gently towards washing off this tragic little scene.

"From what they told me, it was a massive embolism. There's very little you could have done; his chest would have needed to be cracked already to catch that in time."

"He wasn't throwing clots," Cassie mutters. "Just this one. I went as quick as I could, I did... I swear I did."

"Of course." Veronica isn't great at reassurance; she knows that much about herself. All she can fumble towards is what she'd want to hear herself. "You did everything you could."

"I was ready for everything else. I scanned and rescanned for pseudoaneurysms, just in case. He had as much Heparin as was safe, and still?"

"We can't anticipate every twist and turn, Major."

Cassie stops in her tracks, blinks a few times. "You called me Captain before. Why?"

"To get your attention," Veronica replies. "I was reaching, I'm sorry. It really wasn't a case of disrespect."

"It doesn't matter. I mean, it worked. That always irritates me." Cassie shakes her head, and they move off again.

Their steps aren't quite in rhythm, and for a moment it looks like Cassie won't actually leave the theatre space entirely, but they make it to the scrub room with a few squeaks of sneakers against tile. She grips the edge of the sink, leaning over like she might be sick. When nothing happens, Veronica tugs experimentally on the first tie at the back of Cassie's pale blue gown. It gives, and Cassie sighs in something like acceptance.

From there it's easy to untie the rest. Veronica hasn't tied her own since she was an SHO, back when Senior House Officers were still called that. She pulls until the material is balled up in her hands and dunks it straight in the bin.

Death is supposed to be routine, and Veronica would have thought only more so for someone who learned her craft in a war zone. They've had their clashes over technique and procedure, but there's no denying the neatness of the work Cassie has been doing since she arrived. There's not an unnecessary centimetre of incision, not a wasted strip of gauze. Whatever killed that young man in the end, it won't be bad surgical procedure.

"Cassie?" she ventures. It's been too long without talking. Not that it's the same as treating shock, exactly, but the symptoms are the same. "Cassie, I know that you know this, but this wasn't your fault."

The only response is a snort, though seemingly not of laughter.

"I won't patronise you with mortality rates or the unpredictable surgical variables, but his death is not a result of your care for him. He would have died anyway, and sooner, without your intervention." Said just like every bland pamphlet on the subject, ever.

The sound that breaks out of Cassie makes Veronica stumble back in alarm. Not quite a scream, nor a sob, but something raw and jagged. If not for the tears that hurl themselves down pale cheeks, Veronica might still be in the dark. Instead, she does what she's always done when presented with someone else crying: she reaches out with both arms and pulls Cassie close. Even if it provides nothing more than an absorbent surface, it's something.

Cassie doesn't wriggle away or attempt to bolt. She clings to Veronica as if she's the pool wall after twenty lengths of butterfly, every bit as breathless as the sobs continue to rise in her throat. It wouldn't do to offer words of comfort, even something as banal as promising that this wretched feeling will pass with time. Which, admittedly, is about the extent of Veronica's repertoire when it comes to these matters. She opts instead for stoic, solid, and silent. That's the same courtesy as she'd hope to be extended in return.

Pauline returns with Adrian as requested, and they enter on the opposite side of the room. Veronica nods in acknowledgment, angling her body a little more to block Cassie from view. They all understand the privacy of grief.

"I'm sorry," Cassie is muttering, over and over again. "I'm sorry, so sorry."

Veronica is about to gently correct her, but there's no gap in the torrent of *sorry sorry sorry* until a new word pops out with them. "I'm sorry, Jan."

Okay, even allowing for the fact that she only operated on him once, Veronica is sure the poor man's name is Steven. Clearly, something else is in play, and she has no idea how to ask.

"Maybe this is one to shower off, hmm?" Showers are safe, hard to talk during, and private. Veronica very much likes the sound of that, if only because it gives her a decent excuse to retreat and gather herself.

"No," Cassie says, pushing away from Veronica and heading into the locker room. "Not yet."

"Oh God, you're one of those, aren't you?"

"One of what?" Cassie's reply is snappish.

Veronica holds her hands up in surrender. "The exercise ones. Go hit a tiny ball hard against a wall, punch a few bags of sand... You run, don't you?"

"It's still light out," Cassie says, which is true despite the time orthopaedics took over their lunchtime surgery and the recovery time before Steven threw his unexpected clot. "Once around the park will do it. Thanks for... I should go." She already has some gear out of her locker, retreating into the bathroom.

Well. Another time that would read as lack of gratitude, but grief comes out in strange ways. Determined to do right by Cassie, Veronica decides to wait it out. She could get back to her own patients, but honestly the ward is running as smoothly as it ever does, the new staff bedded in, and the patient load only middling.

Instead, she steps back into the scrub room, flipping the light off as she goes. Watching in silence, it's a form of last rites to see the padding removed, heavy with blood as it's tossed into waiting kidney basins. Instruments are gathered onto waiting trays, ready for their re-sterilisation. The huge pale blue sheets crumple to nothing in strong hands, filling the plastic bag that handles all non-sharp waste. Veronica didn't notice the anaesthetist on her first pass through, but he's duly going through his own part of the ritual.

Veronica lingers long enough that she walks back in to find Cassie's discarded scrubs on one of the benches. Tutting under her breath, Veronica picks them up and folds them out of habit, ready for the dry-cleaning sack in the corner. She happens to check the labels and sees that Cassie doesn't have her name penned in. Most of the senior staff have their own sets of scrubs embroidered over the chest pocket, but no doubt the impatient Major hasn't seen the need to do anything other than pull from the central store of waiting clean scrubs.

Fishing around in her own locker, Veronica finds a laundry marker and writes *C. Taylor* on the labels of both. This way they'll be returned directly to this room, and they did seem a good fit. Next time they speak, maybe the personalisation order form will be a good distraction.

There's no reason to do anything now beyond returning to her day. But in the spirit of doing something she herself would appreciate, Veronica collects two clean travel cups and her purse and heads for the park via her usual coffee stop. It would help if she knew Cassie's regular route, but everyone entering from this side of Hyde Park on foot makes a beeline from the tree-lined path towards the Serpentine. It seems to mark a reasonable way around, but Veronica doesn't make a point of looking for a flash of blonde in the distance.

Instead, she waits on a bench by the Diana Memorial. Not her taste, with how it just seems to flow into the ground, but a popular spot nonetheless. The flowers are gathered every other day it seems, but the blooms laid in memory are still fresh. Twenty or so years on and the former princess is still remembered.

Back in theatre lies a pleasant and brave young man with no one to mark his passing but the doctors and nurses who treated him. It's an imbalance that she's gotten good at ignoring. Except for days like these.

She sips at her coffee, still scalding, putting the other cup beside her to deter the occasional weirdo who thinks talking to strangers is somehow welcome or acceptable while out in London. Beside it is a bottled water grabbed on a whim, in the vain hope that something will make Cassie feel better at this point.

It's nice to be outside; that's enough to focus on for now. Sip the coffee, watch the occasional jogger or speeding cyclist. A gaggle of toddlers led by harassed au pairs. Veronica can be patient.

Before too long, the heavy footfalls on her stretch of packed gravel start to slow. Where everyone else has passed, this runner is coming to a halt. Cassie, presumably. As a kindness, Veronica doesn't look round. She simply holds out the bottle of water and waits.

Then the bottle is gone, fingers brushing her own. A moment later, Cassie slumps onto the seat beside her, and Veronica does her best to keep looking straight ahead.

CHAPTER 12

"So," Cassie says, although it isn't really meant as the beginning of her thoughts. More like, it's all she has words for at the moment. Veronica is handling this perfectly, and it's maddening that Cassie doesn't know how. It's easier to form words now, because Veronica isn't staring at her, looking for clues as to what pieces have come loose this time. "This is the thingy, isn't it? The memorial for, uh…"

She can picture the woman, blonde and glamorous, but the name won't come.

"Princess Diana," Veronica replies, finally turning just enough to make eye contact. "It wasn't intentional, just a nice place to wait."

"I really am okay, you know."

"It's really okay not to be, you know. We do allow the occasional human emotion here. Not that I'd know, obviously."

"Obviously." Cassie offers the weakest attempt at a smile, sees in an instant that she's fooling no one.

She should have known Veronica wouldn't be the gloss-over-and-move-on type. Some scenes can be ignored: a patient whose gown flaps too much in the back, a crying relative at a suddenly empty bedside, a Cabinet minister showing up with false promises and a camera crew. A surgeon freezing in theatre will never make that list.

Cassie doesn't owe this woman anything but a brief and meaningful thank you, but this is a collision course. She recognises those when she sees them now. It's the gut instinct that told her to get in the second car of a convoy and not the first. To check one last time for a forgotten lap pad before closing. She has to explain herself, and for once she actually wants to. "I've seen a lot worse than that. Lost men from my own unit, people I worked beside for years in close quarters."

"I can only imagine. Still, we develop that callous, don't we? My ex-wife used to tell me, when things had rather deteriorated, that I had scar tissue where my feelings ought to be. They never really understand in the end."

Cassie reaches for her necklace, counting the tiny stainless-steel beads like a rosary of sorts, until her fingers close around the discs. It's about time she told someone. If nothing else, it might buy her some future privacy.

But why not wait to talk about it with Pauline, with her brisk good humour and kind eyes? Except nurses are notoriously tougher than doctors; it's a cliché for a reason.

Instead, Cassie finds herself baring her well-guarded soul to someone who seems to disapprove of her, whose sudden patience for how Cassie's conducts herself feels too good to be true.

"So I suppose you've worked out that it's not just about the sergeant."

"I had. That doesn't mean you have to tell me anything more than that." Veronica reaches out, her hand firm when it grips Cassie's forearm. Her hands are soft, but there's that slightly chalky quality that comes from spending too much time in latex gloves, the powdered residue becoming part of the skin after a while. "But if you wanted to, well, I would listen."

"There's a reason they don't let us treat our family members," Cassie begins, before amending. "Loved ones."

"Doesn't stop most of us," Veronica reminds her. "We write prescriptions, we call in favours from friends. Danny always says I'd send him to school if his leg fell off. I told him only if we staunched the bleeding first."

Cassie stands, grabbing the coffee now that her water is drained. She tosses the empty bottle in the recycling side of the bin.

"Do you mind if we walk?"

Veronica nods, getting up and setting out on a determined course. Cassie falls in step, trying to get her bearings. They cross the road through the park and head towards Hyde Park Corner, with its daily rabble of speechmakers, some saner than others. Not that they'll make it that far, probably. Grownups don't get to just walk out on their jobs.

"Don't get me wrong, it's not one big happy family on active duty." Cassie almost wishes Veronica would take her arm like she'd seen her do with Dr Hyatt-Wickham. Something about the slower pace makes falling seem like more of a possibility.

"People you could quite cheerfully slap are in your face for weeks on end. But even the worst of them, when shit goes down…they end up feeling like the only people in the world who give a damn. You have to trust them with your life. No choice on that part. Seeing someone from that world, even a stranger, it brings a lot of things back all at once."

As they walk, Veronica doesn't interrupt or question, simply nods in acknowledgment at each pause. As though she's saying *I'm still here.* It gives Cassie the wherewithal to go on.

"I couldn't save her." Cassie has to say it now, or she'll lose her courage. "Jan, she was a translator. We so rarely used women, but she was good, could make anyone talk to her."

"Was she…?" Veronica waves her hand to fill in the blank. "Is that too personal?"

"I'm not used to being 'out'. I know it's no big deal now, in a big city like this. The army isn't bad about it, all things considered, but fraternising is still an issue. We had to be discreet. And when the enemy nearby is the Taliban, you don't want to paint any more targets on your backs. You know, I might have brought this up sooner, but I wrongly assumed you were straight."

"You thought I was straight?" Veronica's mouth quirks up at one side, fighting a smile. "I don't know when I've ever been so offended, Major."

"The kid threw me, that's all."

"Hmm." Veronica considers her next question, and Cassie wants to blurt something out just to divert it. It's always too revealing, when Veronica asks her something. "So when you say you couldn't save her…"

"I'm sure you saw the sort of thing on the news. Moving from one base to another, they didn't let us bed in for too long, and we were needed in so many places. We had scouts, there were all kinds of detectors, but in the end it was the luck of the draw."

"One of those IEDs?" Veronica presses. "Bloody nasty business. I'm sorry."

"It was the crash. The car in front took the worst. I got out unharmed, but the impact in the front seat was too much. She, uh, I mean, I tried with the mobile kit but it was too much damage. Triple A, the autopsy confirmed in the end."

"And you blame yourself for not being able to treat an aortic aneurysm? In the middle of the desert with no real surgical kit? While still reeling from the accident itself?"

"I just—"

"Listen here." Veronica stops right in front of Cassie, grabbing her by the bare upper arms. Her fingers are warm, making Cassie realise how cool she is in comparison. Strong, too, though that's not unusual with all the hours of surgery Veronica must have under her belt. There's something grounding, though, in being touched. Cassie feels the floating feeling start to recede.

"I'm listening," she says, for lack of anything wittier. The thump in her chest, the dull ache of missing Jan and finally sharing some kind of memories of her, it feels like something she can handle head on, now that Veronica has quietly slipped into her corner. Those dark brown eyes and the serious set of her jaw brook no argument: Cassie is being supported here, and she can deal with this.

"You might be a damn fine trauma surgeon, Cassie Taylor. For all I know, you might be the best this country has to offer. But you are not— hear me on this—not a miracle worker. We save who we can and we mourn the rest, but you don't get to take the blame just because you cared about them."

Cassie's throat is tight. The tears are threatening again, just like the dark grey clouds overhead. It's a struggle, but she forces the words out. "Rationally, I know you're right."

"Actually, I'm always right." Veronica hasn't let go yet. "It's usually quicker to just accept that going forward."

"Duly noted."

"How was Peter in there? Need me to have a word?"

Cassie shakes her head. "I fight my own battles, thanks. And he was just doing his job. More professionally than I was." Her phone beeps, and then the surgical pager that the NHS insists on clinging to follows suit. The boxy little thing is a real throwback, but like everyone else, Cassie has learned to use it simply as a 'bleeper' that grabs the attention and using her actual phone to find out what the hell is going on. "Incoming," she adds, though they both know it.

"Listen, you don't have to go back in there." Veronica is sincere about that much, but Cassie turns away, forcing Veronica to almost stumble in coming after her. "Will you at least call for me if you need another pair of hands?"

"Best thing for it is to get right back on the horse." Cassie wipes the last of her tears from her face. The call of the operating theatre is rising inside her again, despite it all. "Thank you, Veronica. Truly."

"Just helping out a friend," Veronica assures her, before catching what she's just said. The woman looks a little stunned to even have thought it, never mind said it aloud. Still, this is the unflappable Veronica Mallick, and she styles it out with a stiff smile and a wave of her hands. "I won't try and keep up with you. Go on."

Cassie gives a stilted little wave of her own, before turning back towards the hospital, kicking up her heels on the first few strides. It's probably her imagination, and she hates how it sounds like something out of a self-help book grabbed on impulse at the airport, but she does feel just a little lighter for saying it all out loud.

And the rest? Well, that's what work is for. She'll be elbow-deep in a surgery within the hour, and that's the best place for her.

CHAPTER 13

VERONICA DIVES HEADFIRST INTO THE rest of her week, and in typical St Sophia's fashion, it's too busy for her to spend much time wondering how Cassie is recovering from her momentary freeze.

The nurses' network does its bit when it comes to gossip, so Veronica can stay safely in her own domain—or at least in meeting after meeting, punctuated by the odd surgery—while keeping tabs on what's happening across the way in Trauma. It sounds very much like business as usual. A rash of car accidents, a few motorcyclists who picked a battle with physics and came off worse, and the usual weekend spate of stabbings and drug-fuelled fights.

AMU has done its bit, admitting and treating and filtering to more long-term wards as needed. It might not be the same high stakes and energy, but it's been bloody frantic all the same. What it always comes down to is that there are a finite number of beds and other resources, but a seemingly infinite flow of bodies.

And of course, there's always those initially minor issues that get much worse out of nowhere. The sudden bleeds or organs failing that nobody can predict. It puts all the staff in crisis mode, just when they thought they could catch a nap or sit down for five consecutive minutes. They're all beyond knackered at the end of the day, surviving on caffeine and determination alone, but they get the few hours in a proper bed to recharge, and then do it all again.

That's Veronica's excuse for being a little dazed while she pores over her tablet, leaning against the nurses' station. It's a ground zero for all information that flows into the department, and for the gossip along with it. There's something going on with one of the agency nurses and that orderly who always lingers too long around Veronica for her liking.

Before she can overhear much of interest, there's some jostling at her elbow. She recognises that faint perfume, almost a cologne really.

"Well hello, Major," Veronica says without looking up. Her new article is in the *British Medical Journal*, and she just wants to scan it to make sure nothing crucial has been edited. They really can be the worst kind of sticklers, stripping every last vestige of personality from the words.

"Have you seen this form I'm supposed to have signed?" Cassie asks. She's been in a visible mood for days. Workwise she's been busier than ever with surgeries, working long hours to operate on as many people as possible. They all seem to have hung in there, which will go some way to easing Cassie's guilt.

Still, juniors are running scared and registrars are looking over their shoulders. The Morbidity & Mortality conference had been brutal, a room full of indifferent men offering useless suggestions of how they'd have operated differently.

"Had to come in on my bloody day off because Travers left me more voicemails than I could listen to," Cassie continues, having rifled through a pile of papers on the nurses' desk.

When Veronica looks up, sarcastic rejoinder ready and waiting, the words die on her tongue.

No scrubs today, oh no. No messy blonde waves falling in a sort of bob. If Veronica hadn't just heard that slightly raspy voice for herself, she would have assumed this was another person entirely. If she'd been concerned about finding Cassie attractive in her usual workwear, there's a whole new crisis at seeing her in what Veronica assumes is a dress military uniform.

The black tunic is spotless, the maroon sash at the waist almost swashbuckling set against the gold braiding at the shoulders. White gloves are off, half-tucked into that sash that serves as a belt. Coupled with the A-line skirt, the terribly shiny shoes, and the hat tucked under one arm, it's really a lot to take in.

Cassie's cheeks are pink from rushing, and although her hair is pinned back, strands are already escaping. Would that be points off on parade ground inspection? Do medical officers have to go through that rigmarole? Veronica finds herself brimming with questions.

Until, of course, she remembers the reason for the purported day off and the formal dress.

Get it together, woman.

"You should tell him that no one checks voicemail anymore," Veronica says, nudging Cassie towards the clipboard that needs a signature from all department heads before lunch. "You look very smart."

Cassie shoots her a sideways glare, suspicious. "I could have worn service dress, but brown doesn't feel right for a funeral. The rest of his regiment agreed."

"Quite suitable for a hero's send-off," Veronica offers. "I suppose you know some of them? A few familiar faces?"

A blank look in return. "Oh no." Cassie looks back at the form. "Our paths never crossed, but it doesn't matter. It's not exactly a social occasion."

Veronica considers the day ahead. Most of it to be trapped at her desk or stuck in God knows which meeting it is this afternoon that's swallowing a huge red chunk of her calendar. She looks down at her fuchsia-coloured skirt. That won't do at all.

"Listen, give me five minutes."

"For what?"

"Five minutes. Wait here."

If Veronica has learned anything in the past couple of months, it's that the quickest way to handle Cassie is with action, not words. Darting into her office, she surveys the dry-cleaning bags hanging on the back of the door. Perfect—a black blazer and trousers. Not quite a suit, but close enough. With the pale grey blouse she's already wearing, it almost looks like she planned to crash a funeral all along.

A quick reapplication of lipstick, a brush through her hair, and Veronica is ready to accompany Cassie. Assuming she hasn't bolted in the meantime. Heading back onto the ward, Veronica can't deny she's pleased that Cassie is still there. Even if she is checking her watch with tangible impatience. No doubt one of those shiny shoes will be tapping.

"Well, come on then," Veronica says, chancing her luck a bit further. "We don't want to be late."

"You... We... Wait, what?"

"We'll just hop in a cab, I think. No one wants to be bothered with the Tube on days like this. You have...everything?"

"But—"

"Come along, Major. Really, I thought your sort were all about punctuality."

It works. It actually works. Veronica sets the pace in her heels, and Cassie strides right along with her. They head out onto Praed Street, a passing black taxi with its light on sparing them the short walk to the Paddington station rank. Only when they're pulling out onto the Edgware Road does Cassie finally find her voice.

"Why are you doing this?"

"I assume you're finding a way to take it as an insult," Veronica answers. "That I somehow think you're not up to this, probably because of last week. Well, before you go assuming the worst, that has nothing to do with it."

"No? Why, then?" Cassie sits stiffly on the backseat beside her, catching the driver's eye in the mirror more than once.

Veronica wonders if his curiosity will get the better of him before they reach their destination.

"Respect," she says.

It's as simple as that. For the soldier whose death resulted directly from his act of decency. For Cassie, who carries burdens that no one seems to know much about. For all the people like them, who'll visit war zones and face threats that Veronica knows she would never dare to. Maybe, just in some small way, for her long-departed father, and his love of all things historical and military. No matter how he railed against the colonial forces and their oppression. She almost smiles at the thought.

"That's hard to argue with."

"I'm sure some of the nurses would have come too," Veronica adds. "Are you handling all of this yourself?"

"We have—that is, there's a department in the Armed Forces. Just for this kind of thing. Mostly they deal with overseas, bringing everyone back for their families. But Steven was only in the process of leaving. No little red book yet. He's not officially discharged. I just signed the forms and helped with the formalities."

"Makes you think," Veronica says as they roll to a stop at the traffic lights. "There but for the grace of whatever. Who'd really miss you when you're gone, that sort of thing."

"Well, I'd say that's obvious for you. You have a son, for starters. An ex-wife who's probably still at least a little bit in love with you, if she has any sense."

"You'd make her laugh with that."

"Still. Beats my scattered cousins and army mates. Enough for a small buffet, maybe. The half-brother I've met a handful of times." Cassie's actually ticking them off on her fingers. "Maybe if I stick around here long enough, some staff will come out of politeness."

"Hitting the pity drum a little hard, aren't we?"

Cassie shrugs, looks out the window.

"I have my sister," Veronica starts making her own list. "We see each other for lunch when we absolutely can't avoid it any longer. She moved to Miami, and God knows I won't go there if I can avoid it." That gets a snort out of Cassie. "Cousins, yes. I do the rounds on the big holidays, but it's hard to get enthused when you're an atheist."

"Your family are Hindu?"

"On my dad's side, yes. My mum's were devout Christians. That's what she was always running away from. I suppose I get the aversion from her. I don't hear from them much. I suppose I stand out too much in a group shot."

"You wouldn't think that still matters," Cassie says with a sigh. They're making good time along the Westway now, central London soon giving way to the endless suburbs. "It reminds me I should have made more effort with Jan's family. I promised at the funeral that we'd stay in touch, but I went back to Germany the next day. Somehow the letters don't just write themselves."

The driver interrupts then. Maybe the conversation is too maudlin for him.

"Excuse me, but you're in the army?"

"I used to be," Cassie answers. "Army medic. Just off to a funeral."

"Ah. I figured with the Kensal Green address and all. I'm sorry for your loss."

"Thank you." Cassie sits back further in her seat, fist clenching and unclenching.

Veronica strikes up conversation about the traffic to prevent any further questions, the risk of any sore spots being prodded.

She's running out of small talk when they reach the crematorium. There's not much traffic around as Veronica hands over a twenty and tells him to keep the change. They step out onto the pavement, no one else nearby.

Cassie puts her hat and gloves on with practiced ease, opening the simple black holdall she's carrying, pulling a slender sword with its own belt from it, and fixing it around her waist with the sash.

"I hope that's ceremonial," Veronica says. "I didn't come prepared for a swordfight."

"It is." Cassie sees a man in the everyday brown uniform lurking in the reception area and leads Veronica over to him.

He meets her halfway. "You must be Major Taylor. We spoke on the phone," he says.

Veronica leaves them to their introductions after her own brief round of polite handshakes, before the army chaplain calls them into what Veronica would instinctively call a chapel. Rather, it's a multi-faith space, bright and welcoming. Rows of benches, a presentation sort of area at the front. Instead of a screen and a projector, there's a coffin on its stand, draped in a Union flag and a bouquet of half-closed lilies.

She waits for Cassie to enter, gauging her reaction. When she doesn't seem to get any more upset, Veronica leads them to an empty bench on the left-hand side.

Slowly other people filter in, most of them men. Someone Cassie greets as "Lieutenant Commander" shakes both their hands, and there are nods of acknowledgment for Cassie from most people who enter. Whether it's rank or they know how she took responsibility for their fallen brother, Veronica isn't sure.

Steven's heroic story had made the national and local news, partly because London news is always treated as national, and partly because of the pure tragedy of it all. Veronica saw mention of it in the Metro, caught a few words about it on the evening news, too. It's right, that his sacrifice should be noted. There's at least one set of reporter and photographer in attendance, but Veronica hasn't looked around to see if any more have joined. Some police have joined the mourners, and Veronica recognises the paramedics who brought the sergeant in—Alan and one of the newer recruits.

The service is simple but incredibly moving. A Bible reading, a rendition of *Abide with Me*, and some stirring words from an officer and a fellow soldier in turn. Cassie sits ramrod straight throughout, hands clasped in her lap. When the senior officer mentions the exemplary care at St Sophia's, Veronica lays her hand on Cassie's forearm. Not a flicker this time.

Out of habit, she looks away as the coffin recedes behind the curtain. Not seeing it won't make it any less real, but Veronica can't seem to help it. She's surprised to feel Cassie's hand on hers, a brief squeeze of reassurance through those stiff white gloves.

The single bugle from the back of the room startles them both, and honestly it's a little loud for the space. Still, everyone stands for the solemn notes of *The Last Post*, offering salutes while Veronica clasps her hands behind her back.

When it's all over, she waits to the side while Cassie says her solemn good-byes and accepts a final round of thanks.

"I don't know about you," Veronica says, squinting in the mid-afternoon sunshine. "But I could go for a bloody big drink right about now."

"Lead on," Cassie agrees. "And Veronica?"

"Yes?"

"Thank you. Again. That's becoming a bit of a habit." Cassie looks like she's about to apologise, so Veronica simply cuts her off.

"I'd say any time, but you know what my schedule's like. Still, whenever I can, should you need a shoulder, et cetera."

She doesn't see the kiss coming. Cassie is quick on her feet, and they're not terribly far apart to begin with, but even so the darting press of lips against Veronica's cheek catches her off guard.

"Tube's just over there," Cassie says, pointing in the direction while studiously avoiding eye contact. "Let's go get that drink."

CHAPTER 14

"You know, I'm sick of everywhere around work," Veronica announces once they're safely on the Bakerloo line. "Did you want to change first? I can't think being in bars in uniform always goes over well."

"No, not everyone is glad to see us. I could do without an undergraduate's lecture on the ethics of war today, that's for sure." Cassie isn't kidding. It's not as bad now, but on her first couple of trips back from Basra and Helmand, the anti-war sentiment had been running high, looking for any outlet. She doesn't always agree with the reasons for war, but she's always felt the duty to care for the young men and women risking their lives.

"Well, there's always my local? If you can stand Maida Vale—I know it's not everyone's cup of tea. Suits me, though. And I can grab you a top or something, though you're quite a bit fitter than I am."

If Cassie believed it were possible, she'd accuse Veronica of nervous babbling. As it is, Cassie almost swallows her tongue at the unexpected compliment. "I actually have jeans and a T-shirt in here." She gestures to her trusty holdall, hat and sword already returned to storage. "So the nearest place to do a quick change would be great, yeah."

"It was a lovely service, I thought."

If Veronica is resorting to cliché, Cassie is going to give her a break from having to make conversation. She nods, but doesn't say anything to keep the chat going.

They only have to travel a handful of stops. Cassie keeps an eye on the map to chart their progress. Maybe she should blow it off and head for Paddington. Get back to Swindon and get some proper sleep after last night's tossing and turning. Not that she ever sleeps well in the house. It feels far too much like a mausoleum for that kind of relaxation.

Maida Vale isn't exactly what Cassie's expecting. Not that she knows what she's expecting really. The exit is on a corner, one of those retro Tube stations that looks as if it's been there since the trains were first put on the tracks. The deep red tiling on the outside walls seems polished, though surely it can't be. There's a miniature high street in one direction, a car-lined residential cutting across it.

"I actually live over there," Veronica says, gesturing to the cars and the modest townhouses behind them. "Angela and I got in just before prices got ridiculous. But the real haven is around this way."

One thing surprising Cassie is how she barely gets a passing glance. They really weren't kidding about how unshockable Londoners can be.

"Good, won't be the first time I've changed in a pub toilet. But I must insist that dinner's on me."

"Chivalry? I think that uniform goes to your head, you know. You might regret that once you see my bar tab."

"I think I can take it," Cassie says, taking in the antiques shops—more than one, naturally—and the local branches of a bank or two, side by side with newsagents plastered in Oyster card logos and posters for shows that even she knows aren't running anymore. "NHS wages might not be the top of the tree, but it's a nice step up from the army."

God, Cassie squirms even talking about money. Growing up with almost none, it wasn't until she joined the army that Cassie really had money of her own. Cassie doesn't have the first clue how to go about selling it, what it will mean to have that money along with her new salary to put towards a home of her own. Her first permanent one, after all this time.

The other officers teased her about it. They used army loans to get good mortgages on properties in sleepy villages close to their home bases, but she'd been based out of Germany more than anywhere at home. With Jan, they'd only just gotten to the 'when we finally go home' talk before everything went wrong. Now in her late thirties, Cassie finds herself faltering at things she would have dealt with in her early twenties, a generation before.

If this is how it feels to put down roots, it's fucking terrifying. People like Veronica make it look so easy, the natural progression of things. Maybe Cassie should be asking for advice, but there's already been so much help with work, with settling in.

The pub is exactly the kind of upmarket gastro place that Cassie expects, and being right about that relaxes her in an odd way. "Mine's whatever beer looks coldest," she says over her shoulder while heading to the loos.

That bravado doesn't survive the quick look in the unflattering mirrors once she's changed. The fit of the jeans is flattering at least, but the T-shirt has done a few too many runs in the laundry, its RAMC logo faded against the olive green. Her tiny ponytail, held in with clips behind her ears, is all coming loose. Cassie shakes it out, running her hands through it, still wet from washing her hands.

Almost presentable. She's quick but careful with folding her uniform, the shoes not quite going with the pale blue skinny jeans. The test, the one she doesn't realise she's issuing, comes when she strolls back out to join Veronica at a booth in the corner. The lighting is almost romantic, and the beer glass is tall and twisty, condensation running down it like an invitation. She hasn't been this thirsty outside of an arid desert.

Which is all a distraction from the test. As soon as she gets in range, Veronica looks up. Cassie braces herself for the brief half-smile, barely a glance, before Veronica gets back to a menu she probably has memorised. If that's what she does, then this is absolutely two new friends having dinner.

What Veronica actually does is enough to make Cassie's knees almost buckle. Instead of a flicker of a look, it's a moment of recognition, then a long, dragging glance that makes Cassie wonder for a second if she remembered to put clothes back on at all. It can't last more than a second or two, but it's an eternity where Cassie has to relearn her name and the process of how to walk. That she slides into the booth, nonchalant, is something of a miracle.

"I got you some Dutch thing or other." Veronica indicates the perfectly apparent beer. "Somehow English ones are always a little disappointing."

"I had you pegged for a red wine sort of girl," Cassie says, raising her glass for them to clink together. "Shiraz?"

"I dabble with it, but Merlot usually gets my loyalty points. We can still split a bottle if you like?"

"Gives me a headache," Cassie replies. "What's good here? God, I feel like I ask you every little thing. Aren't you sick of me yet?"

"It just plays into my natural bossiness." Veronica takes a long sip from her glass.

Cassie crosses her ankles and tries not to dwell on that particular flash of an image.

"And I'm told I'm not exactly subtle about when I've had my fill of someone," Veronica finishes.

"Is that why Travers scuttles away from you in the hallways?"

"He has been known to try my patience. Problem is finding him half the time. I handed in my budget the other day and it took longer to get his signoff than to find him. Even then, it was like he wasn't expecting them."

"Funny, because he came chasing me. Even offered to help me."

Cassie almost ends up wearing a mouthful of red wine at that comment. Startled, she waits for Veronica to explain.

"Oh God, he actually did that?" Veronica looks genuinely shocked. "You must have some kind of supernatural power. Or you're his type and he's…oblivious."

"I don't look that gay, do I?"

"You know fine well how you look," Veronica reassures.

Cassie tries not to beam at what seems suspiciously like a compliment. A chipper waitress interrupts them, and it's a much-needed respite.

"But you know, that casual chic combined with the whole macho-army-medic thing…" Veronica continues.

"Shall we order? I'll have the burger, thanks." Okay, that was definitely a compliment. Cassie doesn't know quite what to do with herself. Better to just focus on her order. Can't go wrong with a burger and chips. That will go down well with the second pint she orders with it.

Veronica orders the fish something or other, and another large glass of Merlot. When they're alone again, all talk of Travers is done. It turns rather serious, and Cassie feels the urge to run.

"You are holding up okay? Not because I think you're some delicate piece of china, you understand. Rather because that would be a lot for anyone, considering."

"Fine. One funeral is much like another, in the end. I laid some demons to rest last week. Today just felt like… What's that awful American term for it? Closure."

"I think we use it here now, you know. My good friend Edie is just mad about it."

"She's one hell of a shrink. I told my army bods to use her work, if they can." Cassie takes a drink of her beer, trying to formulate the words. "I like to think I can fix any kind of physical trauma, or have a bloody good go at it. Most of the time, I don't see the guys I patch up until months after. They've usually accepted it by then. The discharge, the prosthesis. That they'll never see their kids' faces clearly again. Time's the great healer. But so much of what she said at her talk made me realise how much work that has to take."

"She is rather brilliant," Veronica says. "But you can never tell her that. Edie's quite out of control as it is. I'd set you two up on a friend date, but I don't think the universe would thank me."

"I think you might be more than I can handle as it is." Cassie wants to bite it back the second she says it, but Veronica just smirks.

"You're probably right."

CHAPTER 15

Hangovers aren't getting any easier with age. Turning forty had been a particular milestone in that regard, not that Veronica had let it throw her off stride in the red-wine-consumption department. She'd just had to get more responsible about water and aspirin before bed. The worst part is how she always wakes up earlier, as though she doesn't start her days early enough as it is.

Wide awake just after five, she runs through the rest of the evening on her way to the shower. Only the guest room door being firmly closed reminds her that she has company. That puts a certain spring in her step, and she's downstairs in her dressing gown, hair still damp, half an hour later. Cassie seems the early-rising kind, and it seems important she have the offer of coffee and a proper breakfast.

Sure enough, she appears in the doorway with a sheepish expression before the coffee pot is half filled. The Batman dressing gown, with its gaudy yellow belt, is quite a look on her. Veronica is careful not to linger where the hem only hits mid-thigh.

"I see Daniel has been storing his things all over the house again?"

"No, I brought this with me," Cassie jokes. "I'm nuts about, uh, I want to say Spiderman?"

"No, his stuff has the webs all over, I'm reliably informed." Danny was a bit easier in the comic-book phase. "The bat should be something of a clue."

"Right." Cassie frowns at the black material. "Turns out I'm not as funny as I think I am before breakfast. But thank you for letting me stay."

Veronica opens the fridge to retrieve some milk and yoghurt. The fruit is already chopped into some bowls, and there's a plastic container of muesli out on the counter.

"It was the least I could do, after talking you into those extra drinks. I was glad of the company, honestly."

"And the hospital didn't burn down in our absence? Mine was planned, but you just took off."

"Alas, our colleagues are too competent to let it get too out of hand. Might be trickier from next week, once Peter leaves," Veronica says. "Help yourself. I can cook, if you fancy some eggs or something?"

"Now you're just spoiling me." Cassie sits on one of the high stools in her dressing gown and T-shirt. "Honestly, I mostly grab a protein bar and a coffee, so this is already miles better."

Veronica hesitates before taking her seat. Unlike Cassie's towelling number, her own robe is silk and makes her slip right off these stools. It would be more modest to stay standing, but she pulls the fabric out of the way and takes a seat as gracefully as she knows how. Her legs get an appreciative glance that makes it all seem worth it at least.

"Did you really tell me last night that Travers is taking a personal interest in your budget?"

"Yes, why?"

"It's just so unlike him. I think I actually dreamt about it." The coffeemaker beeps to signal a full pot, and Veronica decants it into two large mugs and slides one over to her guest. Her legs apparently merit a second lingering look. Good. "There's always gossip he's a little…something."

"Something?" Cassie parrots back at her.

"Not shady, that's too strong. But a couple of years back we were over budget on some Estates project. Then all of a sudden it was fine. I suppose that's good management on his part, but at the same time, he doesn't really seem the type?"

"Are you saying I should watch my back with him?"

"I'm saying, if you don't mind, I might do a little digging today. Find out why he's taken such an interest in Trauma. One benefit of working in the same hospital since I started training is that I do know almost everyone."

"I'm sure that's not necessary," Cassie says, blowing off the concern again. "I'll tell you one thing, though. Staying here last night has made me all the more determined to get my finger out and find a place of my own. No more train commutes from hell."

"Oh, house hunting?" Veronica perks up at the thought. "Strangely, one of my favourite things. At least for other people, when I don't have to do all the paperwork and hand over a ton of money at the end."

"I haven't really started looking."

"I'm still friends with the estate agent who found me this place; I can give her your email?"

"There you go again, saving the day." Cassie hides a smile with her coffee, not very effectively. "But that would be a big help, thanks."

"If you're itching to go for a run, I think I have some tragically unused gym things upstairs."

"You do?" There's a hint of teasing in the question. "Well, if the shoes fit, that takes care of me getting to work."

"I miss that," Veronica says. "The whole double-your-wardrobe thing of living with another woman. I don't suppose you really needed double the fatigues, did you?"

"Not really."

They're both done with breakfast, so Veronica shifts everything to the sink ready for the cleaner later. "Well, follow me, Major. Let's see if we can get you kitted out."

Veronica doesn't really think the whole "let me take you to my bedroom" thing through, not until Cassie is holding back in the doorway like they've just opened up some Egyptian tomb. Her gaze goes everywhere, though, to the unmade bed and the pile of clothes draped over a chair. Not dirty enough to need laundry but worn once so not clean enough to hang in the wardrobe again.

"Won't be a second," Veronica says, stepping into the small dressing room off the master bedroom, the one perfectly organised part of her house. The spice rack might be missing some key jars, and the less said about the mess of cables and fittings in the garage the better, but in this small room of rails and drawers, there is order to combat any chaos.

There's her actual exercise gear, of course. Not a large section, but weekly Pilates and a couple of sessions on the treadmill keep Veronica fit enough for long surgeries. She has no interest beyond that. It takes checking a few different drawers before she remembers the things she's thinking of will still be in a bag. Danny's favourite shops to drag her to are the ones full of overpriced sneakers and logo-heavy T-shirts. It's indulgent, but it's one of the few things they can still do together without bickering, and so Veronica agrees almost every time he suggests it.

That bag from the last trip to the hell on Earth known as the Nike store on Oxford Circus is what she needs. A couple of running vests, some capri leggings, even a new sports bra. She turns around only to see Cassie slipping into the relatively confined space along with her.

"Oh! Sorry! I wondered where you'd gone," Cassie says. "I have a bad habit of missing the bit where people say 'Come with me' so I wondered if I had."

She's very close. Veronica holds the reusable shopping bag out like a shield in front of her. "Now, I'm a seven in shoes. I hope that's close enough?"

"Perfect," Cassie replies. "Should I…"

"Just behind you." Veronica gestures to the wall of shelves that holds her slightly obsessive shoe collection. The newish Air Max pair are on the bottom row. "Grab those and I'll see if I have those barely visible socks somewhere."

Cassie picks up the shoes and accepts the bag. Veronica feels herself pulled into an unexpected hug. "Thank you," Cassie whispers. "For everything."

Patting her on the back, Veronica lets the warmth spread through her. She hadn't realised until right now how out of the habit she's gotten. It had been a slow decline between her and Angela, easy affection the first casualty in their dissolution. Daniel is in that awkward teenage-boy phase where any attempted contact makes him contort like a gymnast just to get away from it. "It's nothing, really. But yes, you're very welcome."

"I should go change, let you have your morning back."

"You're welcome to crash anytime," Veronica says as they part. "Well, as long as you're stuck out in Swindon. *Mi casa, su casa*, as the Spanish would have it. Now get going. Some of us need more than five minutes to look effortlessly put together all day."

"See you at work, then." With that, Cassie is gone.

Veronica finds herself almost sad about the loss of her presence. Maybe Edie has been right all this time. Perhaps Veronica is just a little bit lonely.

Still, there's a busy day ahead. No time to worry about how Cassie's going to look in that very fitted running gear.

A burst appendix right after she gets into work ends up taking more of Veronica's morning than she expected, but once she's out of surgery it doesn't take too long to get on the trail of Travers.

She corners him on his way out to some lecture at their university campus that's also part of the Trust. He looks less than thrilled to see her.

"Yes, Ms Mallick, I did get your budget for next year." He holds his hands up to ward her off. "I'm sure I replied to that message."

"No, Wesley, it's not that. Not exactly. I just had an idea for something a bit different, and I wondered if I redo the whole thing, could you advise me on a point or two? Just how to get some big items approved, that sort of thing." Throwing in a little charm can't hurt. "And it's Veronica to you, you know that."

"Well, Veronica, as flattered as I am…you know I'm not the details man. I'm Mr Big Picture, the original blue-sky thinker. I'd be happy to check it over when it's done, but ins and outs are really decided more at your level, if you see what I mean."

"You're right. Let's just leave it be til next year, hmm?"

"Probably best."

It's far from definitive, but a very different picture to what Cassie mentioned. In fact, Veronica has only ever known Wesley Taylor to insert himself in the business of department heads when he wants something. Usually to get funds siphoned off to support another troubled part of the organisation. Where other people would doze off at the whiff of financial impropriety, a little bit of Veronica comes alive. Sniffing out something potentially scandalous and nipping it in the bud will do wonders for her future as CEO of the Trust.

By the time lunch rolls around, she's booked in for a cholecystectomy and they've discharged or relocated at least a third of their occupied beds in the Acute Medical Unit. The prospect of whipping out a gallbladder has brightened the afternoon considerably; she's just going to polish off a salad at her desk in preparation.

Two minutes into the thirty minutes she has to herself, of course there's a knock at the closed door. She can't help smiling when it opens to show Cassie.

"I got these cleaned at the one-hour place down the street. Thanks a million." She holds up a clear dry-cleaning bag with the running gear. "And the shoes are in this." After handing over the regular plastic bag, Cassie hangs the clothes on the back of the door next to some clean dresses.

Veronica opens the bag out of habit, though she knows her running shoes will be in there. She smiles at a rather nice bottle of merlot stashed between them.

"That wasn't necessary."

"Tough."

"Oh, since you're here, I spoke to Travers about my budget. He couldn't get off the topic quick enough. I'd say he is up to something, or you've *really* caught his eye. If we prod at him a little, he'll probably give himself away. Always thought he was a bit of a...you know..." Veronica taps the side of her nose with a fingertip and makes a sniffing noise. Drug problems amongst doctors are, sadly, not rare. It's usually the high-pressure ones who succumb mostly easily—the A&E consultants and one of Cassie's predecessors in Trauma.

"The thing is," Cassie replies, shoving her hands in her scrubs pockets and looking at the ground, "I think I maybe don't want to rock the boat?"

"Oh?"

"It's just, I'm still technically on probation. Every new start is on a shaky peg for a few months. It would be a shame to piss off the big boss and have to begin my fresh start all over again."

"But Cassie, surely—"

"Really, let's just leave it for now. I'm starting to really like a lot of things about St Sophia's and I don't want to be kicked out for making accusations."

Veronica wants to argue the point, but it's clear that Cassie's mind is made up. Still, if Travers is cooking the books somewhere, he'll show his hand eventually. There's no reason Veronica can't keep snooping on her own time, either.

"Fine," she agrees, holding her hands up. "Thank you, for the wine. I'll save it for after my choley."

Cassie lights up at that. "You're doing more surgery lately. It looks good on you."

"Yes, well, someone reminded me that surgery is why I do all this in the first place. It's what I like about St Sophia's, you could say. My reason to stick around. Yours too, I suppose."

"Hmm? Oh yes." Cassie opens the door to leave. "That and the people. That really makes a difference." Then she's off, with just a glance back over her shoulder.

Interesting, Veronica thinks, picking up her fork and stabbing a thin slice of radish. Which people could Cassie possibly mean?

CHAPTER 16

FOR A WHILE IT SEEMS like Travers is everywhere she turns. He attends meetings he has no place in. He drops by Cassie's office with inane questions and countless interruptions. There's even an operation or two disrupted by him talking to her from the observation gallery.

Cassie puts in a request for more agency nurses, and it's immediately declined. Strange, given that there's room in the budget for exactly that. That's annoying more than anything because it's getting harder to give her staff the small accommodations here and there that keep them happy.

She gets an invoice for the nurses anyway, but before she can call someone to complain, Travers is doing his creepy rounds again, taking the agency's bill from her and promising to resolve it as the hospital's point person on all things financial.

Another time Cassie would be grateful for the help. Now she just feels tired and worried, right down to her marrow. She certainly never used to feel this way.

"Fine!" Cassie pushes Veronica's office door opening without knocking. It clearly startles her, and she jumps in her seat at the interruption. "You win."

"I mean, I always do," Veronica says in that drawling way she has sometimes. "But what specifically did I win at this time?"

"He's such an infuriating little shit." Cassie can feel a real rant building as she starts to pace, shoving the door shut on her second lap of the room. "Everyone else I mention it to is like you—he doesn't want to know, not a numbers man, basically incompetent at all of our jobs. Then every other day he's asking me questions, poking around my files, and just sent a 'new template' for me to work from. I don't like it. I don't like it one bit."

"I don't think I've ever heard you say that much all at once before," Veronica answers once the silent starts to stretch on.

Cassie can't stop moving. Right now she's a shark, and to stop is to die where she stands. Motion is comforting and keeps her head quiet enough to think. She gets the distinct impression she's making Veronica dizzy, judging by the way she pinches the bridge of her nose.

"He thinks he can take advantage of me. It's probably why I got the fucking job. Assumes I'll just snap a salute and let him sell me down the river. He's doing something with money for my department, and I can't seem to catch what."

"God, you're really in a tizz, aren't you? Major Taylor has a temper."

Cassie shoots Veronica a glare. She's really not in the mood to be mocked.

"Come, sit," Veronica says, maybe as a peace offering.

Cassie does, but her leg is bouncing as soon as she's stationary in the visitor's chair.

"You know, I haven't opened that wine yet. Shall I let it breathe?" Veronica asks.

Fuck the headache. Cassie nods in agreement, not trusting herself to speak again yet. She folds her arms over her chest and waits for Veronica to come up with some brilliant plan. That's what she does, right? Fixes everything?

It's only mildly alarming that Veronica has a corkscrew in her desk. She has some friends for Cassie's bottle of wine, too, if the clinking when she pulls the desk drawer out is any indication. Not too far gone, though, if they still only have coffee mugs to drink the stuff out of.

They're pouring the second mug's worth when Veronica comes at the subject properly for the first time. "We could be imagining it. What has you so sure now?"

"I suppose the heavy-handedness of it all. I actually sat down and did all the bloody work over two days, cancelled surgeries I was looking forward to and everything. Suddenly there's a new template needed. I get the impression that whatever I do submit is going to get changed."

Veronica nods, leaning back in her chair and clasping her hands over her stomach. She's a vision in blue today, the cerulean shade vibrant against brown skin. Her hair is back in a French twist, not a strand out of place despite the evening hour.

"Why you, then?"

"Newness, I suppose? Although what if your boy Peter had gotten it instead?"

"I was thinking about that. He's better than me at financials. Maybe that's why Travers was so keen they not go with the obvious, internal choice."

"Right." Cassie tries to keep the hurt from her voice.

"Not that he was the right choice just because of that," Veronica amends.

Now that Wickham is off to Kensington, Veronica has seemed a little snappier with everyone on the wards. She must miss him.

"But any newbie would need time to learn our ways of doing things," Veronica continues. "No two Trusts are the same, apparently."

Cassie finishes her second mug of wine, wishing for something pale and frosty instead. Instead, Veronica has her covered with a fresh bottle of something red. It'll do. It's not like she has to drive home.

"How goes the house hunting, despite all this?" Veronica asks.

"Your agent is pretty keen," Cassie tells her. "She crunched the numbers for me and everything. We're looking at some places on Saturday. You're more than welcome to tag along, if you really do enjoy stuff like that."

"Well, no other plans that I know of," Veronica replies, considering. "Sure. Where are you looking?"

"Not too far from you. I said running distance from work, so…"

"We might end up neighbours, then." Veronica sounds almost pleased at the thought. "That's worth a second bottle if nothing else, surely?"

"I'm game if you are."

They sip more slowly now, relaxing into the low light of the desk lamps and the creature comforts of Veronica's office. Cassie wants to turn hers into something like this. A place she can greet her staff and hide away from the world as needed.

When they've caught up on the rest of the hospital gossip, Cassie makes a move to rise. "I should get going. Trains aren't as frequent this time of night, and there's nothing gloomier than waiting around the train station."

"Well, not for much longer, hopefully," Veronica offers.

They both stand at the same time, Cassie reaching for Veronica's mug to clear them away to the staff kitchen across the hall. Veronica moves around the desk, apparently with something important to say.

Suddenly Cassie notices how close they are. "Oh." She doesn't know what else to say.

"Whatever Travers is playing at, he won't drag you into it. I won't let him. Understood?"

Cassie blinks a little as Veronica lays her hands on her upper arms again. It's supposed to be soothing, but it makes her breath catch in her throat, her heart beat a little faster in her chest.

"If you say so."

"I do. You'll get home safe?" Her eyes, dark and unreadable, never leave Cassie's face. Lips parted, all Cassie can hear is each of them breathing, slightly out of time. There's something in the unguarded look between them that says *yes, this is it*. She leans in, closing the distance inch by painful inch until her lips are just about to—

A shriek of laughter in the corridor outside. Juniors pulling off some prank, maybe, or someone stayed behind after visiting hours without getting caught. It's enough to have them springing apart like magnets.

"Right, train. Got to go." Cassie doesn't give Veronica a chance to call her out or make excuses for her. "Goodnight."

CHAPTER 17

THE TAXI RANK IS POPULATED mostly by braying city types and giggling girls daft enough to go home with them. Veronica keeps an instinctive distance without surrendering her place in line. When slipping into the cab, she pops her hopefully visible white earphones in, pausing only to give her address. She's in no mood for small talk.

There's no point pulling out the journal that rests unread in her lap for the short journey. She skips a few tracks on her phone until something classical with thundering percussion and no words fills her head. All the better not to think to.

Just as she gets out of the taxi, dreading an empty house, she sees her ex waiting. Leaning against the garden wall, Angela makes for a tall silhouette, but one Veronica can still recognise anywhere. Those broad shoulders, the regal tilt to her jawline—it couldn't be anyone else. The soft cloud of her afro is gone these days, but the close-shaved look is just as striking on her. It's nice to still see some of what Veronica loved about her in stolen moments like these.

"He'd better be in there." And thus the nostalgic spell is broken. That passes for a greeting when it comes to her ex-wife these days. Angela doesn't bother adding a hug or any kind of physical contact to her words, not the easy way she always used to.

"Danny? He didn't say anything about coming here. And you could have called if you were looking for him."

"Well, he's not answering the door and I don't have a key. He's an hour past curfew and his phone's turned off. Yours is just ringing out."

The obvious reply is a sarcastic one, and sure enough Veronica can almost feel it queuing up on her tongue. She summons one last scrap of energy, and her better instincts along with it.

"Well, let's see if he's here. Sorry about the calls, I was in a late meeting." She opens the front door and can feel the emptiness of the house from the first step. "And then we'll go looking, if you drive."

"Out partying, were we?" Angela accuses, but her heart doesn't seem in it.

"Couple of glasses with a colleague having a tough time, if you must know." Veronica slings her light coat over the bannister and heads upstairs, looking around. No shoes kicked off, no schoolbag full of homework dumped in the hallways. She calls out for Danny, getting no response, as expected.

Angela isn't satisfied. "Can I go upstairs and check? Just for my peace of mind?"

Veronica nods. What does it cost her at this point? She's trying to ignore the chill down her spine, the creeping dread she's only known since becoming a parent. She listens to Angela's progress by footsteps, only moving when she hears them reach the stairs.

"I found this?" Angela says when she gets to the bottom. There's a little red book in her hand. "I thought it looked a bit like a school book, but it says Cassandra Taylor inside the cover? Who's she when she's in our home?"

"A home you haven't lived in for two years, Ange."

"I thought it was Daniel's, okay? I'll mind my business." Angela holds up her hands in surrender, before tossing the book at Veronica. "I suppose I'll have to go looking for him now."

They don't say it, but the weighted look between them expresses a hundred worries about raising a brown-skinned son in London. No amount of choosing a safe neighbourhood or the right school is protection enough. As parents they've worried over every scraped knee and bruise, right through to the reality of his teens where gangs and knives and drugs are lurking in even more places than anyone imagines. On top of that, there's the risk of him being stopped or roughed up by the police, just for not being white enough in the wrong place at the wrong time.

Daniel knows all this. They've talked him through it a hundred times between them, and his uncles and cousins on Angela's side have stressed that they don't have the luxury of skipping curfew, going off on their own, or neglecting to check in. There's too many horror stories, and Veronica has certainly seen enough of them filtered through A&E on a weekend.

It's so late on Thursday that it's a yawn away from Friday. She could sleep where she stands. And yet the knot in her stomach of pure panic, the spiralling weight of it, is waking her up again by the second. They need a plan. Action helps; useless fretting does nothing.

"He'll head home, if anywhere." Veronica leads Angela back to the kitchen and its kettle. Two cups of strong tea, just a splash of milk, coming up.

"Mrs Okosha from next door is keeping an eye out. She's up with her husband's coughing anyway, so she'll call if he comes home."

The kettle starts to heat, and Veronica goes through the motions of fetching cups and tea bags. "I assume you checked the website for delays? If he's just stuck on a train somewhere, or there are overnight roadworks."

"Vee, please. I'm not that desperate to see you, so you have to understand if I'm coming here, I'm already worried. For good reason."

"Then we can take my car and go looking. Tea first to make sure we're both alert. Then we take all his likely routes home. Oh! I'll call work, have them check admissions. And I'm sure Wendy in triage will ask her husband for me. He's a fraud detective or something, but they're all coppers in the end. Nice bloke. You know, considering."

While Veronica's no fan of the police herself, she does see what they're up against whenever they appear at the hospital. It doesn't erase what they've done to her family and friends over the years, or how many needless traffic stops she's had ever since her cars got into a certain price range.

She pours the tea, frowning as Angela adds a lot more milk and two heaps of sugar to hers. "You're supposed to be watching that," Veronica warns, careful to keep it light. "A diabetic coma won't help anyone."

Angela rolls her eyes, taking quick sips of the tea. She never did wait for it to cool. "Drink up, then, so we can get going."

After half a mug, Veronica straightens. "Okay, come on." She moves across the kitchen to dig the car keys out of the drawer. "I swear, if that little shit is chatting up a girl somewhere with his phone turned off, he's grounded for a year."

"If he's chatting up a girl, he gets it from you," Angela chimes in, taking the offered keys for Veronica's Audi. "This new?"

"Trade in," Veronica fibs. They don't have alimony; it's none of Angela's business how she spends her money. But still. "The last one had a steering issue."

"Right." Angela's favourite hobby, when things first turned sour, was telling Veronica the many, myriad ways in which she sold out. From her expensive cars to changing her name, right down to shopping at the posh organic supermarket—which happened to be nearest—rather than getting down to the market for fresh veg and spices as their parents had done, everything was a symptom of assimilation.

Most of the streets are ones Veronica recognises. She grew up further west, and Angela's new place is just outside of Hammersmith, so the routes are logical enough that she doesn't have to offer suggestions or turn on the Satnav. Instead, she turns the radio to a local station she generally ignores, waiting for the next news bulletin between the dusty eighties hits.

Angela slots her phone into the dashboard holder, and they both glance at it every time it lights up with a new message. Clearly she's already put the word out to the loose network of fellow parents and local relatives who might have seen their boy. When they park for the first time, at the McDonald's that Daniel swears he doesn't waste any pocket money at, Veronica makes good on her promise to rouse her A&E colleagues, and their police contacts with it.

"Can't we report him missing already?" Angela asks when they get back in the car.

"You know better than I do that we can't yet. Let's not lose our heads entirely." Despite the tension, Veronica risks reaching across slightly to pat Angela's jeans-clad thigh.

"How many mothers have said that, hmm? Told themselves they were being hysterical. It's a gut feeling, Vee. I know you don't spend the same time with him, but trust me on this, okay?"

"I'm here, aren't I?" It's snappish, and Veronica isn't sorry. "Let's cool it on competing for mother of the year and focus on looking for Daniel."

"Fine."

"Fine."

Later, the car purrs through another junction—Notting Hill this time, because he still comes up this way on weekends—and they scan the pavements for any signs of their son.

———◆◇◆———

The sun has been up for more than an hour when Veronica calls it quits, parked outside Angela's new flat. Of course she bought it a few years ago now, but everything after the home they shared is still labelled *new* to Veronica.

"We'll try your place one more time, in case the neighbour missed him. Then I need to shower and change."

"What for?"

Veronica isn't expecting the challenge. "What for? For work, of course. It's bad enough I'm going to be tired and irritable, I'd rather be hygienic and less crumpled at least."

"No, I mean, you're going into work?" The darker circles under Angela's eyes must mirror her own.

Veronica tries to summon the fondness she felt for so many years for this face. Those high cheekbones, eyebrows with their broad, dark lines. Full lips that Veronica has kissed more than any others. Almost fifteen years together, and one beautiful, cheeky, missing son to show for it. "I have to keep busy. There's only so much we can do."

"No, right, of course. I'll drop you an email or something if he shows up before Sunday?"

"Angela, don't."

"Just go to your fucking hospital, yeah? I'll be here, waiting for him."

"He'll show up. Trust me, he's just going to get the bollocking of his young life when he does, okay? Is there someone who'll come wait with you?"

A nod. "Yeah, I've got people."

Veronica doesn't press any further. Part of her just doesn't want to know. There's a reason she doesn't pull all-nighters anymore. Her eyes feel gritty and there's a low-grade headache, probably thanks to dehydration.

"The hospital is another place he might show up, for better or worse." Veronica is trying not to think about the worse. "Ideally because he knows he's in trouble and he'll come there first to try and manipulate me. Or, well. Let's hope not the other way, yes?"

Angela startles her by leaning across the front seat now their seatbelts are off, pulling Veronica into a hug. Just like that, the bubble in the back of her throat seems to burst, and the first panicked tears come.

"He'll be okay," Veronica murmurs, more for her own benefit than anything. "But please, I have to keep busy. I'll go mad otherwise."

"Go," Angela says, more gentle now. "Just keep that phone charged, and Vee, the very second—"

"I promise. No distractions."

"Good."

With that, Angela unfolds her tall frame from the passenger seat, a swing in the curves of her hips even just dashing up the garden path, waving to Veronica from the door when there's no miracle waiting.

A minute later, Veronica fastens her seatbelt and pulls away from the kerb. It's time to shake the trees a little harder.

<hr />

"How long?" Pauline asks, leaning on the nurses' station in AMU, where she's just been chatting with Lea. "Did you ask in A&E as well?"

"Unofficially his name is flagged at every admitting desk in London," Veronica replies, fussing with her hair as it refuses to stay out of her face. She's going to have to attempt a French braid at this point, if her fingers still remember the patient steps. "And they've had a word with the boys at the Met, but no dice yet."

"Angela okay?" Pauline asks. They've always gotten on well, at least out of shared exasperation with Veronica at one time or another. "I think I had a text from her, but I haven't really checked my phone yet." She fusses in her backpack for it.

Veronica offers them a wan smile. "Now, I know the rules, and you can't technically come running if he does show up here in an ambulance, or dragged in by the feds." Veronica wants to smile that she's picked up Danny's slang for them. "But I would really, *really* appreciate it if anyone catches so much as a glimpse."

"Of course," Lea assures her. "He's one of ours; the rules can be bent a little. It's only for his own good. I just hope he's been out with his friends. You can shout at him then."

"There's a queue for that," Veronica agrees. "Thank you both. As always, I don't know where I'd be without you."

"I knew you'd miss me when I went to Trauma." Pauline preens just a little. "Speaking of, I better get through there before they start asking for some of Ms Taylor's games again. Too many fragile ones for wacky races."

"She's in already? Ms Taylor?"

"Before I was," Pauline replies. "She's getting quite keen on the place, I reckon. You two seem to work well together, when your paths cross."

"Hmm? Oh, I suppose so." Veronica tries and fails to block out the near-miss kiss of the previous evening. "I'll be in my office if anyone needs me. If I'm out at any point, I'm just double checking the A&E waiting room."

"Godspeed." Pauline squeezes her hand. "Your boy will come home."

"He'd better." Veronica steels herself not to cry yet again. "He'd better."

CHAPTER 18

"PAULINE! JUST THE SISTER I was looking for."

"I was through in AMU," Pauline starts to explain.

Cassie waves her off. This isn't a punctuality crackdown. "Of course. Anyway, rumour has it my new bedside kits are finally coming in today. Will they come right here, or is it to stores?"

Pauline is playing with her phone instead of listening, which is unheard of, even in the short time that Cassie has known her.

"I appreciate not everyone is as excited as I am…" Cassie doesn't need to explain that her fixation on the new trauma protocol is more about ignoring what *did not happen* last night, rather than a love of first-aid supplies. "But I did expect it to have registered."

"What?" Pauline looks up then. "Sorry, Ms Taylor. It's just my friend's son… Actually, you know Ms Mallick well enough by now. Her son, he didn't come home last night."

"Right. Well, he's a teenager. I thought they all did what they wanted now? Decay of society or whatever."

"He's barely thirteen," Pauline corrects, looking cross. "And you might think everything short of Kandahar is a peaceful place, but there are a lot of dangers in a city like London when you're a young biracial lad."

Cassie trips over her own thoughts. She's never been good at this, the whole empathy trip. Sympathy and compassion, sure, but never quite thinking in the other person's shoes. It's no great leap for Pauline—she has beloved children of her own. Honestly, Cassie has always wondered if she's a bit lacking in some way, that she has to be nudged into the appropriate level of sadness or panic. She prefers to think of it as being good in a crisis.

"Of course. I wasn't thinking. Is there anything we can do to help?"

"She's hoping he shows up here. Angela, his other mum, is at home waiting. Everyone's alerted that can be, short of an official missing person report. That'll go in this evening if he hasn't shown by then."

"Right. Bloody hell. Wait, Veronica is here?"

"Best place for her," Pauline cuts her off, loyalty showing fiercely now.

"I'd feel the same, I'm sure." Cassie is floundering. "Well, I'll keep an eye out."

"Your delivery will come to A&E stores; the supply company usually hits us about two."

"Very good. We're coping here on the ward? All looks peaceful."

"It is, but they're short in A&E today. Might want to send a body down or we'll have them triaging cold symptoms into Trauma again."

"I'll go," Cassie says, seizing on something to be busy with. "If you hear anything, or if anything kicks off here, just beep me."

"You got it. Actually, as long as we stay quiet, would you mind if I go over to AMU? See if I can't help Veronica look for him?"

Cassie nods and takes off to give half a day to A&E. While Cassie would never trade the heightened stakes of Trauma, there's no denying that this is seeing some of her usual types of cases one stage earlier. It's also a lot of staring blankly at people who think minor injuries requiring a swipe of antiseptic are emergencies. Even after seeing a paramedic, receptionist, triage nurse, and then a consultant. Shameless, in its own irritating way.

She ducks out for a coffee when the backshift clocks on, the waiting room down to a manageable number. The hospital coffee shop will do, although there's a fleeting moment when she considers getting the good stuff and taking some to Veronica. She might even appreciate it.

But that means maybe acknowledging that charged moment. Or maybe having another one, which appeals more than it should.

No, Cassie has learned her lessons about dating people she works with. Not getting involved means no more heartbreak, no more terrible guilt to carry around. The whole point in learning to be independent and self-sufficient is that she doesn't need to be caught up in all that nonsense. And on the odd occasion it gets a bit lonely, well, there are dating apps for that. Not that she's ever done more than install them and stare, baffled, at the array of women on there, but still. The possibility exists for detached, almost anonymous sex, nothing that can upend her life.

Nothing that makes her chest hurt just to think about. Or ruins her ability to handle a surgery gone awry.

It's lingering over which flapjack to have with her double-shot latte that does her in. Even though she's not used to the hospital environment entirely, and hasn't worked in a civilian one since her training years, Cassie has quickly picked up doctor blindness. To walk the halls of anywhere so full of sick people, especially when wearing scrubs or any other form of uniform, requires a certain level of obliviousness.

So any other time she probably wouldn't have seen jiggling handles on the fire exit, a sign someone's trying to open it from the outside. She's used to assessing a situation in a split-second, so it just takes the recognition that one of them is Daniel, the fact that it's directly opposite a stores cupboard, and the fact that it's going to trigger an alarm for her to spring into action.

Swiping her pass over the sensor means it opens without the incessant beep beginning, letting the boys stumble inside, almost hitting the ground before they right themselves. Daniel is dressed in casual clothes this time, not his school uniform, but Cassie is already sure. His mate is taller than him by a few inches, much broader, too. His hair is grown out into twists, where Daniel's is shaved in close. Rugby build, but currently bent almost double and cradling his abdomen where some kind of T-shirt is making for an improvised compress.

"This way," she barks at them both, knowing orders get better results than questions. Knowing the hospital better now, she leads them into an overflow room, mercifully unoccupied and technically part of her domain. It will make it easier to deflect nosy enquiries.

Daniel has enough sense to help his mate up onto the examination bed, ripping the disposable paper sheet in the process.

"Going to need a name," Cassie says, although she doesn't reach for the admission forms on the counter. "You can make one up, but that might be too much effort."

"Nigel," the injured boy says.

Okay. Not even close to Cassie's best guess, but different strokes and all that. "What happened here? I'm going to need to move this to examine you, Nigel."

"No!" He protests, clutching at the blood-stained cloth. "We been trying all night, but this is the only thing that keeps the blood stopped."

"I've got better methods, I promise you. I can't use them until I see it. Knife? Or broken glass? What are we talking about here?"

"It was a knife, yeah?" Daniel takes up the narrative, watching the door like a prisoner knowing the guards can't be far away. "Not a fight, nothing like that. A bunch of us were just pissing about, but he slipped and it nicked him."

"Sounds like first aid would have been enough," Cassie says, taking hold of Nigel's wrist and easing the ruined shirt away from his stomach. "Your mum—"

"You gonna grass?" Daniel asks, but there's no bravado in it. He's a scared little boy. "I'm gonna get so much shit about curfew, but if we'd brought him in anywhere it'd be in the computers and stuff."

"No telling tales from me. I can't disclose on a patient. You helped clean him up?" Cassie sees the wound is spotless. Not wide, but deeper than she's happy about. Technically Daniel isn't her patient, and she should march him into Veronica's office right now. Any junior should be able to do a quick scan for internal bleeding and stitch Nigel up.

"Yeah, you think I didn't get *First Aid for Dummies* as soon as I could talk?"

Cassie expected nothing less. "I'm surprised your mother doesn't have you sewing banana skins to get your technique honed early." The look in response says she's not far off the mark.

"Am I gonna die?" Nigel asks. His mid-puberty London accent is tinged with something far away, something Cassie faintly recognises. Her gut says Sudan, possibly. She did some peacekeeping trips there, before it all went to hell. And after.

"Not if I can help it. You risked a lot taking this long to see a doctor." Cassie hesitates. "You don't have papers, do you?"

"My mum doesn't, no. We registered me for school and stuff, but this is different. Anything with knives means police."

"I'm not calling them," Cassie reassures him. "There's no need. You can be treated without worrying. Does your mother know where you are?"

"I texted. She works nights; I'm out before she gets home."

"Were you at his place all night, then?" Cassie asks Daniel. She's going to be grilled on this at some point, needs some facts on her side.

"Yeah, we went there and I kept an eye on him."

"And you couldn't call your mum? One of them?" Cassie has heard enough junior recruits wriggling around with excuses, so Daniel had better not try a weak one on her.

"To have them come round and drag him in anyway? My mums are… Well, they're all about the rules, and how the system will set you free. You've met her; tell me she's not exactly that."

Cassie snorts. He has a point. Surely, though, presented with the facts, Veronica would have taken care of the boy off the books, as simply as Cassie is doing now? Even being on the premises doesn't require paperwork, strictly speaking. She has to assume the son knows his mother better than she does from a couple of months of professional interaction.

And whatever last night was.

"You know she's out of her mind with worry. If you leave him with me and go let her know you're okay, I promise you, I won't put Nigel's name on anything. I'll treat him myself."

"But—"

"He's going to need some blood; he's lost a lot. I'll check there's no permanent damage in that wound, and get him stitched up so the bleeding stops for good, yeah?"

"Then I'll wait til you've done that. Sorry, Doc, you seem like good people, but I promised I'd see him back home without it getting anyone in trouble."

"Then the minute I say he's good to go, you take him by your mother's office before leaving. I'd shake on it, but I'm already in bloodied gloves. Deal?"

"Deal."

She works quickly, most of the basics already stocked. A&E must not know about this room or it would have been raided by now.

"Okay, I just need to get a transfusion kit. Keep an eye on him while I grab a bag from the blood bank."

Daniel and Nigel nod. Nigel's rallying now that the bleeding has stopped.

Cassie leaves the door slightly ajar as she steps out into the corridor. The main bank is up by the operating theatres, but Trauma has its own mini chilled room for blood storage. If she were an F1 she'd be off begging permissions and codes, but there's something to be said for being the boss.

Another swipe of her slightly magical key card and she has access to a couple of pints of O-neg.

When it goes wrong, it does in that awful slow motion usually reserved for crashes and other unexpected collisions. Daniel pokes his head out of the exam room door when Cassie's barely feet away from it, just as his distracted mother turns from the A&E corridor to the junction that splits Trauma and AMU. A literal crossroads, and there's almost the sense they'll get away with it, if not for the way that Daniel hisses, "Ms Taylor!"

Veronica startles at the sound of his voice, a soft cry escaping her lips. She looks to Cassie and her slightly contraband blood next, adding up each side of the equation and coming to a conclusion of, no doubt, blinding range.

"Danny!" she shouts, rushing to him and tackling him with a hug that belies their relative sizes.

All this time and Cassie didn't realise that Veronica would have made a decent rugby flanker. It's a wonder Danny is still standing under the onslaught.

Their conversation is rushed, too fast for Cassie to follow at first. A flurry of *where have you been* and *what happened* and *are you okay* that sounds like pure panic spilling over. There's not much point in running now, but Cassie's calf muscles tense like there might be.

"Sorry, I need to, uh—" Nigel isn't all patched up yet, and Cassie does need to crack on.

It would be better if Veronica focused that sudden, babbling rage and relief on her. Instead, Cassie gets a glare that might well turn a person to stone.

Maybe she should stop and explain the little she knows, show Veronica that Daniel has never really been in danger, that he's been helping in the way any of them might have. Under Veronica's furious scrutiny, though, Cassie finds that words fail her. She continues back into the treatment room, unsurprised when Veronica shuffles right in after her, not letting go of Daniel for a second.

"How are you doing, Nigel?" Cassie asks. Focus on the patient, ease Veronica into the bigger story.

"Sorry, Mrs... Daniel's mum?" Nigel starts out talking to Cassie, but defaults to Veronica's natural, bristling authority. He flounders in the glare of all their attention. The boy's had enough terror for one night, and Cassie is ready to intercede on his behalf. Thankfully Veronica looks back and forth between the two boys, before yanking Daniel towards the door.

When Cassie turns back, Veronica and her son have disappeared down the corridor. She can't follow. There's a job to finish, a promise to keep.

And the definite, horrible feeling that she's fucked up something beyond repair.

CHAPTER 19

THE MINUTE VERONICA PUSHES THROUGH the double doors with Daniel in tow, there's an eruption from the nurses' station.

"I need to let your mother know you're here." Veronica pulls her phone out. "Stay here with Pauline and Lea. I mean it, Danny. No more than five steps in any direction."

"Your mums have been worried sick!" Pauline greets Danny with a visual once over that turns into a full-body hug. "We've told everyone in the hospital to look out for you. I've left Ms Taylor short of nurses in Trauma to help out. You better be in one piece, boy."

Whatever reply Danny makes is muffled, and Veronica ducks away when Angela answers on the second ring.

"He's here. Came in with someone, but Danny's okay. He's okay."

There's no need for introductions or small talk. That's what matters. Veronica tucks herself behind the column that the station is built around, letting it take her weight as the trembling passes through her, shoulders to knees.

"He's not hurt?"

"No, he... I don't even know what happened yet, I found him in the corridor. Should I—"

"I'm coming. We'll... Just wait for me in your office?"

"Of course." Veronica ends the call and brushes away the tears that have welled up again. She's usually more resilient than this, but Daniel has always been the exception. Walking over hot coals would be nothing if he needed it, but the prospect of anything bad befalling her boy leaves her oddly paralysed like this.

"Daniel, we're waiting for your mum in my office. Are you sure you're not hurt? You said you weren't on the walk over, but you won't be in trouble for that. I'd rather know."

"I brought Nigel in. We tried to sort it ourselves, but the bleeding kept coming back, Mum. I'm really sorry. I didn't—"

"Let's take it in here, shall we?" Veronica nods in gratitude at her waiting staff, who go back to chattering amongst themselves. "Now, Nigel is your friend from…?"

"He came to the Arsenal game with us that time? At the Emirates?"

"Gotcha. What were you two up to that you couldn't come to the hospital? If you were drinking, or God help me Danny, if you were on something—"

"Mum!" He holds his hands up, those big eyes radiating hurt at her. "Come on, I know you're not around all the time now, but that's taking the piss."

"Taking the—"

"He hasn't got papers, has he? Nigel can go in the school system 'cause they don't ask for everything, but if he goes on an NHS computer, his mum and him get deported."

"No, that's not true, Danny. And even if it were true, why the hell are you coming to a woman you've met once instead of your own mother? Did you think I'd see him sent back to…?"

"Sudan."

"To Sudan, just because of ticking some boxes?" Veronica's stomach flips. Is that really what he thinks of her? That her morality would take a backseat to stickling for the rules? This is what comes of never getting to be the fun mum, of always being the *brush your teeth* and *eat the broccoli* enforcer. "Danny, if you'd just explained it like you are now… You must promise you always will, in future. I'd never see anyone in trouble because they needed a doctor."

"Yeah, I mean. I guess."

"Danny. Is he okay? Do I need to go and check with Ms Taylor?"

"She said he'll be fine. Can I go?"

"No. No, I don't think so. We're going to have some words about sharing information between colleagues. Have you eaten?"

"Yeah, we had stuff. You got anything to drink?"

"There's bottled water—"

"Mum..."

"Fine, I'll be back in five minutes with one can of fizz. Don't step out of this room unless there's a fire alarm, hear me?"

"Yeah, Mum. Sorry."

"I think you were trying to do something good." She pulls him into one more hug, less bone-crushing this time, and smooths his short hair, pressing a kiss to the top of his head. "Next time you do it with a call first, at least."

He nods against her, and for a minute all that teen attitude evaporates. It must have terrified him, a friend bleeding out. How Cassie is treating the kid in a side room is beyond Veronica at the moment, but she's about to find out.

If there's a record for the time to cross that short distance, Veronica smashes it like Usain Bolt in Jimmy Choos. Cassie is running a portable ultrasound over the young man's abdomen when Veronica comes bursting into the exam room.

The torrent she wants to unleash is like a fizzy sweet on her tongue, but Veronica summons the last of her willpower.

"Nigel, sweetheart. How are you feeling?" Veronica asks.

"Better, miss."

"No, no, we've suffered an Arsenal home game together. It's Veronica to you. Please tell me your mum knows where you are?"

"Nah, we don't see each other until after school now. I've got a few hours." He winces as Cassie prods the fresh stitches, studiously not looking at Veronica. "Thank you for not grassing me up. Both of you."

"If you're ever hurt, you come here and get treated right away. Your mum too, Nigel. We won't report anything to anyone, but you might need something we can't do in a back room. Now, do I need to be worried about you and Danny being stabbed again anytime soon?"

"It really was an accident, miss. Miss Veronica. I'm okay now."

"Yes, but we don't want another night like last night. Danny has to at least call us, even if he doesn't come home." Her hands are shaking as she steps up next to the exam bed, elbow brushing Cassie's and making them jolt further apart on contact. "I'm glad you're feeling better."

She takes his hand and squeezes it. "I'm going to steal your doctor for a minute. You'll be okay on your own?"

"Yeah, I'm good."

Cassie stiffens at Veronica's hand on her elbow, guiding her towards the door. She has the presence of mind to strip off her gloves and dunk them in the waste bin on the way out, at least.

"Veronica, listen—"

"Not. Here."

Veronica drags them down the hall to the first empty space she can think of: the surplus linens cupboard. There's more floor space than average, since it's only for the rare time they stay in storage long enough to build up an overflow.

Cassie retreats to the corner, backing up against the shelves like Veronica may take a swing at her. It's almost tempting, if Veronica had the first idea how to throw a punch. She is not going to let Cassie play the victim now, not when she's squarely in the wrong.

"First of all, you are one hundred percent, completely in the wrong, Ms Taylor. Whatever excuses you're about to offer will not change that fact. I know the nurses told you, like they told everyone else in the building." Veronica feels the head of steam building up after hours and hours of holding it all back, and *fuck* it feels good. "We may disagree on patient care, on the best training methods, or what constitutes an acceptable midday snack."

"Veronica—"

She holds up a hand, the swipe of it to cut Cassie off is a little too vicious, but no matter.

"You don't get an opinion on the safety of my son. On what secrets to keep. How long did you have them stashed away in there, hmm? It's bad enough you can't respect me as a colleague, but I thought we were friends! Or getting to be. Worse than that, however you feel about me, Angela certainly deserved to know as soon as we had any confirmation that Danny was okay."

"You're right, and—"

"Will you stop interrupting me?" Veronica advances on Cassie then, just two steps, but enough to make her tense for a fight. "If my son or

118

anyone else connected to me shows up at this hospital again, I'll thank you to keep out of it, or at least send them straight to me. Are we clear?"

For a moment it looks like Cassie is going to give her what for, and Veronica actually relishes the thought. The only thing more cathartic than yelling it all out is getting shouted back at in return. She wants someone to just say it for a change, instead of hiding behind passive-aggressive politeness. To tell her that if something happened to Danny it would have been at least partly Veronica's fault. Her absence, her lack of attention, her blithe assumptions that Angela would handle whatever cropped up.

This could have turned out so much worse, and she'd be living with that for the rest of her life. Veronica sees exactly two ways of dealing with that realisation: either she turns it on herself and spends the rest of the day self-flagellating, or she lets it all out on the convenient person in front of her.

"Crystal," Cassie says eventually, through gritted teeth. "Now, if I can get back to my actual patient?"

She pushes past Veronica, a little rougher than is strictly necessary. In the doorway the urge to bite back must overcome her.

"Because Daniel wasn't my patient. Once I'd dealt with the boy who was, I was going to march them straight over to you, if you'd bothered to stop for a minute and find that out. But no matter how worried you were, my first and only obligation was to the bleeding person in front of me. Maybe you expect everyone else to put your commands first, but that won't wash with me."

"Oh, so this is my fault now?" Veronica hates how her voice rises on the question, positively shrill. "You've got a lot of nerve, Ms Taylor."

"I've also got things to do."

It would be so easy to reach out, to catch her wrist and walk it all back with an apology. But frankly Veronica isn't sure that's wise, given the strange spark between them. She's done more than enough for this woman already, and they can be professional, distant colleagues, just nodding acquaintances roaming the halls.

Better. Safer. Infinitely wise.

Because there's another unfortunate truth hurtling towards her right now. Not about Daniel, or professionalism, or the correct way to treat non-lethal sharp trauma to the abdomen.

No, this truth is that when her cheeks are flushed pink with anger, and her blonde bob is mussed from rushing around, not to mention the sparkle in those grey-blue eyes at the hint of a fight, then Cassie Taylor might be the most gorgeous woman Veronica has seen in a long time.

Which is much, much more than she's capable of dealing with right now. And so she lets Cassie storm off, before doing much the same after a minute's delay.

By the time Veronica makes it back to her office, at a less breakneck speed, Angela is sprinting down the corridor to meet her.

"He's really okay? You checked?"

"I promise." Veronica absorbs the slightly frantic cuddle she receives the way she imagines Danny just handled the one from her. Once, drunk on wine and younger love, Veronica had called Angela an 'Amazonian goddess'. 'Nubian', Angela had corrected, but she feels surprisingly frail and mortal right now. "He's fine, Ange. Not a mark on him. His friend got hurt; he was trying to do good. We'll have to talk about how we handle it, but not just yet."

Angela pulls back eventually, wiping at her cheeks. "I'm sorry. For giving you shit about work, for—"

"Not necessary." Veronica waves it off. "Heat of the moment and all that. Come on, you won't feel all the way better til you see him for yourself."

"We'll talk to him tonight, once we decide," Angela says, taking Veronica by the arm. For a moment it's as if they never broke up and nothing ever got too complicated. "Come around; I'll do dinner. You always were good in a crisis."

A flash of blonde hair on a passing orderly gives Veronica a guilty pang as they approach her office door. As her anger gives way to relief, she realises how hard she was on Cassie, how unfair. That is going to take some fixing, if it can be repaired at all. Pauline comes scurrying to greet Angela, repeating Veronica's reassurances that Danny is fine.

Distracted, Veronica considers if she really can let Cassie off the hook as easily as Angela just did for her. Wasn't Cassie just being a good doctor?

She'll worry about that later. Now there's Danny to rescue from Angela's tear-soaked hugs, and tea to drink, presumably, while they all get back to normal for a while.

Cassie Taylor can be next week's problem.

CHAPTER 20

Smoothing down her leather jacket, Cassie glances at the rest of her outfit. She refuses to dress formally on a weekend, even if she has popped into work to collect her contract and payslips for all things mortgage related. It will probably take months to find a place, especially now she won't have Veronica's guidance, but there are another couple of viewings booked all the same. Finding something comfortable that still says "responsible adult with a real job" is the balancing act. Her jeans are clean, and instead of the usual gym T-shirt she'd favour, a crisply ironed white shirt is the best she can do.

There's a knock at her office door, and she calls a distracted 'come in' without bothering to look round.

"I heard you were in on your day off," Alan says, and he's a pleasant surprise. "I also heard that AMU and Trauma are at war. Two households, each alike in dignity…"

"That decision has nothing to do with me," Cassie replies, aware of how tense she sounds as she says it. "All I did was treat a patient. If Veronica Mallick still isn't speaking to me a week later, I'd say that's very much her problem."

"Well, so long as you're totally chill about it." Alan is teasing, but he takes a seat in her one visitor's chair. He's in civvies, too.

"Just off nightshift?" she asks.

"Yeah, the NHS doesn't believe in social lives. The clubs will have to survive without me two weekends a month."

"That's a perk of being the boss, I suppose," Cassie says. "Not having to work weekends for the first time in years. I do, however, have to go and look at a bunch of overpriced and generic houses. Lucky me?"

They're interrupted by another knock at the door. Before Cassie can invite them in, the door swings open and Alan sits up straighter in his chair.

"Ms Taylor, I wondered if I could have a word?" Veronica, in all her dressed-down glory. Which of course means she still looks smarter than Cassie did the day of her interview, but the soft cardigan and black jeans are both items Cassie automatically wishes she knew where to buy.

"Are you here to apologise?" Cassie is not giving an inch, not after a week of whispers and now outright gossip if Alan has heard all about it.

"You know, I can just go," Alan says, getting out of the chair and edging quickly towards the door. "You ladies have fun now, and remember St Sophia's has CCTV if you were planning on fighting it out."

With that, he disappears out into the corridor.

For a moment it looks like Veronica really is going to stand her ground. Arms folded, she purses her lips as though the apology is a physical, unpleasant taste on her tongue.

"Fine. I'm sorry that I may have overreacted. I appreciate you were trying to look after Nigel. Oh hell, I don't have a rational explanation. Just an excuse. I hadn't slept, I was worried sick, and I acted like a complete cow."

"You do realise that my next stop was absolutely bringing Daniel right to you? For the sake of ten minutes. How is he?" Cassie isn't letting her off that easily, but it would be nice to know if the boy is all right.

"He's grounded is how he is. I really did mean to come and talk to you about this sooner, but it's been one of those weeks." It really has, on all fronts. None of it helped by two bodies of staff loyal to bosses they know are at odds. Cassie forces herself to swallow the instinctive anger that bubbles up in her throat, no doubt accompanied by cruel words. She focuses instead on the fact that Veronica looks less polished for once. Her make-up is lighter, not quite hiding the dark circles under her eyes. It's possible to Cassie's untrained eye that those heels don't technically go with the dress, either. A sure sign that all is not well.

Cassie gestures towards the visitor's seat that Alan has vacated. Veronica's glance at her to make doubly sure sells her contrition. Suddenly exhausted by the tension of it all, Cassie sees the way forward. "Then I accept your apology. What are you doing in on a Saturday? I thought I was the only sad case?"

"Well, I had to collect some things," Veronica says. "And I wondered if you were still looking for a house-viewing buddy? Thought it might be a chance to get back on track, friendship-wise. I know you hate it, but I really can be useful at that whole thing."

It would be easy to deny her, on principle alone. Part of Cassie still wants to, wants Veronica to understand the chest-tightening feeling when a friend turns on her. She can't understand how rarely Cassie gets close to other people, how much more sensitive she is to losing them for no good reason. The week has been endless, assuming that Veronica would never speak kindly again.

Then Cassie finds herself reaching into the pocket of her jacket and unfolding the papers she printed yesterday. "I have two different flat viewings late morning. They're not a million miles from your neighbourhood, if you fancy it."

"Private viewings or those godawful open house things? There's nothing more irritating than trying to quietly fawn over somewhere you're not even sure you like, just to try and stop a bunch of strangers from snapping it up first."

Cassie snorts. "You're really making me want to go."

"I did say… Well, you've made your plans while I was being a heinous bitch about everything." Embarrassment. That's the emotion Cassie's been seeing flicker across Veronica's features for this whole conversation, so out of place that she almost didn't recognise it. Right, that's officially enough of that.

"I think that's a bit strong on the self-flagellating. At worst, you were a mother overreacting. We've all been on the receiving end of that."

"The longer I left it, the worse I felt about it. I should have apologised right away. Let's see what you're going to look at."

"You don't have to come if it's just out of obligation," Cassie says, but she's suddenly hoping that Veronica will insist.

"Oh no, I told you. I actively enjoy this sort of thing. Based on your expression, it's not something you're looking forward to. Unless you've gone off me altogether, that is. As a friend." Veronica's voice is just a little higher, as though her throat is tight. As though she's almost afraid to suggest the idea.

There it is. The reset button Cassie should be looking for. Just friends, who don't lean or get too close, or have huge arguments in their place of work. Friends who do favours, who loan some running gear or bring a nice bottle of wine. Friends, a commodity Cassie is short of these days. The trouble with leaving the army in your early forties, while almost everyone you're friends with stays in, is learning how to start over. Cassie has never been the most popular kid in the playground, and without the common bonds of work, she'd have no idea where to even start.

"I think we should at least give it a try. Friends, I mean. And a friend who helps me find a home would be a valuable one right now."

"That's probably more than I deserve, but I'll take it," Veronica says. "So which one are we seeing first?"

Millie the estate agent greets them both like old friends, even though she and Cassie have only spoken on the phone twice. Veronica shakes her hand her warmly, picking up the small talk effortlessly. No, she and Angela clearly didn't get back together; Danny's doing great in school, thanks, secondary already.

"So this place is actually a bit of a steal." Millie leads them around the side of the house, to where the upper flat has its own entrance. "I crunched the numbers you gave me, Cassie, and we've already got interest on your Swindon pad."

"You do?" Cassie wasn't expecting that. "Wow, I mean that's great. It takes a lot of pressure off if that's already underway."

"You keeping the Maida Vale place, then, Veronica?" Millie asks, unlocking the door with one of a few dozen keys on one big ring, like a school janitor. "In case this one doesn't work out?"

"What?" Cassie mutters, but no one seems to hear her.

Veronica hesitates before answering. "Well, we don't strictly need it in play just yet. Wanted to see what's out there before selling both our places. Cassie's just back from such long service abroad; have to wait and see if she can really acclimatise."

"Yes, she did mention the army doctor thing. Terribly hot, if you don't mind me saying, eh?" Millie actually winks at Cassie, who would be more flustered if she weren't massively confused.

Why is Veronica going along with the misunderstanding that they're together? Someone should say something, or Millie is going to get entirely the wrong idea.

"Now, Millie." Veronica is off again. "Let's save you a bit of work and do the wandering ourselves, then you can give us the nitty gritty once Cassie has a feel for the place."

That sounds close to perfect. Cassie's been dreading a morning of people jabbering at her, trying to feign interest in taps and door handles or whatever the hell is supposed to be the difference between once place and another. Structural integrity, plenty of light, a relatively blank canvas—that's all she wants. It might be nice after all these years to go to a home-décor sort of place and get as enthused about tiles and paint colours as other people seem to, but Cassie doesn't see that happening.

Clean, bigger than a tent, and much less drafty. This place fits the bill on those fronts already. Although the building is quite modest from the street, whoever revamped it had an eye for space and angles. She quite fancies herself the esteemed surgeon in a place like this, with its skylights and white walls. The floors are stripped back, no evidence of whoever lived here before.

"Right, you go left, I'll go right. Meet you back in the hall once we've done a full circuit," Veronica says, always happiest issuing orders.

Cassie supposes she's just glad someone knows what the hell she's doing.

She only makes it from the living room to the kitchen before Millie follows along.

"Been together long?"

"Not...really. I've only been back a matter of months."

"I see. That's why you've been tackling the house solo, hmm? Keep it all in your name in case it doesn't have legs?"

Cassie feels faintly offended on Veronica's part. Then considers her legs, which are quite spectacular, frankly. That's distraction enough for Millie to pounce.

"Should it fizzle out, here's my card. Always had a thing for a lady in uniform." She's still holding it out when Veronica appears in the doorway, causing Cassie to grab at it, no doubt looking completely guilty in the process.

"No good, I'm afraid," Veronica says. "The bathroom is just…yikes. Not worth the amount of work it would take to redo. I mean, have a look for yourself, of course…"

"No, you're the expert," Cassie says, darting across the room to join her. "Second place a bit better on that front?"

"Well, yes, it's a newer build. Quite modern from top to bottom," Millie says, trying to duck Veronica's glare. "It's just one street over, so I'm going to leave the car here."

"We'll follow along, let you get it opened up," Cassie decides. "We'll meet you there. Number 53, was it?"

Millie doesn't look pleased about that either. "Yes. Well, don't take too long. I do have other appointments this morning."

Doubtful, since it's already coming up on half past eleven, but Cassie steers Veronica downstairs and out. St John's Wood was the closest decent area to the hospital within her budget, and Cassie has pored over maps in the past twenty-four hours to get a feel for it.

Veronica still looks faintly annoyed when they make it out onto the street.

"You okay?" Cassie asks.

"You know, if you're on the trawl for dates as well as a place to live, I can always go home."

"What?"

"I saw Millie put the moves on you, even though she thinks we're together. Always been an incorrigible flirt, that one."

"Okay, I'm not the one who implied we were house hunting for our new love nest, so hold on a minute." Cassie doesn't understand what she's supposed to have done wrong here. "Look, let's just get this other place ticked off, and then we can have a much nicer time getting lunch than staring at skirting boards."

"Yes, well." Veronica straightens up and starts walking off. A moment later she calls out for Cassie to follow, because she's heading the wrong way. "Nice neighbourhood, at least."

"Not bad." Cassie looks around, this street far more residential with its large family homes. She could be anywhere, honestly. "I'm not sure modern is going to suit me, exactly. We'll see."

But when she sets eyes on the place, with its For Sale sign only just being posted in the small front garden, Cassie is already halfway to sure. It's one of those eco-friendly builds, with special wood panelling that's all specially sourced, and lots of glass everywhere. It would never stand up to roadside explosions, and that's something she instantly loves about it. She's done her time behind concrete and steel, in darkened bunkers with lights down low to avoid attention.

Millie seems to have forgiven them, opening up the house and letting Cassie stroll across the hall, trying to take it all in.

"You know, this might be just the thing," she says, not sure who's actually listening. Lots of open-plan spaces, privacy from high hedges all around the sides and back. The floor-to-ceiling windows look like something from a swish Swedish design catalogue, and Cassie can already picture furniture, her unpacked boxes of belongings all over it. Even the kitchen screams "come and cook here".

"I've got the reports right here, but there's almost nothing wrong with this place," Millie begins. "The bathroom in particular is fantastic."

Cassie jogs upstairs and takes in the huge shower, walk-in with marble floors, and even a little bench. That will do wonders for the days when her back is playing up a little. The master bedroom looks like a hotel suite, only without a bed for now. The two smaller rooms will make a decent guest room and a small office. She's always wanted a proper space to read journals and catch up on the fiddly admin without being confined to the hospital.

"I'll take it," she announces, as soon as she's back downstairs.

Veronica looks startled. Millie smiles like she can't quite believe her luck.

"I mean, subject to everything being in order. It's just what I've been looking for. And even you won't have complaints about the bathroom, Veronica."

"We'll see about that." Veronica storms off upstairs.

Cassie follows with a *what can you do?* shrug to Millie. "See?" She gestures towards the bathroom.

Veronica has now headed straight for the empty bedroom, with its whole wall of built-in wardrobes. Cassie will never own enough clothes to fill them; she knows that already.

"You can't go all in on the second place you see," Veronica hisses, keeping her voice low. "And dial down the enthusiasm if you don't want to end up paying twenty grand above the offer price."

"I like it." Cassie gestures around the room, hands waving a bit uselessly. "I'm not looking for too many specifics. Gut feeling, this is the place for me."

"You can't just decide like that! Do you make all your decisions this way?"

"Pretty much," Cassie says. "Saves a lot of time and agonising, don't you think? It's like trauma: just do it; worry about it later if there's time."

"That's how you end up throwing yourself at patients with knives, isn't it?" Veronica advances on her, staring at Cassie like she's from another planet. "Or ignoring the plight of frantic mothers to treat injured boys?"

"Listen, I thought we were sorted about that—" Cassie finds herself back against the wardrobes.

"You just decide. Quick, strong, so utterly sure of yourself. What about Millie's offer? Decided on that yet?"

"I'm not going out with her if that's what you're asking. I'm beginning to think you're almost…"

"What?" Veronica makes the single word dangerous.

"Jealous." Cassie throws the accusation out and sees it land.

Veronica is barely inches away, and it's definitely warm in here, for an empty house with no heating on. "Why on *earth* would I be jealous?" she asks, grabbing a fistful of Cassie's leather jacket. "Oh, did you think I'd forgotten about the other night? Our interrupted little moment?"

"That was…" Cassie swallows hard. "That was a moment, then? Not my imagination?"

"Why do you think I was so disproportionately pissed off at you?" Veronica asks. "I'm not in the habit of overreacting."

"No, I can see that." Cassie thinks agreeing is a wise plan right now. "Is this…one of those moments?"

"You tell me." Veronica presses her lips against Cassie's with purpose.

It's almost a tender kiss for a moment, a brief exploration of how it might feel. As soon as Cassie raises her hand and runs it through Veronica's silky black hair, it nudges her into deepening the kiss right then and there.

Open-mouthed, a little breathless, they're clutching at each other as though gravity might betray them at any moment.

And right then, Cassie's suddenly sure of two things. That she wants this house—might even mount a plaque in this room to commemorate this moment. And Veronica Mallick can really, really kiss.

The sound of Millie climbing the stairs brings them back to their senses, but not before Cassie sneaks one last capture of Veronica's bottom lip between her teeth.

"Has she changed your mind yet?" Millie calls. "If not, I can have the paperwork started first thing Monday."

Cassie pulls away, marching right out onto the landing. "Monday it is. I'll give you a call and let you know when I can call in at the office. I'll just take one more walk around, if that's okay?"

"Well, it's going to be yours," Millie says. "I'd say you can do whatever you want. Veronica, you approve?"

"Oh, I approve," Veronica replies, her gaze raking over Cassie with very little ambiguity. She leans in to whisper against Cassie's ear. "I'm already looking forward to being invited over."

The look she gives Cassie then almost makes her knees give out. Oh, she is definitely doomed.

CHAPTER 21

VERONICA'S LIPS ARE STILL TINGLING when they've walked back to Millie's car, somehow hand in hand without either she or Cassie seeming to make a deliberate move to make that happen. They wave the happy estate agent off in her gaudy Mini covered in her company's logo.

"I can't believe you bought a house in less than five minutes," Veronica says. "I mean, I know there are formalities to come, but you really did that."

"I might have bought a house, but I can't believe you snogged me in it!" Cassie comes right back at her.

"Must we use that word?" Veronica's protest is heartfelt. She has never, ever liked it.

"*Kiss* barely seems to do it justice. You had intentions, Veronica. Don't start walking it back now."

"I have no *intention* of doing that. In fact, I'm trying to work out if there's a nice park around here, where two women so inclined might do a bit more of that kissing. Perhaps sharing a bench in a quiet corner of it?"

"One thing I didn't research was kiss-friendly parks." Cassie smacks her forehead in mock frustration. "How could I have been so short-sighted?"

Veronica's phone peals in the quiet street like the bells of Big Ben. That is decidedly not good. In one of her fits of over-organisation she'd set only three numbers to always ring even when her phone was otherwise silenced. Angela, Danny, and the on-call service.

"Is that—" Cassie starts to ask, before her phone starts trilling, too. Still on the irritating default ringtone, at that.

"Sounds like all hands on deck," Veronica says, answering hers with a swipe. "Ms Mallick."

It's not one of the usual phone bank workers; they must be using more temps. "Sorry to call you in on a weekend, but we have a—"

"Can you just email the alert? I'm on my way. Fifteen minutes ETA, give or take."

"Oh, thank you, Ms Mallick. A&E is already expecting overflow."

"Understood." Veronica watches Cassie hum in acknowledgment of the same information. It must be a decent-sized trauma if the existing A&E plus rostered Trauma teams can't handle it.

"Well," Cassie says as she hangs up, already drifting towards the junction with the main road, the better to catch a taxi. "Looks like it's going to be a busy Saturday after all. Wasn't I just saying how great it is to be the boss and have the weekend off?"

"You might have said that. I would never tempt fate so foolishly. Rain check on the bench and the, uh…"

"Kissing," Cassie finishes. "Well, assuming you can restrain yourself during the"—she flags down a passing black taxi with its light on—"cab ride. After you."

Veronica climbs in first, pleased when Cassie slides along to sit closer, rather than sticking to their respective corners. No kissing, alas, but when she lays her hand on the sliver of seat between them, her fingers are soon entwined with Cassie's. Not a simple handhold, because Cassie's rarely that still. Instead, she traces each of Veronica's fingers in turn, lingering over the tips and tracing patterns across her wrist. It's maddening, and more pleasant than it has any right to be.

As they approach the hospital, Cassie slowly withdraws her hand. "I might not be an expert in all things NHS, but I already know about the gossip mill," Cassie explains off Veronica's look. "Ready for action?"

A twinge between Veronica's thighs at Cassie all prepared to do battle is the real answer, but she opts for the safety of a tight smile instead. "Always. Besides, you'll be handling the big stuff; some of us are just making up the numbers on the sprained ankles and bloodied noses."

"It all counts, surely?" Cassie pays the driver and they step out. "Separate entrances?"

"You're rather good at this," Veronica says with some suspicion. "A lot of 'don't ask, don't tell' in your past?"

"That would be, well, telling…" Cassie winks. "I can run ahead, if you don't want people talking."

"Oh, sod them," Veronica replies. "We weren't even talking yesterday. Even my department aren't that good at conjuring up stories. I checked the email, by the way. Looks like we have a bus crash, right into a shop window. It's going to be messy, but no one's saying terrorism yet."

"Shit. Right then." Cassie looks a little awkward, but they cut through the courtyard to their side of the building quickly enough. "I'll just go and get my scrubs on. Never could work in civvies."

"See you out there!" Veronica feels the overwhelming urge to lean in and kiss Cassie on the cheek. The bustle of some passing nurses puts paid to that idea in short order. It's the reset she needs to get her game face on, prepared for whatever is about to be unleashed on them. Assuming most people on the bus have at least minor issues, then the people on the pavement, and inside the shop, the numbers could be quite horrific.

So she makes her way to AMU and finds the ward in full preparation mode. She loves her team, really. They're so competent, particularly under Lea's direction. The locum covering Peter's departure seems bright enough, and he's running through charts to see who they can chase for offloading patients already, which is absolutely the best place to start.

The first rumble of trolley wheels approaches the ward, so Veronica steps aside and picks up a white coat in the process to protect her clothes. She's never been one for the status thing, but she has met one too many bodily fluids in her career to get too devil-may-care about it. A plastic apron is handed to her by Lea as she passes, and by the time that's on, one of the juniors stops and offers to tie it in back. A well-oiled machine.

"Okay, people," Veronica announces, startling the staff who haven't noticed her yet. "Big day; let's keep things moving. Just do what you do best. Anyone who suddenly deteriorates, skip A&E and head straight through to Trauma. Stick to protocols and you can't go wrong."

The patients start coming then, and every time the doors open for a new admit, Veronica sees the more urgent ones being rushed to Trauma. It's going to be one hell of an afternoon.

Veronica waits in Cassie's office afterwards, but almost regrets the decision. There's not a comfortable surface to be found, and Veronica is a little achy after four hours of overtime and an unexpected day on her feet. She's just relieved she came in wearing flats.

The office is as sparse as the day Cassie came to work here—not even a dated motivational poster, or a flyer about blood drives on the empty noticeboard. Cassie has nothing more than an empty travel mug sitting on her desk, right next to the dock for her laptop. It might as well be unoccupied.

"Hey." Cassie speaks from the threshold, always alert and looking just slightly wary that there's an intruder.

Speak of the devil—and in magnificent dark teal scrubs she will appear. *TRAUMA* is stitched in white above the breast pocket, a veritable badge of honour for the woman who looks knackered and exhilarated all in one.

"Hey, yourself. Coping okay on this end of the corridor?"

Cassie shrugs. "It wasn't as bad as they thought. Helps that it was more panic than explosion. Mostly walking wounded. Saw a compound fracture worth a journal article, though." She's lit up like Danny talking about his football sticker album and who he needs to complete it. "Seriously, the first break was—"

Veronica holds a hand up. The one with a bottle of red in it. "Much as a first date with emergency orthopaedics is damned sexy, I think it's a precedent we don't want to set. Do you?"

"You'd prefer it on the floor of my office, swigging from the bottle?" Cassie comes over to join her with a smile, but not before closing the office door.

They sit side-by-side on the bare floor, and Veronica reveals her two paper cups snagged from the vending machine with a flourish. "A Girl Guide is always prepared," she says, trying not to crack up laughing.

"I was in the Guides, you know. Brownies too," Cassie replies, hopefully not too offended. "I bet you were thrown out for being too bossy."

"Rude." Veronica decants the first cups of wine. Thank God for screw-tops on decent merlots now and then. "And actually it was for not respecting Brown Owl's authority."

"Always had a thing for bad girls, me," Cassie says around a laugh of her own. "Are you planning to lead me astray, Ms Mallick?" She turns to Veronica then, and the wine seems completely irrelevant.

Barely setting the cups down, Veronica turns to meet her, hand extended until she's caressing Cassie's thumb with her cheek. "You know, I once told my entire department in a seminar that inter-workplace relationships are the bane of my entire existence. They'd have an absolute field day, if they could see me now."

"Well, they can't," Cassie, ever helpful, points out. "Because I closed the door, and we're well under window height. I really have thought of everything, haven't I?"

"Have you thought about what happens if we—"

Cassie shuts her up with a kiss. This time it's a little slower, almost tentative. A kiss that says *we have time* and that Cassie has no intention of rushing.

Veronica feels the ripple of pleasure roll through her, a miniature tidal wave of promise and expectation. "Good point," she says when their mouths finally part again. Somehow she's gotten up on her knees, the better to lean into Cassie. "Now that it's a more decent hour, we could probably manage a proper date."

"So you're saying no to a quickie in the supply cupboard?" Cassie asks with a lopsided grin, taking Veronica's hands in each of hers. "Tempting though it is, I think I'd prefer doing this properly too."

Then comes the thump on the door. Cassie is on her feet in depressingly little time, smoothing out her unwrinkled scrubs. Since chivalry isn't dead, she extends a hand and helps Veronica the rest of the way up. By the time Cassie goes to open the door, Veronica is aiming for nonchalance in the corner, having stashed the wine in the bottom of the room's only bookcase. She has her hands on her hips and hopes she looks more annoyed than interrupted.

It's Alan, Cassie's paramedic friend. He's never been anything more than civil in passing with Veronica, despite the years they've both worked here. "I was just heading out from a drop and there's some kind of standoff on your ward. I think Cardio are trying to steal one of your patients, and the nurses are *not* having it."

"Damn right," Cassie says with a snort. "Sounds like the boss is needed. Ms Mallick, if you'll excuse me."

"You're excused," Veronica replies. "I'll message you that information you wanted."

"Good."

God, they're ridiculous. Veronica is still a little giddy. She watches Cassie stride off to deal with the next nascent crisis, wheels turning all the while. How long has it been since she went on a real date? Not since the last time she'd been talked into installing one of those godawful apps that seem to be populated exclusively by nineteen-year-old girls and men who don't understand the word lesbian.

She's halfway to calling Edie and begging for a restaurant recommendation, for anywhere that might still have a table for a Saturday evening, when Alan comes back to knock sheepishly on the still open door.

"Ms Taylor said to let you know it's a pseudo. She's going to be in there til midnight or so. You two got plans?" There's a raise of his eyebrow that just screams 'gossip hound'. Time to be careful, then.

"No, I just said I'd give her a lift home." Veronica's lying has gotten a little smoother at least. Not a hint of fluster; she can be proud of that. "Saves me a detour, then."

"Doesn't she live in Reading or something?" Bobby is far more interested than Veronica particularly wants him to be.

"She did. Her new place isn't far from me. I suppose you're on the nightshift, Alan? Well, I'm not even supposed to be working today, so I'd better get off."

"Yeah, you better had." Is that the hint of a suppressed snigger?

Veronica can't react or the game is officially over.

He finally leaves, giving her the chance to retrieve the wine and head off. No point wasting half a bottle. She's free now but with nothing particularly planned. Is it too much to hope Cassie might ping her when the surgery's done? Would that be worth waiting up for?"

No, she decides, setting out on the short journey home. There's no need to be so utterly desperate about it. If Cassie wants to do something tomorrow, well, maybe they'll see.

In the meantime, there's bad television and a serviceable takeout app on her phone. It's going to have to do.

CHAPTER 22

CASSIE TRIES TO PLAY IT cool, but the weight of her phone in her scrubs pocket, even beneath all the layers of surgical paraphernalia, feels like she's carting around a brick.

The operation is thankfully less onerous than her first glance suggested, so even with cascading problems, the patient is ready to be sewn back up before eleven. Not bad going. As she changes and checks the times of the last train to Swindon on her phone, Cassie can't help but flick straight over to her messages.

Thank some kind of deity, because Veronica has caved and sent a text first.

Let me know when you want to cash in that rain check.

There's probably some kind of rule about how long to wait, about how aloof to be, but Cassie has never been great at standing on the sidelines.

How about tomorrow?

What is she doing? What's the plan? She should be getting a move on and making sure she catches her train, not staring like a love-struck idiot at a tiny screen.

The panic abates as soon as Veronica replies.

Yes. Your choice, just give me a time and a place.

Okay, so that part Cassie has to work on. She's going to have to run to make her train now. She looks up, having just reached the staff exit beside A&E, and sees the glow of the faceless corporate hotel that backs onto the hospital, separated by one of those shallow ceremonial pools that serve no purpose.

"Off home, Doc?" Alan strolls up to her, halfway out of his paramedic uniform, down to just the fluorescent-trimmed trousers and the dark green T-shirt. Both arms are sleeved with elaborate, artistic tattoos that Cassie is quite taken with. "I didn't even make it to midnight without getting puked on."

"I really don't envy you on the front line on a Saturday night." Cassie knows she's all but missed her train now. The hotel seems to beckon to her from across the concourse.

"I bet plenty of people said that to you about Basra."

"Oh yes," Cassie agrees. "And Kandahar, and Beirut, and a couple of warzones in Africa while we're at it. You get used to it, right?"

He nods, and makes to move off, apparently in search of another jacket.

"Alan, if you're not entirely wrecked tomorrow—"

"Yes?" He practically lights up. Is this what it's like to have normal friends? Now she just has to see if he's the kind of gay guy who'll be up for a particular challenge.

"Well, I sort of have a date, or I'm going to have one. And since I have approximately three items of clothing that aren't scrubs or army issue, most of which I'm wearing right now, I wanted to brave the, uh, shops."

"Shops, like bargain basement in some shopping centre, or like, doctor-level nice?"

Cassie blushes, glad he probably can't really see it in the semi-dark recess of the doorway. "The second one, I suppose."

"If you're asking me to *Pretty Woman* you, the answer is absolutely yes. I should have surfaced by lunchtime." Cassie is pretty pleased with herself that she's picked the right man for the job. Her instincts are finally realigning for the civilian world.

"Perfect. I'm thinking late afternoon cinema and dinner after. Bit of a Sunday date. Do people still do that?"

"Oh, that's adorable. My last date was a twenty-four-hour rave in an abandoned warehouse, so you've got me beat at least."

"So where should I meet you, for fancy-lady shopping, then?"

"You know Selfridges?"

"I'm going to Selfridges?" Cassie isn't expecting that.

"It's not all designer ball gowns. And there are plenty of other places nearby. Meet me outside there at noon, okay? You've got my number." He pulls her into a quick hug, as though they do it all the time. Cassie could almost get used to this.

"Thank you. And if you don't show, I'll assume you're sleeping off a rougher than usual Saturday on the rig?"

"Oh, I'm not missing my chance to pull a *Princess Diaries* on GI Jane, so I will see you there. Even if I have to drive the ambulance directly to you."

She waves him off as he heads towards A&E where the paramedics have some supplies and clean clothes stashed. All that leaves is for her to decide between the terribly convenient hotel or the gouging price of a taxi so far out of London. The decision rather makes itself.

Cassie secures herself a double room with no view of the hospital, shrugs off the offer of a bellboy for her non-existent baggage, and slinks towards the elevators.

For a moment, just a moment, she considers tapping out a *so I'm staying at the Hilton by the hospital tonight* text to Veronica, but the urge to speed that eventuality along is tempered by the urge not to rush something so potentially amazing.

Not to mention there's every chance Veronica has seen sense by now. She might be safely tucked up at home working on a way to get out of this whole thing. Only she answered quickly enough about the rain check. Cassie can't screw this up by doubting every word and sign like always.

The room is perfectly generic, clean and spacious. The mini bar doesn't have a great selection, but the single malt will make for a decent nightcap.

She strips down to her skivvies and throws herself down on the bed. This will do very nicely indeed.

<hr />

Oxford Street on a weekend is a specific kind of hell, though not as bad as previous times when she's risked a Saturday close to Christmas while passing through. This part of the famous street is dominated by massive department stores and the supersized versions of various brands she just about recognises but has probably never worn. There are signs for Bond

Street, which sounds perfectly distinguished. A quick glance at it confirms mostly jewellers. Not what she needs right now.

Alan almost matches her own promptness, arriving fully five minutes early and looking fresher than anyone after the shift from hell has any right to. He can pull off skinny jeans and a black shirt unbuttoned one button too many in a way that makes Cassie feel dowdy all over again. She's in the same leather jacket, jeans, and shirt from yesterday's house viewing.

"Are we really doing Selfridges?"

"Oh, come on, you don't have to be royalty. Besides, as an army chick you must be all about your fine tailoring. I dated a guy in the navy, and those dress uniforms aren't just any old tat."

He takes Cassie by the elbow, guiding her by the elbow through the heavy doors of burnished metal and glass. "Now, just direct me. Are we femme-ing it up? Or do we just want a sharper version of something between androgyny and soft butch? I mean, play to your strengths and all that."

Cassie rolls her eyes. "Just make me look like not an idiot?"

"Well, I'm not a miracle worker."

They head through the perfume section, and even though no one sprays her directly, Cassie can feel the early stirrings of a headache. Perfume she has, even though she never wears it to work. It's always in her bag along with deodorant and a brush to keep her hair from tangling completely.

"So who's the date? I can't believe you haven't spilled yet, Ms Taylor."

"And I can't believe you're reverting to titles. Behave, Alan!" She deliberately leaves her phone stashed away, not checking Veronica's agreement to a movie and dinner for the fifth or sixth time. "It's very new, so do you mind if I don't fess up?"

"Hmm, upstairs for the lady clothes, come along." Alan leads her to the escalators. "And when we're done, it's cakes and tea down in Dolly's. That's the café in the basement, you tourist."

"Right. Gotcha."

Cassie stares at the grandeur of the store around her. This is going to be an unbelievably long day.

By the time she sinks onto a chair, mumbling out an order for strong tea and chocolate cake, Cassie is officially in one of the stages of shock. She's a little light-headed, fairly sure her pulse is racing, and the giant yellow bags she clutches, one in each hand, won't quite seem to leave her grip.

"Oh, put them down. You didn't go too mad," Alan assures her. "Although I didn't see you having a thing for swish exercise gear. Who knew?"

"Well, I mean, I run." Cassie knows it sounds feeble. "You're sure the clothes looked good?"

"Definitely. Now I've been patient, but you have to tell me who has you so giddy. If you're not naming names, that means it's someone from work."

Cassie's stomach gets that plummeting feeling like a lift skipping floors. No, she can't blow this already. Then again, Alan is a good sort and not a total gossip. Would it be the worst thing to actually confide in a friend? A compromise then.

"If you can guess, I'll confirm or deny. But I'm not just giving her up, I'm afraid. Too easy."

Alan claps in anticipation. "I do love a guessing game. That new night receptionist in A&E? Chloe or whatever her name is?"

"Nope. She's at least ten years too young for me."

"That cardio woman everyone's scared of? She's bi, so the scuttlebutt tells me."

"Is she?" Cassie files that one away for…well, sheer human interest.

The waitress comes back with their order, setting down all the tea paraphernalia as though she's setting out surgical instruments. Cassie finally lets go of her bags, making peace with her uncharacteristic spendfest.

Alan sips at his coffee. "Okay, who else is there? I don't get up to the wards much, but there was that nurse—"

"Nope. Not a nurse. Not a paramedic either, before you turn on your own people."

"Ooh, snobby. Dating another doctor then. In fact, if you're that emphatic about it, it has to be another surgeon. You don't rate the other lot, do you?"

"Now, that's not fair, I didn't say—"

"Wait, it's not Ms Mallick, is it?"

Cassie prays the colour isn't draining from her face, although it sure as hell feels that way.

"Oh my! You've got a thing for hot and bitchy? No, that's not fair. She's just…efficient. Our paths don't cross much. Still, no wonder you wanted to up your clothes game."

With a weak smile, Cassie leans across the table. "I really don't want to wreck this through the gossip mill. I'm not swearing you to secrecy, exactly, but if you could sit on it for a couple of weeks, maybe? If it takes off, I have no intention of hiding it. That's one lesson I *have* learned."

"Now, that sounds like a sordid past. Eat up, Doc. And tell me more."

———

After a quick pit stop at the hospital to shower and change, cramming the bags of clothes into her locker and wondering if she should return at least half, Cassie is ready to meet Veronica at their agreed time. The clocks haven't gone back yet, so the evening stretches ahead of them even when meeting early for the cinema.

It's so different now, organising a social life by text. Cassie knows if she got on social media like people keep nagging her to, she'd be able to chronicle her every movement today. Whereas that usually sounds dull and faintly creepy, the low buzz of excitement in the pit of her belly makes her see the point of keeping a record. If this goes well—and it has to, it just has to—she's going to want to remember every second of it.

Cassie has always been strangely protective of her memories, as though not remembering something good will mean she never has it again. Jan used to say it was the product of a slightly sad childhood. Nothing so terrible she wanted to block it out, but genuine happiness was so rare that it felt like an unexpected treat. These pat psychological explanations have never held much water with Cassie, who prefers to think that people simply are how they are most of the time.

For some reason, that makes her mind drift to Edie, who so impressed her with her understanding of trauma psychological treatment. Who could have dreamed that random lecture while on leave would turn out to be the close friend of the next person Cassie dates? It's hard not to think the universe is having a benevolent laugh at her expense sometimes.

The tickets are crumpling in her grip, so she pushes them into her pocket for fear of tearing them. If Veronica doesn't show up, Cassie is pretty sure she'll go and see the film anyway. It's at one of those quirky cinemas—

Alan's recommendation—where instead of rows of flip-up chairs, the space has been filled with comfortable clusters of armchairs, complete with side tables for a glass of wine and the obligatory cinema snacks. It's a beautifully restored Edwardian building, and hopefully classy enough for someone like Veronica.

The woman in question sweeps in just on the dot of their arranged meeting time, stunning in a dress that Cassie hasn't ever seen on her at work. It's knee length, dark silk with faint floral patterns. The cardigan over it is a perfect complement, just like the strappy heels. Her hair is properly pinned up, unusual but every bit as gorgeous as ever. It shows off the sparkle of earrings at each ear, matching the gold necklace that nestles against brown skin.

Cassie has never been the world's snappiest conversationalist, but right now she's finding it hard to form words.

"You look fantastic!" Veronica says, stealing what would have been a great opening line. "I have to say, Cassie, I didn't know you scrubbed up quite this well. Uniform is one thing, but I think I'm going to need to take you shopping if you've got an eye like that."

Cassie's fitted black trousers are a pretty comfortable choice, and the dressing room mirror did suggest they were flattering. The blouse is a bit gauzy, but with a camisole underneath it Cassie feels decently dressed at least. Alan had been kind enough to let her keep her leather jacket as part of the ensemble—"a classic for a reason, darling"—and the new kicky ankle boots might have a low heel but they would still feel at home on a Harley.

"I can't take the credit, I confess. You know Alan, from B rig?"

"Vaguely." Veronica looks momentarily shamed that she isn't au fait with every person who passes through the hospital. "I didn't know you were pals?"

"Well, like everything else, it's pretty new. He fought off a hangover to get me looking like a competent dresser, though, so I probably owe him more than the cake and coffee I got roped into."

"Ah. So, what are we seeing?"

"You know, I'm not entirely sure. I just saw the posters with Cate Blanchett everywhere, and assumed I needed it in my life."

"Hard to argue with logic like that. Shall we?"

Veronica crooks her elbow, offering her arm to Cassie like some Edwardian lady no doubt did on this very spot almost a hundred years before. There's nothing prim and proper about the flash in her eyes as her gaze drags up and down Cassie again, though.

"Let's," Cassie agrees, linking her arm with Veronica's and leading the way inside.

CHAPTER 23

GUN TO HER HEAD, VERONICA really isn't a cinema buff. Which is to say she can't actually remember the last time she watched a film that wasn't either already halfway through when she was channel hopping, or that she hadn't fallen asleep before the end of.

Still. There's no denying Cate Blanchett is easy on the eyes. There's a faint resemblance to Cassie, in fact, although the good major is a bit more realistically human. No mere mortal could have Blanchett's height and bone structure and smouldering looks all at once, but Cassie makes a damn good stab at it.

With her habitual glass of red, Veronica can't remember ever being so relaxed on a date. Her few and fleeting attempts since Angela have been awkward and stilted affairs, some promising moments of connection that ultimately fizzled out. The biggest relief is not being peppered with questions about *how cool* it is to be a doctor, or worse still, the mid-date diagnosis request, usually from a specialty more troubling than Veronica's own.

As she's had to explain more than once, a general surgeon is a great help if your appendix is about to burst or something has had the bad manners to whack you in the spleen and make the little bugger bleed like it's going out of fashion. Less so if you have an embarrassing question about ingrown toenails or symptoms that put normal people off their dinner.

Cassie seems quite content with her beer, turning to Veronica just before the lights start to dim. "I'm so glad we're doing this."

Veronica smiles in response, glad Cassie is actually talking now. She's been a little monosyllabic since the foyer. It's given Veronica a chance to do plenty of discreet ogling, though, so it's a net win for the home team thus far.

As for the movie? Well, there definitely is one. Five minutes after the opening sequence lights up the screen, Cassie's hand reaches across the small gap between their armchairs and takes Veronica's hand in hers with a gentle squeeze. It's a silent way of asking, "Is this okay?" and Veronica squeezes back in the affirmative.

Any action on screen fades away as Cassie's restless fingers trace and wander again, just as they did in her office. Whether it's a nervous habit or an intentional 'move' of some kind, Veronica has zero complaints. It seems such a simple thing, but Cassie finds every sensitive spot, and more than once Veronica's breathing hitches. Each time, Cassie smirks without looking around, so it's definitely some kind of intentional.

When the end credits start to roll, Veronica finds herself wishing it had been more of a *Les Mis* than a lightweight indie, if only because she wouldn't have to get up just yet. Cassie does seem reluctant to let go of her hand, but when she does in order to stand, she quickly bows to kiss Veronica's cheek. Just as quickly, she's upright again, ready to lead on.

"I hope you weren't too bored?" Cassie asks. "I know not everyone likes these low-budget flicks with lots of smeared mascara and long pauses, but I'd watch most things for Cate."

"Should I be jealous?" Veronica replies, smiling. "What's up next? I believe you mentioned dinner."

"God, I'm starving." Cassie grins at her own confession. "My recommendation was for a Spanish place, sorry, Basque. Small plates, pick-and-choose sort of place? And the wine list is double the length of the food menu, I'm reliably informed."

"Not bad for a new girl. I think I even know the place you mean."

"It's not so far, just down Portobello Road."

"Then let's get going," Veronica says.

The cinema has emptied out around them, and the staff are already pushing through the rows to clear up. It's not exactly a private moment, but Veronica is feeling pretty impetuous.

She steps in close to Cassie, height difference offset by her heels, and presses a soft kiss to her lips. It's not exactly salacious, but it sparks something inside of Veronica. When Cassie kisses back, they lose a minute or two to the soft exploration of lips and teeth and tongues. Cassie's fingers are firm against the back of Veronica's neck, the skin there so responsive to touch. She moans softly into the kiss, and Cassie finally pulls away.

"Mmm. Let's save something for after dinner," Cassie says.

A lesser woman might pout, but Veronica simply sashays past Cassie with a deliberate sway in her hips. She'll play along with this whole dating game, but nobody ever said she has to play fair.

The quiet groan from Cassie as she follows confirms that there's only ever going to be one winner.

The restaurant is dark and cosy in a pleasant way, and they're tucked away in a corner table that gives relative privacy. After their initial order of delicious bits of food on little skewers, they're both relaxing with a drink. Cassie's features are glowing in the soft light. It's almost unbearable, suddenly being so attracted to someone after so long. Veronica has had her passing fancies, and she saw that Cassie was attractive from the get-go, but this is that next level where it makes her downright giddy, almost breathless.

Veronica has the gnawing suspicion she's going to make a fool of herself before long. After all these years of building up her strict and professional reputation at St Sophia's, from the most dedicated house officer to the most responsible of senior consultants, and here she is directing soft smiles at a colleague, like a schoolgirl with a crush.

"So how am I doing?" Cassie asks, changing tack after they've compared notes on the food and wine. "I can't say I've arranged many dates, not under normal conditions, anyway. Do I pass muster?"

"So far, so good." Veronica sets her wine down and reaches for Cassie's hand across the table. "And you? You're not hiding some silent panic that we're going to ruin a promising professional partnership?"

"You have your kingdom and I have mine. Sure, we'll cross paths in theatre, but you'd know better than me if we're, uh, breaking the rules."

Veronica raises her eyebrow quite deliberately. "Because I'm such a good girl? How dull."

"Well, they say it's best to know the rules before you break them."

"Nice save." Veronica finishes her glass. "Smoother than I would have given you credit for, although I suppose you do better under pressure."

"I'm just glad no one's choking on their dinner. Too much of a cliché to have to jump into action, and you wouldn't even be that impressed."

"Interesting. You don't think I'd jump in first?" Veronica can't resist the tease. She has no illusions about who the macho army medic in this equation is.

"No! Of course not, I just assumed. I mean, you could. Or you would. I just thought we were talking about... I've actually had to do it before, that's all."

"And did it impress your date?" Veronica suspects she knows the answer, confirmed by Cassie's blush.

"She didn't hate it, no. Shall we order the next round?" Cassie flags down the passing server. "More red?"

"Always," Veronica replies.

They linger over dessert, crème caramel blowtorched within an inch of its life, and slightly sobering coffees, before they head out into the late evening.

"You know," Veronica says, once they've tipped out onto the pavement, unusually quiet because even London slows a little for Sundays, "since this is technically our second date, I could just invite you back for a nightcap."

"You could." Cassie pulls Veronica closer by the edges of her cardigan.

They're comfortably back in kissing range now, and Veronica thinks it's about time.

"But the last remaining bit of sense in me is screaming that we shouldn't rush this," Cassie finishes.

"How chivalrous."

"No, I just—"

Veronica silences Cassie with a finger over her lips. "I'm inclined to agree. This doesn't seem like something we should spoil by skipping ahead."

"Right, because—" Cassie jumps in as soon as Veronica moves her finger.

"It's just amusing that when it comes to relationships, suddenly you have self-restraint. If I were an abdominal bleed..."

"Lucky you're not, then," Cassie replies, before kissing her soundly. "Walk me back to Paddington?"

147

"In these heels?"

"Taxi it is." Cassie steps towards the kerb, arm aloft and already hailing. "Though we should probably try not to scandalise the driver too much?"

There's a glint in her eye that says she plans on doing exactly that. A pleasant shiver skitters down Veronica's spine.

———————————

With Cassie dispatched to her train with plenty of good old-fashioned necking, as Veronica would once have called it, coming home to an empty house isn't quite so depressing.

She makes herself a green tea, pottering around the kitchen she scrubbed within an inch of its life earlier that morning, the most immediate way of working through her nerves. Now that it's all gone swimmingly, Veronica is determined to enjoy it. Her propensity for self-sabotage is not going to get a foothold here. She won't allow it.

There's no amount of willpower that can stop her from checking her work email, though. Some old habits die hard, and she's conditioned to click on that little blue box every time the red circles reach a number higher than ten.

A lot of pointless circulars as usual, no matter how many she unsubscribes from. A pile of requests from weekend staff—resources drained, complaints, and other tribulations. Better to glance now than be blindsided in the morning.

But then Cassie's name catches her eye. Time sent: an hour ago. About when Veronica is 100 percent sure that Cassie's hands were firmly on Veronica's backside, and nowhere near a phone or laptop.

She could call, of course. Make sure Cassie wasn't sending emails behind her back or under the table. Though given that it's a request for funding to expand the ward, a lengthy bit of text with a bunch of attachments, it seems highly improbable. There are scheduled emails, of course, but it's all Cassie can do to stay logged into the St Sophia's system on her best day.

Has someone in the department sent it on Cassie's behalf? It's unlikely any of them would have the time or energy unless specifically asked. So who's sending emails pretending to be Cassie? Someone with either easy access to her office and computer, or seniority enough to get into her work accounts without raising eyebrows.

Veronica makes herself that last cup of tea for the day instead, stripping off accessories and letting down her hair. She's ditched everything but her dress by the time she makes it upstairs.

They've gotten a little sidetracked on the prospect of Travers having it in for Cassie, but he's the most obvious answer to the nagging question. Tomorrow they'll have to regroup, try and catch the wriggly little bastard red-handed. Her phone pings then, interrupting her train of thought.

Desperately uncool to text so soon, but I had a wonderful time.
C xx

Veronica could mock that Cassie still signs a text that clearly shows up as her, but she's too busy smiling at the little grey bubble to be mean.

Me too x

There. That's effusive for one night. Swapping the dress for the nearest nightie, Veronica crawls into bed. The tea and hardback novel on the bedside table are going to go to waste. By the time her head hits the pillow, she's already asleep.

CHAPTER 24

NORMALLY MASSIVE TRAIN DELAYS AND missing her morning run would be enough to slap Cassie right into a foul mood, but she's still practically skipping by the time she hits the entrance of St Sophia's.

Ridiculous, truly. Then she strides right into an arriving multiple trauma, and that does admittedly take the swing out of her hips, but, as ever, it only gets her heart racing in the best possible way.

A roof collapse at a nearby hotel, of all things. Head traumas jump to the front of the queue, backboards and neck braces making patients look like restrained sumo wrestlers. There's a lot of greyish dust on the worst injured, tapering off as they get to the walking wounded trailing in behind the last of the gurneys, looking shell-shocked without anyone to guide them.

Cassie has to tend to the worst, her internal triage system already dismissing them with the habitual pang of guilt. Luckily they're soon collected by passing nurses and ferried to more appropriate treatment areas. Most will be patched up in the Emergency Department; the ones needing more long-term treatment will filter through AMU.

Two quick patching surgeries later, Cassie finds herself hoping for a borderline case that she can wheel over there and catch a glimpse of Veronica in the process. The date really did seem to go well, from the handholding to the wine choices. The kissing certainly put a tick in the 'not a disaster' column.

There's the small matter of calling the estate agents as well, to get the house-buying ball rolling. Would it be strange to ask Veronica to tag along? It's the kind of moment that should be shared. Cassie seems quite sure of that, even if the rest of the process is murky. She's done the preliminaries, the boring and faintly excruciating process of sitting down with someone at the bank. Now there's something to actually buy, it seems it should be straightforward.

Unlike the arterial bleed this poor fellow has in his left thigh. Cassie knows there'll be a kit for it, there's a kit for everything, but it's easier to nick the hem of a blanket with her knife and tear a strip from it. Tourniquets aren't exactly a fix, but it does slow the blood flow long enough for a quick repair. Anything gushing this fast isn't going to wait for its turn in theatre.

It would be easier with diathermy, but Cassie is able to stitch up the wound in jig time. When her patient starts to rally there on the ward, she wants to punch the air at another life saved. There's really nothing like it, and, since starting in the NHS, her loss rate has dropped tremendously. With conditions and equipment firmly on her side, she's been able to do so much more.

Not that the failures sting any less. Steven still weighs heavily on her, featuring briefly in her fitful dreams last night, his ready smile flickering in and out.

Pauline bustles past in her plastic apron to drag Cassie from her funk. "I hear we've got trouble coming our way."

Sure enough, the next two men through the doors are practically brawling, even though neither can stand exactly upright. Judging by the uniform versus expensive suit, Cassie would lay money on a dedicated hotel employee having had enough of his boss when the sky literally came tumbling down. Situations like these are so often negligence, or rich men cutting corners for even bigger profits. It takes a body count for anyone to be shamed anymore. It's downright Dickensian.

"Enough!" Cassie shouts at them, in her best parade-ground bark. Their lizard brains hear enough of it to respond, staggering to their respective sides of the entryway. "What is going on here? Aren't you hurt enough?"

Pauline moves towards the man in uniform, but he's already lunging back at his boss. Cassie won't risk anyone else getting hurt, and the manager is closer to her, less injured to boot. She jerks him out of harm's way, even as he raises his hands to defend himself.

"You." Cassie puts herself bodily between the two men. "Name. Now," she demands of the fellow in hotel uniform. With men it's always easier to be the bossy headmistress or whatever stern matriarchal figure brings back boyhood shame.

"I'm Robert, Bob really, and he—"

"Bob. You're injured. I need you to walk over there with my nurses and promise me—promise me, Bob—that you won't raise your hands again while you're here. St Sophia's has a zero tolerance—"

"Yes, tell him," the boss chimes in, causing Cassie to round on him just as savagely.

"You can shut it." She backs him against the wall, aware of security bustling in to her right. "Bleeding from anywhere? Short of breath?"

He shakes his head.

"Then my colleagues here are going to walk you back to the Emergency department, where you should have gone in the first place. Hope you like hard plastic chairs. You'll be sitting on one for a while."

"Now, listen here, you smug bitch—"

Cassie doesn't let him finish. She's been assessing him the whole time, the head laceration and the ankle injury the only obvious damage. So when she shoots him an unimpressed glare and he comes at her, there's little remorse in the way she grabs and restrains him, arm twisted up his back.

"We treat the patient in front of us, but I can easily put you out on the pavement where you won't be in front of the nurses and doctors you clearly need right now. So what's it going to be?"

"Ms Taylor?" *Oh, fucking perfect. Travers.* Cassie's rising temper doesn't need this.

"All in hand, Mr Travers. Security, if you could step in?"

They bustle across, muttering no doubt about how she's trying to put them out of a job.

"Ms Taylor—"

"Mr Travers, I'm in the middle of a multiple trauma here. I'm sure this can wait?"

"Afraid not," he says in that posh-boy drawl Cassie has hated from her superior officers for half her life. "Bit of a mix-up, I'm afraid. Girls in my office are lovely sorts, but it seems they forgot to notify you about your conference."

"My what?" Cassie is really gripping on to the happiness behind her adrenaline, but it's receding like an early evening tide. "I really do have to check on the next lot of patients."

"Well, your train is later this afternoon, you see," Mr Travers persists, actually following her behind the nurses' station. "Paediatric Trauma, up in Liverpool. Leaving tomorrow would be cutting it much too fine."

Cassie snaps her head up from the admissions list at mention of the conference. "I thought that was next month. I put in for it, like you told me to, but I'm not remotely prepared—"

"We have cover enough to let you go; that much was organised at least. I appreciate it's short notice, but I'm sure you can get home and pack for a few days up North, and still make your train? The details are all in your email now, thankfully."

"I—"

"It would be so important to the Trust, Ms Taylor. Exactly the kind of impact we were hoping for when we hired you. And your speech isn't until Thursday, so there's still plenty of time to get that ready."

Speech? Christ, this really is going from bad to worse.

"Well, I can always be late," Cassie decides. "I'm sure the train company will be flexible."

"The meet and greet is this evening. You've been earmarked for the VIP table; some former colleague of yours insisted. I'd hate to see St Sophia's looking unprofessional."

"You really have enough cover?" Cassie knows she's conceding, and she does it with a sigh. There goes her hope of a cheeky coffee with Veronica later to compare post-trauma notes and maybe even set another date. Pulling up the email on her phone, she sees a few replies to something she doesn't recognise, no doubt another reply-all chain run amok, something the NHS excels in.

"Leave that to me, yes," Travers insists. "We do have a car service to speed up the process for you. Just head for the west entrance; they'll get you home, packed, and back for your train in no time at all. Do us proud, please Cassandra. I'm quite sure you will."

His grip on her arm is trying for vicelike, but he lacks the upper body strength. Cassie easily shakes him off, adding the same warning glare as she just gave her misbehaving patients.

"Fine, I'll go. It's too important a conference to miss. The speakers alone... Still, I can run my department remotely. Just can't carry my surgical load." It pains her, this new life of meetings and conferences. The sacrifices weren't supposed to come quite so soon. "So if there's anything—"

"Yes, yes, of course."

Travers retreats, no doubt slinking back to his lair.

Cassie sighs, flagging Pauline down as she returns from getting rid of one of the troublemakers. "It appears, Sister, that you're going to have to do without me for a few days."

"Without our fearless leader? However will we cope?" Pauline replies, dry as ever. "Everything okay?"

"Date mix-up with a conference," Cassie says. "That happen a lot round here?"

"Almost never." Pauline picks up the next chart, scanning their admissions, every bed occupied. "Usually it takes half a year to get the tickets and the time off. Still, never say never. Off somewhere nice? I quite fancy Barbados. My sister moved out there."

"Barbados?" Cassie snorts. "Not a place many have mistaken for Liverpool, that."

"Your accent gets stronger just saying that, you know." Pauline might be teasing, but she holds her poker face perfectly. "You'll be back singing the Beatles before we know it."

"They never really were my sort of thing." Cassie pulls her phone from the pocket of her scrubs. It's not as though she has to check in with Veronica, but suddenly disappearing to another county might not look great. The thought of explaining it all makes Cassie weary, and she decides it can be kept for the long, dull journey ahead. "If Ver— If Ms Mallick pops over later, will you let her know I'm off to conference?"

"Why would she be looking for you?"

"Oh, well, I skipped the surgical meeting to handle this, didn't I?"

Pauline raises an eyebrow. "The meeting was cancelled, since everyone was pulled in. But sure, I'll let her know."

"Much appreciated."

Still, a short drive to Euston with someone else at the wheel won't be terrible. It gives her time to pack better and organise herself, pick up a proper little suitcase somewhere along the way. Moving off at short notice is familiar at least, and she ducks into her office to sign some waiting paperwork and gather up her bags. At least she doesn't have to go home and pack—she has all that clothes shopping at work and never leaves home without the essentials. It's a bit ridiculous to be striding out in the middle of day in her civvies, laden down with the weekend's wardrobe update, but it's fairly well-timed. She hasn't been to many conferences, but nobody ever showed up in scrubs.

Since she doesn't have to detour via Swindon, something she could never have managed in the allotted time, Cassie decides to throw caution to the wind and exit via the AMU. No sign of Veronica out on the ward, so she heads directly to the office.

"Looking for Ms Mallick?" a nurse asks. *Lea, that's it.* They had a nice chat last week about the Philippines, since Cassie spent a few weeks there helping with natural disaster planning, running drills for typhoons and earthquakes. "She's in surgery."

"Is she really?" Cassie can't help asking. "Whatever happened to it not being on the roster on a Monday?"

"General's short-handed," Lea answers. "Although I thought that was partly because you're not supposed to be here."

"I'm just leaving, actually." Cassie knows she's drawing attention by being here. Absolute rookie mistake. "Liverpool. Conference. Going now!"

Lea smirks as Cassie turns to leave.

That could definitely have gone smoother.

CHAPTER 25

VERONICA HAS BARELY TOSSED HER surgical gloves in the waste bin when her phone vibrates against her thigh. It can wait. Everything can wait today. She's already been summoned into theatre because general was suddenly short-handed. Which has the added bonus of getting her out of the tedious regular meeting. As Mondays go, this is an exquisitely pleasant one. Less so for the injured folks, but Veronica has long since detangled her guilt over enjoying the ability to heal them.

She's back on her ward before long, intent on checking when the surgical meeting has been rescheduled for. It's a little like bunking off school to have missed it, only to find out the teacher had been off sick after the fact. A waste of perfectly good skiving, if dealing with a gallbladder could be classed as that.

"There you are!" Lea calls out, quite cheerful despite her arms full of blood bags. "You're never more popular than when you go away."

"That sounds terribly wise," Veronica agrees. "Though I suspect it just means people want to annoy me. Who came calling?"

"The good major from Trauma."

Veronica painfully, carefully, forces herself not to react. Not a millimetre of raised eyebrow, not even the faintest quirk of a lip.

"Was she really? Trying to steal our gauze pads again? I've told her where stores are."

"No, looking for you. Didn't leave a message, though. Just said something about a conference in Liverpool and ran away."

"I'm sure she didn't run, Lea."

"Oh, she runs. Some of us cut through the park in the morning now just to get a look. Great legs, don't you think?"

Veronica pretends to be fascinated by the blank face of her phone. She needs to charge the damn thing. Perhaps within the messages an explanation will lurk. "Hmm? Oh, I've never really noticed her legs. We all look the same in scrubs, eh?"

Lea doesn't look as convinced as Veronica would like.

"I'll be in my office."

It seems like an age before her phone is alive again, but Veronica stabs at Cassie's name in her contacts before she can second guess herself.

"I heard you were looking for me?" It'll do in lieu of a proper greeting.

Cassie fumbles into the silence. There's a muffled announcement somewhere in the background.

"Yes. Yes well, no. Not looking for you as such, just..."

"Major, where are you?" Okay, so there's a little thrill in using the title.

"On a train. To Liverpool."

Veronica frowns at the news. "And you didn't think to mention this yesterday? Not that it's my business where you go; I just thought it might have come up in conversation."

"I just found out myself. Our good friend Mr Travers sprung it on me. Something about the girls in the office messing up."

"Nonsense. Those two women run this hospital. Does this have anything to do with your email?"

"What email?" Cassie sounds as baffled as Veronica expected. Which isn't exactly great news.

"The email you sent—allegedly—while we were out last night."

"But I—"

"I know you didn't. Which means someone else sent it from your account, signing off on the preliminary budget."

Cassie goes silent, hopefully working out for herself what that might mean.

"Bloody hell, he really is up to something isn't he?"

"'Fraid so," Veronica says.

"What has he got against me?"

"I've got no idea. It might be a wrong place, wrong time sort of thing. Or maybe he fell madly in love at first sight and he's secretly trying to advance your career?"

That silence is a pointed one.

Veronica tries another tack. "How long are you away? I could do some discreet digging, find out what he might be trying to put you in the frame for. It must be something serious with money if he's so obsessed about budgets."

"You're obsessed with budgets," Cassie points out, not unreasonably. "Are you out to get me?"

"Not like that, no. So how long will you be hiding from me up there? Revisiting your roots while you're at it? Taking in an Everton game, maybe?"

"There's no need to insult me, you know. And I don't even know if Liverpool are playing at home. I haven't been to a game since I was about twelve."

There's a knock on Veronica's office door. "Ah, better go. No rest for the wicked."

"Let me know how the snooping goes?" Cassie asks.

"Of course. I'll, uh, check in. Coming!" She adds for her impatient visitor.

By the time Veronica has answered three obvious questions for one of the juniors and stopped an arterial bleed caused by weak stitching, she almost forgets about her phone. When she takes it off the charger a while later, with freshly sanitised hands of course, she sees the messages from Cassie.

> I'm not running anywhere, just so you know. Second date when I get back?

Veronica smiles. Right to the point, this one. She reads Cassie's next text.

> You might be too busy of course. No pressure.

And her own worst enemy. She types a reply.

> Only if I get to choose the venue this time. Speak soon.

There. Not entirely desperate. A pile of work awaits her, but Veronica feels the thrum in her veins of a puzzle unsolved. It's time to do a little digging on Wesley Travers.

"You're late, for the second time in our entire relationship." That's how Edie greets her for lunch on Thursday.

"You can say friendship, you know," Veronica tells her. "You just think it sounds more dramatic your way."

"Try listening to neurotic housewives all morning and see how much drama you need in your life. Sliced and diced anything interesting?"

"Not so far, no. How's Peter settling in at the Kensington? He did drop me an email, but it was about as enlightening as a solar-powered torch. I gather everything is 'Fine. Good stuff. Good people'?"

"Don't let him fool you, he's missing you desperately. Nobody knows anything, not compared to the almighty Ms Mallick." Edie flags down their waiter. "Bottle of Chablis, darling. Don't give me that face; I can't drink red this early in the day."

"You've gone soft since you had that second child," Veronica accuses. "I've been busy trying to sniff out a bit of a scandal, if you must know. I think Peter might have dodged a bullet not getting the Trauma job."

Edie eyes her over the top of her glass of water as she takes a sip. "Do tell."

"You met our dear Wesley, didn't you?"

"Oh yes, back when GI Jane swept in to steal the Trauma post, I remember."

Veronica must blush at the mention—damn her skin for being not quite dark enough to hide the reaction.

Edie lights up like November fireworks, tossing long red hair back over her shoulder as though preparing to dive in. "Well, isn't that an interesting series of micro expressions," she says.

"I knew having lunch with a therapist was a bad idea." Veronica can't really grumble. "We are not talking about Cassie right now. Yet, anyway."

"Oh, Cassie. Of course. Close personal friend and all that. Silly me."

"Do you want the gossip or not?"

Edie holds her hands up in surrender, and Veronica pauses as their wine comes, two generous glasses poured after she tastes it with barely a wince. It's certainly not terrible, as whites go.

"So come on, tell all. Especially if it's about the dashing major."

Veronica allows herself a brief, withering sigh, before launching into her tale.

"Fucking hell," is Edie's considered verdict when the details are unloaded.

It's taken three days of asking questions, talking to people she barely knows, and having a good snoop around online. "Quite."

"I am glad Pete's out of the picture if all this is going on. I had Travers pegged for a narcissist at first glance, and it's not hard to see he has something of a coke problem. Wish we could say that's entirely rare in the profession. Selling off everything but his flat and possibly even re-mortgaging that suggests a man desperate for cash. It has to be gambling, if he's desperate enough to start cooking the hospital books."

"I just don't understand why he'd want to pin any of the mess on a woman he's barely met," Veronica picks up her thread. "Especially one who's served her country. He's your typical military history nut, with the grandad's medals on the shelf bit, you know the sorts."

"A lot of patriotic sorts get less nostalgic when there's serious money involved. But how much trouble would he have to be in, to risk robbing the hospital, though? I mean, we have our jokes about the NHS bureaucracy, but the accountants know where every penny is."

"Maybe he's picked Cassie, returning war hero, because it would make for worse headlines. He's hoping for a cover up?" Veronica hasn't settled on any logic that particularly makes sense to her, but that has something about it.

Edie glances at the menu.

Good idea. They'd probably better eat something to soak up the wine.

"Yes, *Cassie*," Edie says. "You know, you were hard to get hold of at the weekend. Up to anything in particular?"

"Oh, just a spot of house-hunting. You remember that estate agent Angela and I used?"

"You're moving?" Edie's eyes widen. It's not easy to shock her. "But you love your house."

"I was simply advising." Veronica pauses to order the risotto.

Edie orders the steak with a particular kind of relish that would be unnerving in someone less lively.

"Ms Taylor was the one looking for a house," Veronica continues. "Hasn't had a chance to put down roots since coming out of the army."

"Well, make sure you don't get roped into looking every weekend. The market's a real bastard right now."

"When is it not?" Veronica's just glad she doesn't have to up sticks. "Besides, she's done and dusted already. Putting an offer in on the second place she saw. And if I know anything about that woman, she'll get it."

"Sounds like just your cup of tea, darling." Edie can't resist, but her eyes are kind even as she smirks. She's being the biggest advocate of Veronica finding love again. "But last I heard, wasn't she complicit in kidnapping Daniel or something?"

"A misunderstanding. One you'll be stunned to hear I actually apologised for." Veronica waves it away. The restaurant is pleasantly noisy, one of those high-ceilinged places that used to be a fire station or something. The table linens are spotless and the staff have been friendly, if a little harassed by the lunchtime rush. "Although we did take rather a shine to her new place, if you must know."

"How so?" Edie hunches her shoulders in anticipation, ready to pounce on concrete gossip.

"Oh, making out like teenagers in the bedroom, that sort of thing. Cut short by an incident call, though."

"I knew it!" Edie slaps her hand against the table. "And? Come on, getting details from you is like getting blood from a stone, Vee. No way you start fessing up over just a cheeky snog."

"We may have gone out on Sunday. Some film with that blonde woman you're a bit gay for, you know the one."

"That's no way to talk about my one-day lover, two-time-Oscar-winner Cate Blanchett." Edie's tone is almost scolding. "But continue. Necking in the back row, were we?"

"Not quite, but between that and a nice dinner, we did get a little bit of action."

"So why are you here having lunch with me instead of banging her in the locker rooms? Oh, don't tell me you haven't considered it."

"I have." Veronica blurts it out without meaning to. She's usually so good at keeping her counsel, but this time it's bubbling up inside her. It's so nice to be excited, to be happy enough to want to share the news. Beats complaining about the surgical schedule and school fees, that's for damn sure. "Only as part of Travers' grand scheme, I suspect, she's been shipped off to a Paediatric Trauma conference up north. Which means someone should probably have her back here."

"Have you told her everything you've found out?"

"A lot of it, so far. More tonight I expect. We text a lot, you know how it is."

"Not really." Edie covers the sigh a fraction too late. "Oh, no trouble in paradise. It's just easy to miss that early spell where you want to hear every thought from each other. There's a lot less talk about who's going to pick up sweet potatoes to puree for the littlest one, that's all."

They sit in companionable silence for a couple of minutes until the food arrives. The scent of saffron hits Veronica and soothes her in an unexpected way. Comfort food, then.

"You know," Veronica says, after the first delicious forkful, "if I were some big romantic, I'd rush up there to tell her everything else in person, and formulate a battle plan."

"Why don't you?" Edie tears her steak apart with the serrated knife. "It can't be pleasant up there alone, thinking the Ides of March are coming as soon as you get back."

"Well, I do have a job. And a son."

"Chuck a sickie. For, what? The first time in your life?"

"Edie—"

"Vee, the idea clearly appeals to you. I'm sure Daniel is with Angela anyway, and if he's not she'll take him to do you a favour. You've said for years now that you weren't going to throw yourself at any passing woman. Tell me, is this Cassie just any passing woman?"

It's the very question Veronica has been trying to avoid, but it's bearing down on her now like an express train. She considers, takes a breath, and shakes her head.

"Well, then." That's all the conclusion Edie needs, apparently. "Get that rice down you. And before we leave this table, book the day off and start thinking about what sexy underwear you're packing."

"What?"

"Oh, come on, you're not just going up there to talk strategy, and you know it."

"Have I ever mentioned what a terrible influence you are?" Veronica is hiding behind the question, taking a sip of her unsatisfying white wine. "Just eat your lunch and we'll see."

But her mind is already racing through train tickets and the brand-new lingerie bought months ago and stuffed in the back of a drawer.

It might just be time to spring a surprise.

CHAPTER 26

THE LAST MORNING OF THE conference is something of a damp squib, and Cassie has been warned all week that it would be. All the impressive speakers—which somehow include her—did their song and dance earlier in the programme. With the huge party last night, these past few hours are mostly comparing hangovers and chasing down contact details for future collaborators.

She's still pleased at the amount of response and enthusiasm her presentation generated. Talking trauma with people who deal with it every day, some from military backgrounds like her own, or coming from war-torn countries, has been invigorating.

Except, all the while, Cassie's starting to worry that this job that suits her so well is going to be snatched away. They can't be sure yet if the books are being cooked, or if Travers is trying to run Trauma into the ground, but either way Cassie seems to be in the crosshairs.

Her first instinct is to march right back in there and confront him on Monday. Call him out, hope for a straight answer, and take it right to whichever boss or committee sorts it all out. Only, if it were that simple he'd have been more discreet about it. There are so many things Cassie can't prove: the emails sent from her account, her signature showing up on memos and circulars she'd swear she's never seen.

At least Veronica is on her side. As much as the dating and the kissing and everything else, Cassie feels glad in a bone-deep sort of way that someone has her back. Not knowing most of the players makes it hard to strategize. That doesn't seem to be a problem for Veronica. Every call and text update so far has explained another bit of information unearthed, more hospital gossip mined. It's impressive to see her in action, even from far away. Clearly Veronica knows the hospital the way Cassie knew her way around warzones, all the flashpoints and valuable intel mapped out for reference. It's paying off now as all the whispers and rumours about Travers are being offered up, painting a picture of a man they're right not to trust.

Cassie has the hotel room for another night and an open return ticket. A part of her is tempted to visit her old haunts, but something like that would be nicer to do with company. Something she might like to share with Veronica one day, for example.

Which is rather putting the cart before the horse. Outside of this brewing Travers problem, they haven't spoken much, and last night brought no contact at all. Veronica's last text had mentioned a lunch with Dr Hyatt-Wickham, and then radio silence.

And perhaps Cassie had let herself enjoy a few beers too many. Not to mention the shots those nurses from Newcastle had roped her into. There had been a tall dark-haired girl giving Cassie the eye, as much as her rusty little gaydar could be sure of, anyway, but the lack of interest on Cassie's part had been absolute.

She's always been this way with women. Once one captures her attention, that person becomes the sole focus of Cassie's restless attraction and sexual energy. Other options pale in comparison, even when she's fully aware of them. Now Veronica is the tune running through Cassie's head night and day, while everyone else is a static radio with the sound down low.

Just as she's despairing into her plate of avocado toast, Cassie's phone lights up.

Did you say you were staying at the Marriott?

It's a random question coming from Veronica, who's probably one short surgery and two meetings into her morning already, but Cassie's fingers itch to answer. Still, she makes herself take a steadying sip of orange juice before picking up the phone.

Yes, just having breakfast. Conference is all over but the handshakes.

The interminable three dots torment Cassie for a long minute. Should she have asked about Travers? Veronica might only be getting in touch with an update.

Gone down to the restaurant when you could have had breakfast in bed? I bet you've been to the gym, too.

Cassie is quick to correct her.

I haven't actually.

She sets her phone back down and drains her coffee cup. Only to almost spit the entire mouthful across the table when a voice says right at her ear. "Oh please, the post-exercise glow is blinding."

"Veronica?" Cassie spins around in her chair, not quite believing her ears. "I... You..."

"There's that Cassie Taylor eloquence that St Soph's has been missing so much."

Cassie stands, because that's how you should greet a lady. Or something. "Are you... Did you eat?"

"Yes, thank you. First-class tickets come with a bacon roll and all the coffee a girl can drink. Nice digs."

Veronica sits without having to be invited, because even here and unexpected, she's at ease in her own skin. Cassie envies that more than she's comfortable with.

"Did we... I mean, what are you doing here? And so early? It's barely ten."

"Time enough to go to the gym and lie about it. I got an early train. Simple, really."

"No, I went for a run, actually. Down by the Albert Docks."

"Sounds touristy."

"It's quite lovely, in fact."

"Well, let's just be glad you didn't fall in," Veronica says. "Avocado? Really?"

"What's wrong with avocado?" Cassie demands. It's been bloody everywhere since she came back, and after taking the plunge and trying it, she's become rather fond of the creamy green fruit.

"Just a bit...you know. Anyway, here I am." Veronica slides her hand over the crisp white tablecloth to wrap her fingers around Cassie's.

"Yes. But I didn't know you were coming."

"Neither did I. You can blame Edie for putting the idea in my head. There I was telling her about your work predicament, and somehow we got to talking about the whole dating situation."

Cassie waves down the waiter and orders another flat white. As stalling tactics go it's not a great one. Veronica declines to add anything. All business.

"So it's a situation?" Cassie has to ask.

"Yes. Given that someone's trying to push you out of the place where we both work. Which might change your house-buying plans. Or staying-in-London plans. All these potential things that might change dating from a possibility to… Well. Not being one, I suppose."

Cassie swallows hard around a sudden lump in her throat. It's one thing to have been panicking about these things on a loop inside her head. It's quite another to hear someone listing all the horrid events out loud.

"Aside from my professional and personal ruin, then"—Cassie hopes she isn't barking up the wrong tree—"are you saying that an outcome where dating isn't a possibility would be…"

"Quite unacceptable. Now, while we're asking important questions of one another… Are you staying here tonight? Or do I need to go and book a room?"

"I… Yes. One more night."

"Excellent."

"Is it?" Cassie's voice is almost a squeak. "Only I thought we were going with more of a 'slow and steady wins the race' kind of approach?"

Veronica leans across the short distance between them and kisses Cassie with tender, insistent lips, knocking the breath from her in an instant. "That was one option. But tell me, Major, with everything that's going on, do you really want to put this off? I had you pegged for a woman of action."

Cassie gulps her coffee down in three quick gulps, wincing only slightly at the temperature.

"Action. Good. That I can do." She stands up, extending a hand to Veronica. "Since my room is just upstairs…"

Veronica takes her hand almost immediately, and they're in motion towards the lobby and its lifts without another word.

———

It takes considerable willpower not to kiss Veronica until they're inside the hotel room. Cassie supposes she's rather out and proud these days, as much as anyone ever asks about it, but she's still wary when it comes to any kind of intimacy. There'll forever be that little voice in her head telling her to watch out for a lurking superior officer, a disapproving guardian, or a bunch of leering guys who'll shout out sordid things.

That's the last thing she associates with Veronica, in her immaculate, belted creamy-coloured coat and simple striped blouse and pencil skirt beneath it. Even on the static-inducing hotel carpets she walks with perfect precision in shiny black heels, somehow leading Cassie down the corridor even though Cassie is the only one who has the room number.

It takes three slightly trembling attempts with the white plastic rectangle that's supposed to open the door. Each mortifying whirr and little red light makes Cassie long for an actual key. Once they're in, Cassie is glad she keeps her quarters clean out of habit, and the only sign of her having been there for days is her toothbrush sitting by the sink.

The room is comfortable enough, with a few generic splashes of decoration that substitute for a personal touch. Cassie doesn't get to explain away the décor, though, because Veronica has her backed against the wall of the room's little entryway, and Veronica is really, really good at kissing. Even knowing this from the weekend can't tamp down Cassie's excitement.

With her hands free to wander, she traces the curves of Veronica's body, clutching and squeezing as she likes. When it makes Veronica moan faintly into the kisses, Cassie knows she's an absolute goner. Frankly it's been too long since she's felt this amazing tingling feeling sweeping through each of her limbs.

"Nice room," Veronica says, her voice barely a murmur against Cassie's cheek. "I can't tell you how relieved I am that this isn't happening in some tent somewhere."

"Excuse me," Cassie answers, trailing kisses down the side of Veronica's neck. "But you were there when I put an offer in on an actual house."

Cassie prides herself on giving every bit as good as she gets, even daring to be a little more aggressive than she might normally on the first time with someone new. It helps that this is their own private haven, away from prying eyes, to do with exactly as they will. Cassie's first decision is to slip Veronica's light coat from her shoulders and toss it vaguely in the direction of the open wardrobe.

Veronica responds by hooking her fingers through the belt loops of Cassie's brand-new smart black trousers and pulling her even closer.

"Still, this will do for now."

It's hard to think of anything else to say as Veronica's hands move to the buttons of her own blouse, undoing each one with that steady surgical precision, before dropping it gently to the carpeted floor. Her bra is black but gauzy, barely there at all in the parts between the lace trim. Cassie hears a faint whimper before even realising that it came from her.

They kick off their shoes, and they land who knows where. Cassie, eager to keep up, pulls her simple grey top up and over her head. The bra is more functional than frivolous, but she doesn't mind much the moment Veronica's fingers skim over the thin fabric. Cassie realises all over again how good they look together as they stumble together towards the bed, Veronica's darker skin contrasting beautifully against her own pale complexion.

When she's pictured this—and God, has Cassie pictured it a lot this past week and before—she rather assumed she'd be taking charge. Women have always expected that from her, not so much asking as folding themselves into the less dominant role by default. That has been incredibly fun, perks of the title and the position and all that, but when faced with an equal like this, Cassie finds her inherent curiosity wondering what it's going to be like if Veronica starts calling the shots. Right about the same time she finds herself on her back with Veronica lightly pinning her in place.

And Veronica has her first shot all right, seeking out the sensitive spots on Cassie's collarbone as though provided with a map. She can't help but react, arching into the caress of Veronica's mouth with growing enthusiasm, feeling the wetness between her legs increase with each passing second.

"I thought you'd like that," Veronica says, and she's so quiet compared to the harsh way they're breathing already, the want making Cassie's chest tight and her head a little dizzy.

It's not long before Veronica has Cassie's trousers slipping down her legs, joining the other discarded clothes on the floor. Cassie makes a happy sound somewhere at the back of her throat as Veronica's fingers massage their way back up her bare legs, especially when they encounter the more sensitive skin of her inner thighs.

"You," Veronica says as she leans in for another quick kiss on the mouth, as though she's missed Cassie's lips during her brief absence and can't resist another visit. "Are one gorgeous lady. I guess you know that. I see it in the way you walk. But I think it's worth mentioning."

"You're not so bad yourself," is as much wit as Cassie can muster in return. What would the rumour mill at St Sophia's have to say right now? If they could see their Head of Trauma, skin flushed and chest heaving with anticipation that the most capable surgeon in the hospital will keep touching her, keep kissing her? Cassie can't remember the last time she felt this alive, and maybe it takes someone else who understands the realities of working with death to bring it out in her.

Drawing Veronica down into another deep kiss, Cassie busies her hands with undoing the wisp of material masquerading as a bra. It's easily slid out of the way, and Cassie tries to contain her sharp thrill at the new but welcome sensation of Veronica's breasts against her palms. A real handful— or two—in every sense of the word.

Moving on instinct now, Cassie's libido finally overwhelms her analytical side. She can't stay entirely passive, so she starts to make more deliberate progress in exploring Veronica's body, letting throaty moans of pleasure guide the way. Cassie progresses from gentle stroking of her nipples to more determined flicks that Veronica is very vocal about enjoying, dropping her head as though faintly embarrassed to be experiencing such pleasure. By the time Cassie allows her mouth to wander towards one hardened nub, she's confident in her ability to get this right.

Sensing her advantage, Cassie flips their positions, guiding Veronica onto her back. The sheets that had been freshly made up are already mussed beneath them. Letting her mouth trail more purposefully across Veronica's gently rounded stomach, Cassie is able to slip the silky black underwear down Veronica's thighs in a relatively smooth movement, leaving her completely naked in front of Cassie. Rational, objective thoughts be damned, because with her dark brown eyes sparkling and lips wet, Veronica looks so completely fuckable that Cassie can't think of ever wanting anyone more. There's a pang, then. The guilt. The little clench of her heart that she wasn't braced for.

No, she wants this too much to let the past come roaring back. Cassie is moving on, and she's doing it with a happy heart.

Because this isn't just about loneliness and a chance to spend time beside another warm body. This is a choice. This is choosing the woman who's captured Cassie's imagination since the first moment they laid eyes on each other.

"Well, then," Veronica teases just a little, "what did you have in mind for me?"

There's a moment's hesitation, because it really has been a while since Cassie did this. She presses determined little kisses along Veronica's prominent hip bones, down to the neat patch of dark curls between her legs. Lingering for a second until she can pluck up her remaining courage. Cassie's quickly very glad that she does, because Veronica is so wet already that it's flattering, mirroring the arousal pooling between Cassie's own thighs and soaking through her underwear, the last thing she has on.

And oh, the taste is intoxicating.

Although her intention is to draw this out for as long as possible, Cassie can't resist the stronger swipes of her tongue over Veronica's clit that draw out the most emphatic reactions. The instinct to tease and torment seems too strong, but before long, Veronica's coming against Cassie's mouth, hips jerking in a syncopated rhythm. Pausing for just a second, Cassie then slips two fingers inside, stroking Veronica steadily to an even stronger second climax.

Proud of her efforts, Cassie is slow to withdraw her fingers, licking them clean before kissing her way back up Veronica's still-trembling body.

"You did say we were throwing the 'go slow' plan out of the window," Cassie says.

Veronica gives a dazed little smirk in response. That appears to be about as much as she can express, as Cassie falls down next to her on the bed. They kiss, soft and leisurely, with Veronica seeming to relish the taste of herself on Cassie's lips and tongue.

"You really know how to get to the point," Veronica says when her breathing has regulated again.

Cassie rests her hand right above Veronica's steady heart, aware of its faster beat.

"Christ, I needed that."

Cassie almost swears out loud at how much she still needs, but she buries the thought in a firm kiss to Veronica's shoulder. "I'm just getting started," she says, but Veronica is already on the move.

CHAPTER 27

VERONICA PLACES HER HAND ON top of Cassie's, which is resting over her heart. It's been so long since Veronica did anything this impulsive, and she suddenly sees the appeal of acting on a whim.

She pulls Cassie up to a kneeling position, taking up position behind her. Veronica enjoys pressing herself against Cassie's back, dragging her hard nipples over the soft skin. Cassie arches into the focused touch of Veronica's fingers as they cup Cassie's breasts, alternating strokes of the thumb and soft pinches of her nipples. Cassie seems more than a little worked up already, so Veronica indulges in rougher treatment, squeezing harder and twisting just enough to make Cassie cry out with pleasure.

Veronica lets her right hand slip down towards Cassie's slick and swollen centre, her fingers slipping beneath her fitted blue briefs without bothering to remove them. Her movements are strong and direct, seeking out Cassie's clit until she's grinding herself hard against Veronica's fingers.

Cassie doesn't try to hold back any longer, crying out and reaching behind her to press an open-mouthed kiss against Veronica's cheek as she climaxes, and it's even better than she was hoping.

Not that Veronica stops there. She lets Cassie relax in her embrace, kissing the base of her neck, before pushing her gently forward on the sheets. Face-down against the crisp white cotton, Cassie grabs at it as Veronica inserts two, then three fingers inside her, building from slow strokes to a fast thrusting action that has Cassie bucking back against her hand. Using her free hand at the base of Cassie's back to steady her, Veronica smiles at the sight before her.

Cassie comes again with a sharper, louder cry. She slumps down against the sheets, her ragged breathing finally beginning to slow as Veronica pulls her into a hug before dragging the comforter over their naked bodies.

"That was—"

Veronica cuts her off with a kiss. "I know. For me too."

They spend a few minutes like that, bodies still learning each other with random caresses. When Cassie rolls into her, Veronica feels the tickle of those long eyelashes blink against her skin. They're as close as two people can be in that moment, and Veronica finds herself surprisingly tearful. Nothing she can't hold back, of course, but it's so delicious to be this close and not find it irritating or suffocating.

"Well," Cassie says eventually, and Veronica takes her cue to wriggle free and slide out of bed.

She doesn't go far, sussing out the location of the minibar in the perfectly generic wooden panels on the wall. She plucks out a bottled water, waving it in Cassie's direction. When she nods, Veronica tosses it over and pulls out another for herself, draining it without pausing between gulps.

Feeling a little self-conscious, and with the slight chill in the air, she soon returns to the bed.

Cassie is propped up on one elbow to drink, opting for careful sips instead. "Get what you came for?" she asks a moment later, throwing in a wink for good measure.

It has no business being that adorable, but with the mussed blonde hair and rosy pink cheeks, that's the overall effect.

"I'll say." Veronica watches Cassie for a moment, wondering if the moment will come.

Sure enough, an internal storm cloud passes over Cassie's lazy grin.

"Listen, I didn't rush you into anything, did I?" Veronica asks.

"No. No! I was very much going after what I wanted. Still want. Would want again, given even a fraction of a chance."

"Babbling?" Veronica shouldn't tease, but it's honestly irresistible. "I meant to ask, if you've been with anyone since…"

"An ill-fated attempt or two. More beer and optimism than any kind of moving on. It's strange; for just a moment there it still felt like I was cheating on her. On Jan. She'd have been the very first to mock me for that."

"Well, I won't be the second. Are you sure you're okay now? It doesn't have to be all basking in the afterglow, or whatever."

Cassie laughs softly.

"Nothing very rational about feelings, is there?" Veronica leans back against the stack of pillows. "Travers must be feeling guilty—this is a much better suite than I got in Birmingham." She gestures towards the sitting area in the other half of the space, with its huge sofa and even bigger television mounted on the wall.

Cassie groans, and when she rolls over this time, it's to press her face into the mattress. "I'd almost forgotten again."

"Well, I was going to help you anyway," Veronica says. "But consider me even more motivated now, Major."

"You really do enjoy calling me that, don't you?"

"Oh, only in bed," Veronica says with a smirk.

"Don't you dare!" Cassie warns, but when she surfaces it's to slide her way up Veronica's body, capturing her lips again.

The kiss tastes cool, from the chilled water, but that strange sensation soon passes.

"Am I keeping you from the end of your conference?" Veronica asks when they settle into a side-by-side position, rubbing her thumb over Cassie's cheekbone. Her bone structure really is something out of Greek sculpture. The breasts are holding their own, too, though smaller cup sizes do have that advantage over gravity. Definitely winning on the arms front, though, with both present and well-defined.

"Oh, today it's mostly watching the walks of shame from the party last night, I'm sure."

"Really? I've never done any such thing, of course. Clearly I've been going to the wrong conferences. And how many offers did you have?"

Cassie raises an eyebrow. "One or two. I think there's a nurse from Newcastle still hoping she'll get my number. Seemed a little too interested in my methods for wound cleaning in the field."

"Don't think they have a lot of battlefields in Newcastle, unless you count the city centre on a Saturday night. But tell me, is that going to be a factor? How many interested nurses am I going to be beating off with sticks?"

Veronica is well aware how petty she sounds, but somehow in her bubble of first dates and grand conspiracies, she forgot that anyone else might stake a claim. Generally she hates that possessive talk, treating women like prizes to be won, or property to be defended. Then something like this clicks and suddenly she's Xena, Warrior Princess, ready to ride into battle against any possible foe.

"Do you know where I want to be right now?" Cassie asks, expression almost entirely innocent.

"Downstairs to give out your number?" Veronica answers, her voice getting higher as Cassie trails her fingers down Veronica's abdomen.

Cassie pauses, fingertips pressed against wet, sticky curls. "Right here," is her reply, as her fingers slip lower and begin to work.

Veronica tips her head back and sighs in contentment.

By the time they feel a break is necessary, via a long shower that's not much of a break at all, Veronica is wrapped up in the hotel robe and perusing the room-service menu.

"God, a steak sandwich sounds like heaven, but I'm supposed to be cutting back on red meat." It's a small complaint, but a valid one.

"Indulge yourself." Cassie leans down from where she's just finished drying her hair, tying it up in a neat little ponytail before kissing Veronica's neck. Most of the hair falls loose again; it's still too short to be properly tied back. "I'll have one too. Make sure they send up so many chips that Davidson in Cardiology would have us struck off too. With mayonnaise."

"How continental."

They content themselves with fooling around until the knock at the door and the table is wheeled in. Only when they're alone again does the subject turn to work.

"I think we need a strategy. One that puts you on the offensive sooner rather than later, to get all military about it."

Cassie gives an indulgent smile, dipping her French fry in mayonnaise with a certain quiet glee. "I've been going over and over what we know. There's definitely a hole in my department budget, nothing to do with the little I've signed for or requested. I mean, it's been a few months. I've hardly had time to spend anything."

"No, this part of the year is all about burning through what you've stockpiled. And stealing from other departments, preferably while they're distracted by stealing from you."

"So far we know Travers has sent at least one email from my account, budget-related. He seemed very keen to get me out of the hospital this week too, leaving it to the last minute so I couldn't get suspicious or snoop around once I knew."

"What would he have done if you'd said no, I wonder? If you had childcare, or a phobia of trains? Some kind of Merseyside curse preventing you from ever returning?" Veronica winces as the horseradish stings on the tip of her tongue. She takes a long drink from her glass of soda and lime. "Speaking of, fancy a bit of a tour later? I could do with stretching my legs."

"You stretched your legs just fine when we—"

"Cassandra, please."

Cassie wrinkles her nose. "Nobody calls me that; please don't. Anyway, from what you've found out this week, at least a few people working directly with him think he's having financial troubles. More than a few think he has a pretty serious coke habit. In your emails you said that nurse was going to come back to you about the men hanging around looking for Travers?"

"He never got proof, but he's pretty sure they were some kind of bailiffs. The rumour was Travers took something from petty cash to pay them off in the short term. They haven't come back, that anyone knows about."

"And we still don't know why me." Cassie slumps against the cushions. "Travers and I have no history. No one in common that I know of. Unless he pegged me for a lesbian at first glance—which is possible, I suppose—I can't see how homophobia is a motive. And it isn't some kind of anti-war statement, because he's more into the military pomp and circumstance than I am."

"I spoke to Edie about that." Veronica takes Cassie's hand in her own. "She wondered if it wasn't a case of any person would do—it just had to be in a department with turnover. Less likely to be any scrutiny from someone learning the ropes. If you hadn't swept in to take the job, it might just as easily have been Peter."

"But he's…"

"A fellow posh boy? Fully paid up member of the straight white men club? Yes, but he's not bad as they go."

"Ah yes, your protégé. So the question is, assuming it's not that personal, what happens if I march in there on Monday and pull the alarm?"

"Well, don't pull an actual alarm; the last full evacuation was in a thunderstorm. Now, Travers seems to have been a little sloppy so far, but we have to assume he has a contingency. Some sort of insurance that he can blame you and get away with it."

Veronica sets her plate down and checks her phone. Besides the usual email alerts and a forward from Angela about Daniel's school timetable, it's all quiet on the southern front.

"You know, all this plotting and planning isn't going to do much. We're only going to get results if we confront him." Cassie sounds more than a little fed up.

"Or it might tip him off that you're aware, so he can cover it all up before you prove anything. At best he might blab something he doesn't mean to. I imagine you can be quite intimidating when you corner someone, but we have to be more strategic than that."

"I don't intimidate you, even when I'm really trying."

Veronica leans in to kiss her. "No, but Wesley Travers is no Veronica Mallick."

"If we're right, they'll fire him. Won't they?" Cassie asks. "Because the idea of him just getting a tap on the wrist, having to watch my back forever more…"

"Planning on sticking around that long, are you?" Veronica doesn't mean the question to sound so loaded. "I wasn't entirely sure you wouldn't panic and re-enlist at the prospect of trouble like this."

"Buying a house. Making a move with you. Rearranging my whole department." Cassie counts the commitments on her fingers. "I've got running routes I like in the park." That makes four. "And Daniel's going to need a reference for the RAF at some point, so I'd better stick around for that."

Veronica rolls her eyes, pleased all the same.

"We can plot about how you confront Wesley later, but I wasn't kidding about stretching my legs," Veronica says. "Let's finish this off and get dressed."

Cassie tugs the belt of Veronica's robe in protest, letting it fall open. "You sure about the clothes?"

"Well," Veronica replies. "There is plenty of afternoon left."

CHAPTER 28

MONDAY CREEPS AROUND FAR TOO fast, but Cassie is braced and ready for it. Returning to London on Saturday, they went straight to Veronica's house, with Cassie returning to her place in Swindon late on Sunday afternoon. Even that was a wrench. There's a pile of paperwork waiting for her about the new house, the mortgage, a hundred other things.

That's all going to have to wait until she's sure she can defend her job. Hopefully that won't take long, since she's just made an appointment to meet with Travers after his lunch, his secretaries eyeing her warily the whole time.

Maybe it's the spring in her step, or waking up a full hour earlier than necessary, but she slips into Veronica's office about five minutes before she usually arrives to leave a travel mug of piping hot coffee and a granola yoghurt something that's entirely up her street.

Part of her wants to wait and steal a few kisses to start the day, but that's just greedy at this point. Besides, if she can sign off a couple of things now, she can get in on a rescheduled liver resection before the tedium of the weekly surgical meeting.

At least she will get to make eye contact with Veronica at it. Maybe even pick the seat next to her and find out just how distracting she is. Jean would never forgive them, though, for disrupting her meeting.

By eight she's ready to get off the ward and into theatre, but a familiar face peeking around the side door stops her in her tracks.

Daniel Mallick.

"Tell me your mothers know where you are," is how she greets him, grabbing him lightly by the elbow and walking him back out into the corridor. "Or do you have another wounded friend for me?" She doesn't want to scare him off after all.

"I need a form signed. I was waiting for Mum. She's talking to some nurses about stuff, so I thought I'd come say hi. Mum says I owe you an apology next time I see you. So, you know, sorry."

He doesn't appear to be treating her any differently, but Cassie is almost sure the change in her relationship with Veronica is written all over her face.

"Apology accepted. But Daniel, it's a big and scary world out there. I'm not going to patronise you about that. If you ever find yourself in trouble, tell your mum. But if you absolutely can't, I will always help you out. Okay?"

"Yeah, okay."

"I mean it, kiddo. I'll even take the heat from your mums if I have to, but I'd rather that than you or your mates not getting treatment when you most need it. Not that you will need it, but...you know what I mean."

"My mum hasn't given you this back yet," Daniel says, pulling her discharge book from his pocket. "She said she meant to, but I found it and I thought it was pretty cool. 'Cause I'll get one like this in the RAF, won't I? Then I kinda thought about it, and maybe you, like, needed it."

"Yes. Well I had been looking for it, but I didn't think to ask when I came around on Saturday." Cassie hopes she isn't blushing.

"You came round?" Daniel frowns at her. "Mum never said anything."

"Right, well, I'm really glad to have this back, Daniel." Cassie takes the book from him. "Thank you. It's quite important to me."

"Maybe next time you're coming to Mum's I'll be there?" he asks, and there's a complete lack of guile. "I know you didn't fly planes or nothing, but I figure a lot of stuff is similar. Mum thinks it's some kid thing, but I swear to God I'm serious."

"Well, that's a good start." Cassie pats him on the shoulder. "Veronica has my number, if you want to chat about it any time. Or, like you said, next time I come over."

"Cool." Daniel turns, ready to head down the corridor. "I mean, it won't be long before you're round, will it? 'Cause you're dating my mum?"

Cassie looks down at the floor. Despite the long crack in the linoleum, the ground refuses to open up and swallow her. She has no read on the situation, no indication if Veronica has told him or the kid just pays attention.

"Daniel, I—"

"It's okay. I'm not one of those whiny little kids that wants to get his parents back together. My mums are happily divorced, so it's all good."

"Right, well—"

He cuts her off again. "Only, Mum might seem really tough. Like nothing bothers her, and that whatever you do, she already planned for it. That's what she does with me, like, all the time, yeah? She'll kill me for telling you this, but she gets hurt too. I've seen her cry about some mad stuff. Just don't be one of the things that makes her cry, okay?"

Cassie nods. "I won't do that, Daniel. I can't... I need to talk to your mum more about all this, but whatever she says to you, that's how it's going to be."

"Cool. Anyway, I gotta go get my form signed. Or I can't go swimming."

"Good luck with that," Cassie calls after him.

Well. That happened.

"Ms Taylor?" One of the scrub nurses comes out of the ward past her. "We just wanted to check if you still wanted that liver op, or if we should call in one of the locums?"

"I'm coming." Cassie picks up her pace. "Can I get a refresh on the patient details?"

⎯⎯⎯ ✦◄✦►✦ ⎯⎯⎯

Cassie slides into the surgical meeting right as Jean calls it to order. The seat next to Veronica is already taken by Davidson from Cardio, so Cassie fixes him with a glare while he isn't looking. She doesn't much care for the way he leans in to talk to Veronica, but it's clear from her indifference that he's making no headway with his Monday morning banter.

Just as Cassie is smiling at her look of boredom, Veronica looks up. As their eyes meet, Veronica has a radiant smile of her own.

Subtlety, thy name is woman.

There's a brief interlude when Cassie gets into an argument with the Head of Neurosurgery over correct immobilisation of spinal injuries. He claims recent admissions from Trauma haven't been up to his standards. Cassie puts him in place by pointing out they were suitable for transporting a patient on a helicopter under fire, so they'd likely survive a long corridor and three floors in a lift.

It's worth it for Veronica's smirk.

All too soon they're funnelling out of the meeting, bumping elbows amongst the crowd.

"Saw Daniel earlier." Cassie keeps her voice low.

"Ah yes. Seems the little Columbo has been putting some pieces together. Or he's a lucky guesser."

"I think I handled it okay."

Veronica waves to Jean, who's being swarmed by the oncologists. "Really? He said you forgot how to speak at one point."

Cassie groans. She's just never going to get to play it cool.

"Did you get your meeting with Travers?"

"Right after lunch," Cassie replies. "Which I'll be having at my desk, since I blew off paperwork this morning to slice up a liver."

"What have I told you about having dessert first?" Veronica says. "I have a thing, but call me when you get done with your meeting? I can be around."

Cassie reaches for her hand and squeezes, since no one can see while they're still in a throng of surgeons.

"I'll let you know."

They part ways at the junction for their respective departments, and Cassie tries to tamp down the fizz of nerves that's settling in her stomach. It used to feel like this, getting in the car to visit outposts, to move from base to base. She's gotten good at hiding it, at using the adrenaline to fuel her during long days.

She's going to confront Wesley Travers and find out what the little shit is up to, once and for all.

He's languishing behind his desk when she enters; the "Come in" sounding almost distracted.

Cassie appraises him again, looking for something she might have missed before, some extraordinary quality that marks him out as a worthy villain of the piece. Yet again she's presented with a middle-aged man in combover denial, pasty of complexion and in a badly fitting suit. The shirt looks expensive, and that's some kind of school tie. Someone else might recognise it at a glance, but Cassie has never gone in for that boys' club bullshit. There's only one type of uniform she finds worthy of that kind of display.

"Ms Taylor. What's the good word from Trauma today? Please, take a seat."

In her scrubs and trainers, Cassie rarely feels underdressed. His wood-panelled office is out of step with the rest of the hospital, decorated to intimidate subordinates and impress donors. She hates it. It reminds her of faculty offices, the sorts she only got invited to when topping her classes.

"I had just a few questions about my budget, Mr Travers."

"Now, I thought between us we had that resolved. It is submitted, after all."

He leans back in his chair. Either he's got an airtight plan, or he's completely underestimating her. Which is a bit bloody insulting, if it's the case. All the same, Cassie has spent her life being underestimated. Maybe it's time she ensures Travers is the last person to make that mistake.

"Yes, but in the interests of thoroughness—"

"I'm sure someone from the Finance department could run through any particulars. I can put in a word with one of them for you, if it's a tutorial you need for next year's?"

"When did you decide to send the email as me?" Cassie can't handle the pretence anymore; it's been making her feel almost queasy. "I never worked in counterintelligence directly, but that strikes me as an avoidable risk."

He sits forward at that, almost springing out of his ludicrously oversized leather chair.

"Well, well." He steeples his fingers, as though taking instructions from a low-budget Bond rip-off. His fingers are trembling. "Not as oblivious as you look. Well, if you've noticed it too then I suppose it confirms my working theory."

"I'm sorry, what?" Cassie hates having the brakes slammed on a train of thought. The last thing she expected was Travers agreeing with her.

"You've worked out what she's up to as well." Travers gives her only a dismissive glance. "Let me guess, she rushed to your side, offered nothing but support once you realised someone was tampering with your emails? I don't have to tell you, she has friends and allies everywhere. Bending IT to her will would be no problem."

"Now, hold on a moment. What are you talking about?"

"I pay attention to what goes on in my hospital," Travers continues. "Word is Veronica Mallick is intent on making you a friend. Didn't you find that curious? Considering how differently you approach your jobs? Not to mention that it all coincided with emails supposed to be from you, that you never sent."

"What are you trying to say?" Cassie doesn't like this conversation one bit. It's like he's been expecting her. Like he knew exactly what she would say before she ever set foot in the room.

"I'm saying that with me out of the way, the popular choice for Deputy CEO is Veronica Mallick. Which is convenient, since that's the next step on her particular ambitious to-do list."

"What does that have to do with anything?" Cassie fires back. "Veronica's well aware that you've been cooking the books."

"Oh, *Veronica*, is it? But you've got it backwards, Ms Taylor. She's using you as a pawn to unseat me." He looks so wounded. "She's so very clever, you know. Clever enough to direct you to me, when in fact she's the one hatching plots in this hospital."

"So you're saying that you're not out to get me? Or at least to frame me?" Cassie says back to him, trying to process his counter accusation. "And that, what? Veronica Mallick is?"

Travers stands brushing off the front of his tweed trousers. "Draw your own conclusions, Ms Taylor. Now if you'll excuse me, I have another meeting off-site. Good luck if you do decide to take on Ms Mallick. Rather you than me."

He strolls out of the office completely unruffled, leaving Cassie sitting there in the visitor's chair. Can he really be right? Has Veronica been stringing her along in some elaborate plot? It has to be nonsense, after what they've shared in recent days. *Right?*

Cassie checks her phone and sees the *In my office all afternoon* text from Veronica.

It's just another complication if Travers is going to point the finger from Cassie to Veronica and drag their brand-new relationship into it to boot.

Whatever happens next, it's time for a long talk with Veronica.

CHAPTER 29

VERONICA IS GETTING MORE THAN a little impatient by the time Cassie finally darkens her doorstep. The lunchtime shift changes are all complete before she makes her appearance.

"Well, you don't look particularly happy," Veronica says.

Cassie gives a vague nod to say that she's heard, coming into the room and carefully closing the door behind her. In a couple of strides, she's folding herself into the visitor's chair, raising one knee and hugging the leg close to her. "So I went to see Travers."

Veronica bites back an impatient remark. "Yes, I gathered."

"You know, he didn't even attempt to deny it? Just sort of looked at me like I was a pain in the arse for daring to figure it out. No movie villain speech about his motives, no justification. He's just...doing this. I thought he'd at least deny it to my face. He's just too slippery. I don't know how to fight someone who simply refuses to play fair."

Cassie takes an envelope from the pocket of her scrubs and unfolds it, smoothing it out against her raised leg.

"Did you get anything useful from him?

"Useful?" Cassie shakes her head. "Interesting, sure. His actual response, in fact, was to point the finger at you."

That's enough to startle Veronica up and out of her chair. *What the hell?* "He did *what?*"

Cassie leans back a little, as Veronica starts to pace.

Does she really think I'm guilty? The thought of Cassie, who's she's spent all this time trying to impress, would believe the worst of Veronica, is making her feel almost queasy. Her limbs seem cumbersome and unnecessary, and each time she reaches the wall she seems to have the turning circle of an ocean liner.

"He pointed out a few things. That if he's fired, you're the likely first choice for a big promotion into his job." Cassie stands, approaching Veronica cautiously. "That even though we didn't get along, as soon as I started talking about budgets and my suspicions, you got closer to me. I don't know if he knows we've slept together, but I think it was implied."

"So you're saying—"

"Travers suggested that I'd been played by someone altogether too smart and competent. Someone who knows the hospital and its politics intimately. I mean, who does that describe, if not you?"

Veronica raises a hand to her chest, as though the futile gesture will protect her heart. To be accused by that ginger worm from the executive suites is one thing, but for Cassie to buy his deflection hook, line, and sinker is quite another. Then again, if she's turned against Veronica, why is Cassie here and telling her everything? Is there still a glimmer of hope, especially considering Veronica hasn't done any of the shady deeds she's being accused of.

They're less than a foot apart now. Cassie holds out the envelope.

"What's this?"

"My resignation," Cassie says. "I've laid out the facts as I understand them in there. It's the only way I can be sure to trigger an investigation. I've also said I'll go to the papers if they try to hush it up."

"Cassie, wait—"

"Yes?"

"So you really do believe him?" Veronica asks it as a ragged whisper. The hope she had is flickering out by the second. Still, she has to know. The masochist in her needs to know if it's going to start hurting now, and how much.

"What do you think?" Cassie tilts her head, ever so slightly. "Of course not!"

"Oh, thank God!" Veronica doesn't care that anyone could walk past and see, she grabs Cassie by the shoulders and yanks her into a full-body hug. "You had me terrified, you idiot!"

"Well, it didn't hurt to make doubly sure." Cassie's hands slip lower, a cheeky squeeze of Veronica's bum. "I've gotten to know you, Veronica. In a choice between you and him for the villain of this piece, there's no doubt who it has to be. Shouldn't we be careful of, uh…?"

"Sod it." Veronica reaches without looking for the blind cord, dropping it on the window in the door. The very second they have privacy, she's kissing Cassie. Once, twice, losing count as kiss blends into kiss and they hold each other close.

After a moment, Veronica asks, "Not to spoil the party, but what does this mean now, for your job?"

"That his best hope is thinking we'll turn on each other. He probably thinks women always do. Or at least that I'll be too scared to say anything when I can't prove who's behind it all."

"Doesn't sound great." Veronica wishes she had one of her instant solutions for it all, if only so they could get back to the kissing and the touching without all the gloom hanging over them. Even then, her "instant" solutions are usually the product of weeks or months of hard work and planning.

Something she clearly doesn't have time for, judging from the knock on her office door.

"Yes?" She only opens it far enough to be seen. Sure enough, hospital security are there, two of them flanking Jean.

"Ms Mallick, I'm afraid I need an urgent word," Jean says. "There's been a serious complaint made."

"Has there, now?" Veronica wouldn't have given the weasel that much credit, but he's clearly sounded the alarm already.

"Veronica, it's okay." Cassie pulls the door the rest of the way open. "Hello, Jean. I'll assume Wesley sent you. Veronica has done nothing wrong, and I'm more than willing to answer to any accusations against me while we're at it. There's something rotten in the management of this hospital, but the problem isn't with your department heads."

"Ms Taylor—"

"It's actually still Major Taylor, though that couldn't matter less. If you'll excuse me, I've actually got an appointment with our esteemed CEO, Mr Pedersen. My union rep is meeting me there."

"You do?" Veronica asks before anyone else can.

"Yes, and I'd really better get moving." Cassie pushes past Veronica, pausing when one of the security guards thinks that's his cue to still come after Veronica and manhandle her out of there. "I'm going to pretend you didn't just do that, Harry. Nobody lays a finger on Ms Mallick until I'm done with Pedersen, are we clear?"

"Why don't I just come back later?" Jean asks. "Seems like someone's chickens are coming home to roost if Ms Taylor's on the warpath. I think we can stay out of it until the dust settles, don't you? We've more than enough to be getting on with."

Veronica shrugs at her, nodding at Cassie who strides off down the corridor. "Yes. Sounds like a CEO problem to me. Will that be all?"

The group outside her door departs and Veronica closes it firmly, pressing her back against it and letting out a steady sigh. Cassie's dived into action again, this time with even less of a plan than her confronting of Travers. Veronica can't help feeling that this lack of planning, the utter departure from strategy, is going to make all this a living hell.

<hr/>

An hour passes and still no sign of Cassie.

Veronica has had quite enough of waiting, and the panic of thinking she'd be blamed somehow for all this has her nerves jangling even now. No, she's always been one to fight her own corner, and for those…people she cares about. Today is not going to be the exception.

Jean has the decency to put her questioning on hold, sensing that there's something amiss with all these sudden complaints. Cassie's take-charge routine hasn't exactly hurt, and Veronica has been left to roam her modest office and try to see a way out. Only she's running out of ways to distract herself. Her in-tray is empty, her pens are lined up by colour, and she's finally tackled the uncharted territory of the 'miscellaneous crap' drawer at the bottom of her desk, the hiding place for all the things even Veronica at her most organised doesn't have the heart to deal with. She checks one more time that her phone isn't on silent, leaning against her desk.

Eventually there's only one thing left to do, and that's march into Wesley's office herself. It's one thing to let Cassie fight her own battles, which she has admirably. It's quite another to let the smug little twerp come after Veronica and her career, one she's worked her arse off to keep quite spotless.

"Wesley. No, don't get up," she greets him, strolling into his office and closing the door behind her. She doesn't hurry, forcing herself to look almost bored as she comes across and drops herself into the visitor's chair.

"You know, I could have sworn I just sent the Head of Surgical Services and security to talk to you, Ms Mallick. It seems you've been playing around with the budgets, and setting someone else up to take the fall."

His patronising little sneer is so smug that Veronica almost immediately loses her cool. Only a lifetime of holding her tongue to defeat overconfident men with too much power over her allows her to keep the peace.

"I've always enjoyed that dry sense of humour of yours," Veronica says. "I think we both know who's been cooking the books, and I've never been much of a chef. Oh, you've been subtle—no doubt about that. But I saw your long game right from the start, and I've been leaving you to it while it's been serving my own interests. Until you tried to drop me in it, at least."

"Excuse me?"

Oh good, she's actually surprised him.

"You're not seriously saying you're rooting for the Head of Trauma to fail?" Wesley stares at her in disbelief.

"I've wanted rid of her from the start. From before then, even. I pushed for Peter in that role, you know I did. I did everything to get him ready, short of taking the damn interview for him. She comes in here, turns everything upside down. Laughs in the face of the way we've been running things. I've never been so insulted." She scrunches her face in the most long-suffering expression she can think of, the expression usually reserved for Danny's unwashed football kits and self-diagnosing patients with too much Google access.

Wesley comes out from behind his desk, regarding her with no small amount of suspicion. Veronica stares him down, not flinching in her supposed offence over Cassie.

"For someone insulted, you've certainly been hanging around with her a lot."

"Know thine enemy. Didn't you tell me that, back when A&E was trying to swallow my department?"

He preens. Pride really does go before a fall, or Veronica's hoping like hell that it does.

"If anything, I was helping you," Veronica continues. "Keeping the major distracted, giving her something to concern herself with outside of work. And how do you show gratitude for that, Wesley? By framing me." She tuts, for the added disappointed governess effect. God knows it always works on the public-school drips.

"Oh, I wouldn't worry about that. The beauty of blaming you, Veronica, is that no one would really believe it. Your record is exemplary. Sure, there'd be whispers, but ultimately the goal was to cause enough murkiness around Taylor that they'd pay her off and bump her out to the sticks somewhere." Some of the tension has leached out of his shoulders, and as he talks his hands are back to their usual fussy, expressive gestures instead of the balled fists when she first approached.

Veronica shrugs and gives him a sharp look. "Well, a little bit of fraud isn't going to get the job done. Money was a good way to go, but it's so easy to pretend she just didn't know, or made an innocent mistake. They'll slap her on the wrist and have someone supervise her spending. No. I want her gone, and I want Peter back where he should have been all along."

His eyes light up at that. Finally she's hit on a motivation that Wesley understands: pouting over not getting one's own way.

"You really are a terrible loser, Veronica." Wesley almost beams at her in his moment of understanding. "Well, I don't like losing, either. That's where you underestimate me. You always do that, Veronica. You think because I don't choose to get my hands dirty on the wards that I'm not a real doctor like the rest of you. Or that because I'm currently deputy that I won't make a fine CEO some day."

"Wesley, I've never—"

"No, it's fine. If that's how you have to think to compete with me, so be it. But I'm not some scheming second-year thinking up pranks for the new kid. There's almost a quarter million in dodgy transactions with Taylor's name attached. There's no chance she's walking away from that, whether you're in the frame or not."

"See, this is why I had to leave it to you. You had the idea, and you're the one to execute it." He's lapping it up as he leans against the front of his desk, hands clasped in front of him. Veronica feels sick, but pushes on. "A man like you, no one thinks twice or questions his integrity. Someone like me? Well, as hard as I work you know there are still people who only see the colour of my skin, or the fact that I sleep with women. That's why pointing the finger at me was your backup. I see that now. Clever move."

"You're selling yourself short," Wesley says. "I chose you because you'd weather any allegations, putting the blame back on the new girl by default if it came to it. Still, Taylor will be out on her backside soon enough. Then perhaps you and I can look to the future here at St Sophia's. Do a little house cleaning elsewhere?"

"Trouble is, Ms Army Medic is already talking her way out of it. Already pleading her innocence to anyone who'll listen. It won't be the first time the Trust has looked the other way when it comes to financials."

"You don't really think that's all I have planned?" Wesley scoffs. "Oh dear, you really haven't given me anything like enough credit."

He's so secure in his status, his privilege. He's a wealthy white man, albeit one with debts he's had to steal to cover, and not for one minute does he see this rebounding on him. Veronica wants to punch him in the teeth.

"And what else can you do from this office, Wesley? Give her some nightshifts? Take her best staff away?"

"No, what you people on the ground never seem to realise is that you're all incredibly vulnerable. When doctors make mistakes, it costs the hospital and the Trust dearly. So what's the best way to get rid of a doctor?"

"I don't know what you mean…" Veronica suspects she actually does. The man has gone from secure in his ivory tower to coldly unhinged in the span of this conversation, and every nerve ending is screaming at her to start backing out of there. Fast.

"Doctors doing bad admin can be fixed. Doctors who don't provide correct patient care, who lose a patient or two that they absolutely shouldn't, well…they get shipped out much quicker. It's the liability."

Her blood runs cold. He can't be saying what she thinks he is. Veronica just has to hold her nerve a little longer.

"So you're saying—"

"That a few extra patients suddenly not making it, due to something that looks negligent? That would be Act Two. Taylor gone, the Trust not looking too hard for fear of further scandal, and I've cleared my own financial tight spot in the process. It's quite brilliant."

"How would you make it happen?" Veronica sounds every bit as stunned as she feels. "It's not that easy, not really."

"Well, since you're so determined to be helpful, perhaps that's where you come in. You two operate together. What if you nicked something on her side of the body cavity while she wasn't quite looking? She'd blame herself, and so would the post mortem."

This, somehow, feels much worse. This is a bone-deep, rising-from-the-toes dread. The worst part is that she didn't even see it coming. Her body seems to be rejecting the very idea. It's like she wants to throw up, but she's forgotten how. In all the years she's held a scalpel, not once has she looked at a life hanging in the balance and wondering "what if?". Saving them has been her only job, her only priority. To do anything other than that, for any reason, is beyond unthinkable.

He carries on, as though he's only suggested they host the Christmas party somewhere different this year instead of something so sickening, so far over the line that there's no hope of clawing him back.

"You should check your email, though. I've had a draft of some of those Cassie emails she didn't send stashed in there. Doesn't make you look great, but if you're coming in with me on this, it's only fair we get rid of that little distraction."

Veronica pulls out her phone and checks. Sure enough, the first item in her drafts is a copy of the email she received during her date with Cassie.

She has to focus now on getting out of this room. Someone who could so casually suggest a spot of murder by malpractice could be capable of anything. Except now, even more than when she walked in, Veronica has to convince Wesley that she's on his side. God knows what he'll do if he suspects otherwise.

Veronica purses her lips and pretends to consider his offer. Can she really bring herself to say it? Or will he notice she's wavering and lose his temper? The seconds seem to drag as she puts on a show of mulling it over.

"What would you have done, by the way? If I hadn't been wise to your bigger scheme, and hadn't come in to see you today? I assume there was another plan."

"Of course." Wesley puffs out his chest again at the opportunity to brag. "But I can't give away all my secrets, Veronica. I'll save that for when we're further down the line in this new partnership of ours."

"If it comes to that," Veronica says, hoping she won't have to stall for much longer. She should have prepared for longer before barging in on Wesley.

There's a faint commotion outside the door. He's going to clam up now, and Veronica moves towards the doors.

"Now, Veronica," he calls after her as she retreats. "Don't get cold feet on me now, I've just shown you some good faith."

The last three words are amplified through Cassie's phone as she shoves the door open, striding in with security hot on her heels.

Taking a step back, Veronica slowly lifts her phone out of her pocket and shows it to Wesley. The fact it's already on a call, and recording, is clear from the phone and microphone symbol. She called Cassie on her way over, told her to keep the line open and on speaker, and listen in with Mr Pedersen or Jean, or any kind of official witness.

It only takes him a second to put the pieces together, and he howls like a cornered animal as they all crowd into his office.

"You bitch!"

For all she was bracing herself, Veronica doesn't see his wild-eyed lunge coming.

He's only a matter of inches away when Cassie comes flying in to tackle him, as sleek and tense as an arrow finding its mark.

THUD.

She makes impact. Wesley gasps. The bruising blow to his ribs drives all the air from his lungs, if his pained expression is anything to go by. Cassie's bruising tackle sends him crumpling to the ground like a sack of potatoes. The woman has follow-through.

Then the persistent idiot actually tries to get back up to take a swing at Veronica, but Cassie puts paid to that with a shove, followed by her foot stamping down on his wrist. She doesn't lift her boot until security are on either side of Wesley, ready to scoop him up and out.

He pouts and whimpers like a petulant child as the guards pull him roughly into position, each of them taking an arm and ready to drag him if necessary.

"Bitch!" He spits at Veronica once he realises they aren't letting go any time soon.

"Oh yes, I can be," she says. "But better a bitch than a thief. And a potential murderer."

"I want. My. Lawyer." Wesley pouts around each word, holding his wrist where Cassie made impact. "Not that you can prove a thing! Secrets recordings aren't admissible in court!" he persists, even as security start to drag him out.

"No, but they really narrow it down so the police know who to arrest," Veronica calls after him. "Not much room for doubt there. Pompous moron."

"You okay?" Cassie is in front of her suddenly, Wesley forgotten as she runs her hands up and down Veronica's arms.

"I will be. Fuck, he was really going to hurt people just to cover up his theft. Like it's not bad enough he's stealing from an underfunded service in the first place." Veronica feels hot and cold all over, like the evening before getting the flu in earnest.

Cassie pulls her into a hug, and to hell with witnesses because it's all that Veronica needs right now. She holds back tears, but only just. There'll be time enough for that later. Travers hasn't just sickened her; he's broken her heart. Veronica has always wanted to believe the best of her colleagues here in the trenches of the NHS with her.

Bad enough each successive government expects them to perform miracles—without queues or waiting time, of course—on tuppence and a shoestring. This is effectively stealing a transplant from a dying man, a cancer treatment from a woman in critical condition, the difference between a child who lives long enough to grow up or not.

"Not really one for the damsel-in-distress role, are you?" Cassie says, looking out at the busy reception area where everything is about the usual level of chaos. "But bloody hell, marching in here on your own."

"I'm just glad you understood what I barked down the phone at you. I didn't even wait to see if you'd heard me." Veronica sees now how much her plan had really been flying by the seat of her pants. "And I should probably be offended that he really thought I'm as twisted as he is."

"I think he liked the idea of you being in the gang with him. It can be a lonely business, all this plotting. Thank God he didn't come after my patients," Cassie says, her shoulders high and her jaw set firmly. "That, I could never forgive myself for."

"Let's get out of here." Veronica doesn't want to be in his office, doesn't particularly want to be anywhere near the hospital right now. Her chest is tight, and her eyes are stinging. The revulsion and panic she's been fighting for the whole conversation won't be held back anymore.

She crosses to the small leather couch in one corner. Sitting down before her knees give out altogether, she lets her head fall into trembling hands and starts to cry.

CHAPTER 30

ONCE VERONICA HAS CAUGHT HER breath and cried it out a little, Cassie leads her back to their end of the hospital and finds a quiet bay on the Trauma ward. Behind the blue curtain, Veronica finishes the job of pulling herself back together, and Cassie has to admit that it's something of a privilege to see it in action. Veronica has proven to be a remarkable woman, one that Cassie's lucky to know, never mind be involved with.

"I'm so, so glad you're okay," Cassie keeps her voice low as she leans in for a slow, tender kiss. "Now we know what he was plotting, I should never have let you face him alone."

"Well, you did too." Veronica isn't going to be written off that easily. She had a horrible conversation, not a knockdown fist fight, after all. "And *let* me? That will be the day, Major. Although I do appreciate your rugby-league skills."

"Please," Cassie says with a scoff. "I'm a union girl, all the way. I just hope I broke his bloody wrist."

A moment later the curtain draws back a little. Pauline gives them both a reassuring smile.

"Dr Pedersen says he can come down if you like, but it might be better to talk in his office. He'll make himself free as soon as you're ready."

"Didn't you…?" Veronica turns to Cassie.

"He heard almost everything," Cassie replies. "Before your call we'd been talking—there were already suspicions about Travers. He's been taking out loans, second mortgages. Some of the companies called HR to verify his income."

"Where is he?"

"Travers?" Cassie confirms. "He's in a cell at Paddington Green. They reckon he's a flight risk, with his money and connections, so no bail is likely."

Veronica nods. She grabs Cassie's hand and pulls her closer. "Thank you."

Cassie clears her throat, since they still have company. Pauline is making her excuses, but Veronica simply turns to her while very deliberately kissing Cassie on the cheek.

"Go on," Veronica says with a sigh. "But if you won the office sweepstake, I want a nice bottle of red from your winnings."

"Of course, Ms Mallick." Pauline retreats as the very picture of professionalism, but there's a squeal and loud giggling the moment the curtain closes again.

"So we're out, then?" Cassie frees her hand so she can cradle Veronica's face with both, before kissing her very gently on the mouth. "I think I like that."

"Good," Veronica says. "Shall we go and see what Pedersen wants? Then I don't know about you, but I fancy getting the hell out of this place."

"Deal."

Later—much, much later—Cassie finds herself staring up at Veronica's bedroom ceiling. There's a tiny mark on the otherwise spotless white paint, and having noticed it Cassie can't bring herself to look away. She's aware of Veronica beside her, propped up against the pillows in her silk kimono, flipping through a journal with a much-deserved glass of Pinot Gris. Cassie is aware she's sprawling, still unapologetically naked.

"So 'outwitting the bad guys' sex is pretty great. Making a mental note," Cassie says to break the comfortable silence. "Though I could live without another fright like that, honestly."

"Yes, next time you can be the one trying to make friends with the murderous embezzler," Veronica agrees, taking a sip of her wine. "Since you were the one being framed, I think it's only fitting that I swoop in to save the day. I'm very competent, you know."

Cassie turns just enough to press against Veronica's thigh, as it's the nearest bit of exposed skin. "I'm just glad I get to keep coming to work.

And seeing you there. I'd have been really mad if I'd had to hand in that resignation. Your plotting and planning saved the day, where my storming into argue with people? Not so much."

"Well, at least you're gorgeous when you get all *man the barricades.* Speaking of acts of bravery, I think I'll tell Angela about us tomorrow," Veronica says, putting her journal aside and draining her glass. "Otherwise Daniel is going to start blackmailing me for 'keeping my secrets'."

"And that's a big deal?" Cassie asks, unsure of the territory. "I mean, as long as Danny's okay with us, that's what I was worried about. And everyone at the hospital knows, on our wards, at least."

"Yes, but there's something about telling your ex that makes it more official," Veronica replies, nudging Cassie with her foot. "You sure you're ready to take all this on? Teenage son and all?"

Cassie pulls herself up to sitting as well, so they're exactly side by side against their respective pillows. "I think I'd put up with a whole classroom of them, to be with you."

"Why, Major. You're getting romantic on me."

Cassie leans over to kiss Veronica soundly. "I'm a born romantic. Deal with it."

"I can hear your mind working from here," Veronica complains a moment later. "Out with it, before it ruins what's left of our evening."

"It's just saying everybody knows about us," Cassie says. "But then Pedersen told us he wants to combine departments into a Critical Care facility, making us co-leads, and didn't seem to have the first idea that we might be together. Can we... I mean, is it possible we could do both?"

"I don't see why not, if we sign all the proper forms." Veronica looks across at her in the lamplight. "I don't care who knows how I feel about you. And we've more than proven that we make a good team."

"Right. Um, how you feel about me?" Cassie doesn't mean to sound so unsure. How to explain that she feels too lucky? That it shouldn't be possible to have all this? She left the only life she knew with a broken heart, and now at St Sophia's, Cassie finds herself with both purpose and...yes, love. Not quite ready to express out loud yet, but love all the same.

"Don't go fishing. But...yes. Assume that all those feelings are positive. Positive enough to shout it from the rooftops, more or less."

Cassie smiles into Veronica's shoulder for a moment. "Good, then. I'm feeling pretty positive about you as well. You know, it's not that late, and since you've already put your bedtime reading down..."

"Well, look at that," Veronica says, shifting position so they can kiss again. "Major Taylor had another bright idea."

ABOUT LOLA KEELEY

Lola Keeley is a writer and coder. After moving to London to pursue her love of theatre, she later wound up living every five-year-old's dream of being a train driver on the London Underground. She has since emerged, blinking into the sunlight, to find herself writing books. She now lives in Edinburgh, Scotland, with her wife and three cats.

CONNECT WITH LOLA

Facebook: www.facebook.com/lolakeeley

E-Mail: divalola@gmail.com

OTHER BOOKS FROM YLVA PUBLISHING

www.ylva-publishing.com

THE MUSIC AND THE MIRROR
Lola Keeley

ISBN: 978-3-96324-014-0
Length: 311 pages (120,000 words)

Anna is the newest member of an elite ballet company. Her first class almost ruins her career before it begins. She must face down jealousy, sabotage, and injury to pour everything into opening night and prove she has what it takes. In the process, Anna discovers that she and the daring, beautiful Victoria have a lot more than ballet in common.

IRREGULAR HEARBEAT
Chris Zett

ISBN: 978-3-95533-996-8
Length: 261 pages (94,000 words)

When drummer Diana Petrell leaves her rock-star life to return to ER medicine, she won't let anything stop her—not even falling for aloof mentor, Dr. Emily Barnes.

Emily isn't happy having to babysit an intriguing resident with a ten-year gap in her résumé. But then the lines blur.

What happens to their careers when Diana's secret comes out?

A lesbian romance that asks how much we'd risk for love.

WHO'D HAVE THOUGHT
G Benson

ISBN: 978-3-95533-874-9
Length: 339 pages (122,000 words)

When Hayden Pérez stumbles across an offer to marry Samantha Thomson—a cold, rude, and complicated neurosurgeon—for $200,000, what's a cash-strapped ER nurse to do? Sure, Hayden has to convince everyone around them they're madly in love, but it's only for a year, right? What could possibly go wrong?

FALLING HARD
Jae

ISBN: 978-3-95533-829-9
Length: 346 pages (122,000 words)

Dr. Jordan Williams devotes her life to saving patients in the OR and pleasuring women in the bedroom.

Jordan's new neighbor, single mom Emma, is the polar opposite. Family and fidelity mean everything to her.

When Emma helps Jordan recover after a bad fall, they quickly grow closer.

But neither counted on falling hard—for each other.

Major Surgery
© 2019 by Lola Keeley

ISBN: 978-3-96324-145-1

Also available as e-book.

Published by Ylva Publishing, legal entity of Ylva Verlag, e.Kfr.

Ylva Verlag, e.Kfr.
Owner: Astrid Ohletz
Am Kirschgarten 2
65830 Kriftel
Germany

www.ylva-publishing.com

First edition: 2019

Credits
Edited by Lee Winter and Amanda Jean
Cover Design and Print Layout by Streetlight Graphics

Made in United States
Orlando, FL
22 April 2024

46059075R00131